The Perfect Family
A Crime Thriller

• • • •

By Denise Weiershaus

I0679760

Editing: K.M. Hotzel

Cover Design: James, www.GoOnWrite.com

Content Warnings

. . . .

This story contains explicit content, profanity, and topics that may be
sensitive to some readers.

Dedication

· · · ·

To all the indie-authors out there who don't believe they can make it.
Yes, you can!

Chapter 1 – The Hospital

Stella

THE CLASSICAL ELEVATOR music penetrated Stella's ears and pierced her brain. If it was meant to be relaxing, it was having the opposite effect. She felt nervous and on edge. Trying to keep her fingers from fidgeting, she squeezed both hands into fists and stared at the slowly increasing digital red number next to the metal door. Tight spaces weren't exactly Stella's comfort zone. Being caged-in like this, with strangers, put her anxiety in overdrive.

At a snail's pace, the elevator went up the hospital floors, stopping on every level. Somehow Stella had managed to take the slow elevator, the local, and now she was trapped with strangers invading her personal space, including one happy chappy who couldn't stop smiling at everyone. His face glowing with pride, he held onto a white string tied to an enormous floating balloon that read *Welcome to the World*. Stella wondered how he'd react if she burst that stupid balloon with the nail file in her purse.

The elevator finally announced level eleven with one of those chirpy pings that made Stella roll her eyes and spared the world's-greatest-dad from losing his floating gasbag. She couldn't get out of that horror show fast enough and pushed through the opening doors into the overly bright space of the Intensive Care Unit.

With determination, she gripped the handle of her silver suitcase and made her way towards the nursing station, her black pumps clicking loudly, announcing her arrival. Busy typing something into the computer in front of her, the elderly nurse behind the counter only recognized the unknown visitor once Stella cleared her throat. Her gray head lifted, revealing a name tag that read 'Marsha'. A set of exhausted but sharp eyes met Stella and she immediately felt a connection with this woman. Weariness was something they had in common. But while endless nights caring for others probably caused the dark circles under Marsha's chestnut eyes, for Stella, memories stubbornly continued to crawl their way into her mind. Usually at night. Leaving her tossing and turning night after night.

"How can I help you, hon?"

With Marsha's unexpected term of endearment, Stella tensed again, all connection lost. She had never understood why some people thought it appropriate to be this affectionate towards someone they'd never met before.

"Hello. I'm Stella Woodworth. My mother is a patient here," she said and pointed at the visitor badge they had given her at the front desk on the ground floor.

Marsha's eyes widened. Stella had almost forgotten the power behind her family's last name. Or was it because of the money her father had pumped into this hospital? The name Richard Woodworth was listed first on a golden plaque Stella had seen hanging prominently at the entrance which showed the patrons of this hospital. This place was one of countless others in the city that bore her father's mark. Too many, in Stella's opinion. It was so easy to forget about these details when one lived on the other side of the world.

"Of course, Miss Woodworth. Just give me a second and I'll get you to her room." Marsha swiftly accessed the computer system, the sound of her slender fingers clicking on the keyboard filling the air.

Stella clung to the edge of the countertop, waiting for the hospital system to spit out whatever information Marsha needed when she heard a familiar, raspy voice. She turned to find a short, older woman with hair neatly tied together at the back of her head coming towards her. Stella immediately smiled at the woman who had helped her with her homework for years and had always given her an extra cookie fresh from the oven.

"Grace!" Stella sighed with relief and leaned into a hug she knew to be warm and comforting.

"Thank you for coming so quickly."

"Of course. Thanks for letting me know." She stayed in the embrace of her family's housekeeper a little longer, having missed the familiar feel of her.

When Grace released her grip and stepped back, she held Stella at an arm's length, her eyes sweeping over her from head to toe, taking in every detail. "Let me get a good look at you. You look tired. Have you eaten anything?"

Grace's motherly concern brought back memories of a life Stella had almost buried, but had her chuckle nonetheless.

"I came straight from the airport and didn't have time to check-in, let alone eat something," Stella said with a nod towards her suitcase.

"That's no excuse. You know you need to take care of yourself, right?"

Although Grace's concern was directed towards her, it was also a subtle mention of her sister Megan's lifelong struggle with an eating disorder. She was touched that Grace still tried to make sure everyone was okay. Her parents could have learnt so much from Grace. But right now was not the time to dwell on squandered parental opportunities. She was here for something else.

"How is she?"

The change on Grace's face was answer enough. The mixture of worry and anxiety made it clear her mother's state was worse than she had expected.

"I don't know how this could happen. She was alright the evening before and when I came in the next morning, I found her on the floor. She didn't move and-and, Stella, I thought she was dead. I was terrified."

Stella felt the need to take Grace in for a supportive hug when a throat cleared next to them.

"Miss Woodworth, I am Doctor Abelson. I am taking care of your mother and can take you to her now."

In front of her stood a middle-aged white man with thinning hair, a paunch slowly spilling over his beltline and with a face as expressionless as the white hospital walls. Stella shook his hand quickly and let Dr. Abelson guide her and Grace to room 1176—a corner room with an enormous window facing west, in which her mother lay.

She knew what suicide looked like, but she wasn't prepared for this. A tube vanished inside her mother's mouth, helping her to breathe, exposing her bottom teeth and emphasizing the dryness of her chapped lips. White tape held the whole thing in place, sticking the tube to her mother's pale cheek. Next to her, an infusion bag hung on a metal holder, liquid entering her mother's system drop by drop, while the small blue metal cap covering her left index finger monitored her vital signs.

A gasp escaped Stella when she moved towards her mother. Or what was left of the once vibrant woman she had known, who had entertained at countless fancy gala receptions but who had always left a goodnight kiss on Stella's forehead, no matter how late. All Stella could see now was a ghost disappearing into the white hospital linen that covered her body up to her chest. Her body looked as if someone had drained it of every ounce of blood, making Stella wonder if she had misunderstood Grace earlier. Had her mother cut her wrists instead of taking pills?

"What happened?" Stella asked as she moved closer to her mother's side. Afraid to hurt her, she briefly hesitated before reaching out. When her fingers touched her mother's hand, it felt rough, like over-recycled paper, yet strangely delicate and fragile.

Dr. Abelson turned on the tablet he'd taken from the nursing station, but without looking at it, he explained, "When the paramedics reached your mother, her blood alcohol level was 0.18%, which is a lot. Combined with the Oxycodone and Doxepin that were found in her bedroom and those we found after pumping her stomach, we are fairly sure it caused her liver failure."

Liver failure?

"Due to swelling in her brain, we had to put her in an induced coma to give her brain and body time to rest."

"Brain swelling and coma? How much did she take?" Stella asked.

In the back of the room, Grace stood quietly next to the door, fidgeting anxiously.

"At her age, taking pills with such an alcohol level is never a good idea," Dr. Abelson continued. "Your mother was incredibly lucky."

He meant well, but if this was his idea of what luck looked like, her mother was in a pretty desperate position. She felt her eyes prick, but swallowed back her emotions. There was no time for tears.

"So, when will she wake up?" Stella asked, absentmindedly twirling a stray strand of her mother's gray hair around her finger the same way she had done as a child—tucked into bed and cuddling into her mother's warmth while she listened to the bedtime story she read to her. When she had left her family more than a decade ago, her mother's hair had been a vibrant shade of golden blond.

"We don't know."

"Come on, Doctor. You need to be able to tell me something, right?" she asked with a glance at the tablet he was hugging. Surely, there was something in there he could translate to her. As the assigned doctor, he should be able to give her more than silence.

But he didn't. The physician merely kept looking at her with pity in his eyes.

"I mean, what is your strategy here, Doc? What are the next steps you are planning on taking?"

Stella felt annoyance brewing inside her as she watched pity spread across his face and his mouth dropping inch by inch towards his chin. It made her fingers tremble, so she kept them gently on her mother's forearm, waiting for a response from the man who held her mother's life in his hands. Any sympathy Stella had for the man, who probably worked twenty-hour shifts and dealt with his fair share of aggravated patients and family members, vanished after his unexpected comment.

"I understand it can be difficult for members of the family to accept the faults of their parents. And I understand you haven't seen your mother lately," he said.

Stella's head shot up at the inappropriate statement. "What is that supposed to mean?"

"Nothing. Your father mentioned you weren't living close. Somewhere in Asia?"

Of course he had.

"China." Her answer was spiked with the guilt she always felt when asked why she had put an entire ocean between her and her family when she had moved to Hong Kong.

Dr. Abelson nodded as if he had figured out her whole life. "Well, I assure you we're taking good care of your mother and that we—"

It was then that Stella saw a faint ring of purple dots that formed a neat chain around her mother's neck. They were half covered by her mother's hair. Easy to miss for the untrained eye.

"What is this?" She interrupted Dr. Abelson, pointing to the almost imperceptible hematoma.

He leaned closer, frowned at her, and let out a surprised, "Huh."

She found his silence more unsettling than his apparent lack of concern for her mother.

"Is this normal?" she asked the doctor, who at this point was barely looking at her, never mind her mother's bruises.

In the back of the room, Grace made the sign of the cross.

"I haven't seen this before," Dr. Abelson said.

"Maybe that tablet you are holding on to can help you with that?"

She could have said this with less sarcasm, but after her thirteen-hour flight and no sleep, Stella didn't feel like being the reasonable person. She wanted her mother's doctor to give her clear information about her current condition and suggest his intended course of action.

Reluctantly, Dr. Abelson turned to the tablet and retrieved her mother's information from the electronic medical records. His index finger scrolled slowly through the data in front of him. With every second that passed, the intensity of Stella's anger increased. Incompetence was at the top of a long list of things she couldn't tolerate, and Dr. Abelson's so-called professionalism showed strong signs of someone who did not know what the fuck was going on.

After he had inspected all the information, he closed the tablet and looked at Stella. "It has not been mentioned in her medical file."

That's it?

That's all he had to say?

"What kind of hospital is this? Is this what you mean by taking good care of my mother?"

Dr. Abelson's friendly demeanor changed to something resembling annoyance. He looked like Stella's sister Megan, rolling her eyes dramatically whenever their father had pointed out her mistakes at the dinner table. In Megan's case, it had rarely been her fault. In this case, Dr. Abelson clearly didn't want to accept his ineptitude.

"Miss Woodworth, I will need to examine this further, but we can't dismiss the possibility that this was self-inflicted."

His unprofessional diagnosis, which by his own admission wasn't based on an examination, outraged Stella. She was upset by this situation and his words that hung in the air, which perhaps was the reason she had taken such a dislike to this doctor and why she couldn't leave it alone.

"You want to tell me she tried to strangle herself?" Stella asked, looking at Grace, who shook her head from left to right in the same disbelief she felt.

Sighing, Dr. Abelson continued through clenched teeth, "I don't know what she did because I wasn't there. But from a medical point of view, there are no indications at this stage that someone tried to harm her. I assure you, we will continue to evaluate her and do everything we can to take excellent care of her."

I assure you, my ass. Something was off about this guy. The way he kept checking his watch. Did he think he needed to be somewhere more important? People had told Stella she could be too pushy sometimes, but how could he have missed these bruises?

"If you have no more questions, I need to continue my rounds," he concluded and turned to leave.

And Stella let him. She wouldn't be able to get anything worthwhile out of him, anyway. She would have to talk to his superior. Ask for a second opinion. Demand answers.

When the door closed behind him, Stella let out the breath she had held in and focused on the riddle in front of her.

What happened to you, Mom?

Grace's warm hand curled around her shoulder, and Stella noticed the same concern reflected in her eyes that plagued her heart.

"Has *he* been here?" Stella asked.

Grace shook her head.

Shocker, Stella thought and wasn't surprised. Her father had never been one for emotionally tough situations.

"Megan knows, but she hasn't said if she'd come," Grace said, which astounded Stella.

She knew her younger sister wasn't on good terms with her father. Stella understood why. She'd never hold it against her sister that she wanted to stay away from his toxicity. That she wouldn't come to see their mother stung, though.

Out of the corner of her eye, she saw Grace shift nervously from one foot to the other. When she turned, Grace chewed the inside of her cheek, and Stella frowned at seeing her nervous habit.

"What is it?"

Grace paled. Her lips kept moving, but nothing came out. This scared Stella more than if she had shouted at her—which she had done a few times when Stella was younger. Grace wasn't usually afraid to say what was on her mind.

"Grace?" Stella pushed.

"Stella, I don't believe it," Grace whispered.

"What do you mean?"

"Your mother has been very happy recently. And I mean joyful. Content. I hadn't seen her like this in years."

The idea of her mother being happy felt alien to Stella. She had always played her part of the happy housewife, putting on smiles like ball gowns at all the right times. Yet true happiness wasn't something she associated with Beth Woodworth.

"Trust me, she would have never done this to herself."

Slowly, Grace's statement settled in. Her mother didn't have an easy life with her father. None of them had. She understood the pressure that came with being a Woodworth. She also knew about wanting to ease the strain of living with a man who owned half of Manhattan and considered his own family his property as well.

But she trusted Grace. If anyone knew her family better than herself, it was Grace. If she was sure her mother didn't do this, she believed her. But what was the alternative?

"What are you trying to say, Grace?" Stella's gaze shifted back to her mother and the blue marks that might indicate something more than an accident.

Suddenly all noise was sucked from the room and only the churning of Stella's stomach echoed in her ears when she asked, "Are you suggesting someone hurt her?"

Chapter 2 – The Mansion

Stella

STELLA HAS NEVER BEEN one to wait for answers to magically appear to her. If she needed something, she found it easier to get it herself. Over the years, this practice had proven to work well for her and ensured she never had to rely on anyone else. In this situation, though, where her mother's life was at risk, she had to reach out to someone who could help her find out what happened. She couldn't do this alone, especially not if Grace was right and her mother didn't attempt suicide. So, Stella decided to drop her luggage in the boutique hotel she had booked, call Grace, and inform her she would be over in a few minutes to pay her father a visit.

Growing up, talking to her father without scheduling an appointment had been a challenging task, and it was still almost impossible today. Even after his wife almost died, his work still came first and always would. Some things just never changed.

For more than an hour, Stella amused herself by chatting with Grace, watching her fold kitchen towels and wash dishes before she started dinner preparations.

At some point, Stella made herself comfortable in a leather chair in the hallway of the place she used to call home and stared at the oil painting in front of her. The gigantic family portrait spanned the entire wall and showed her mother sitting calmly and poised in a green velvet chair, both hands demurely folded in her lap. Perched on the left armrest was fourteen-year-old Stella, frozen in time in her red Sunday dress, a fake smile painted across her face. The same smile she had trained to perfection for any public family gathering.

On the right side of the portrait, her sister Megan stood as stiff as a poker. Her porcelain skin and golden mane had always drawn everyone's eyes to her, even though she rarely smiled and detested the attention. Above them all towered the master of the house and family, Richard Woodworth. Her father. His hint of a smile was almost as perfect as Stella's. A stranger wouldn't realize that the smile on his face was that of a self-important narcissist. With his dark and piercing stare that never truly matched the smile he had put on, it wasn't a loving father and husband who looked at you, but the devil. To others, however, this portrait depicted nothing less than a perfect family. How easy it was to fool people.

This portrait hadn't always been like this. Originally, there were five figures in the painting, but after Jonathan was gone, Stella's father quickly erased him. While most of the family was mourning over a son and brother, her father thought it was the right thing to expunge even the memory of Jonathan from the family. Jonathan wasn't able to take over the family empire, so he was taken off the walls and his name never again left her father's lips.

Suddenly, the temperature changed around her. Maybe a breeze brushed over her, but Stella felt a chill in the air that made the hairs on her skin stand on end.

He had arrived.

Moving her head first to the left, then to the right, she loosened the tension in her neck with a series of cracks she felt ripple down her spine.

Once upon a time, she had convinced herself she was adopted, or that he wasn't her real father. Unfortunately, as much as she wished he were not, the evidence had confirmed the man approaching her was her father.

He strode in as if he owned the world, confidence dripping from his expensive tailor-made suit. Like a suit of armor, he only took it off on rare occasions, like when he played a round of golf with his buddies.

He saw her and his grim face grew darker, before he passed by her and opened the door to the room that held his home office. He vanished without saying a word to Stella.

So much for a welcome back.

Leaving the door open was his way of letting her know to follow.

Stella took in a deep breath and lifted herself off the leather chair. Without thinking, she straightened her black slacks and blazer before following his unspoken command.

Inside his kingdom, she found him settling in behind his desk, arranging his navy tie before addressing her for the first time.

"Close the door behind you." His voice was arctic cold. No love, no joy, not even the pretense.

"Hello to you, too," Stella replied, which earned her a frosty stare.

For a second, she wondered how long she could keep this up without blinking, but then again, she didn't want to drag this conversation out longer than it had to be. Once she had closed the door, her father's gaze went back to the pile of papers in front of him.

His office was every bit the New York old school business stereotype that he was. Wood paneling adorned the walls and a big, solid mahogany desk greeted all those who visited the patriarch. He even shunned the obligatory family photographs. No distractions.

Stella walked over to the floor-to-ceiling windows and looked out at the city below her. From the sixtieth floor, even a metropolis like New York seemed small.

"Sit down," he commanded, his eyes glued to the documents in front of him, which he swiftly signed with the black Montblanc that bore his initials.

Everything he owned had a *RW* stamp and Stella was convinced that, if given the chance, he would have branded his family like cattle too.

"Thanks, but I'd rather stand," she replied defiantly over her shoulder, crossing her arms in front of her and gazing outside.

When he didn't reply and the sound of pen on paper stopped, she eventually decided to be the adult. She rolled her eyes before she turned to face him and was met by a piercing stare she had seen on him all too often when he tried to intimidate his opponents.

"I said sit down!" his baritone commanded.

Her stomach flipped, her body remembering what she had been taught to do, but she didn't want to. She didn't want to give into his need to control everyone, especially her. She was a grown-up woman now. She had created a successful life for herself.

I don't have to take your shit anymore, she thought as she walked over to his desk and sat down in one of the two chairs in front of him. Better to get this over with.

Taking a moment to actually look at her father, whom she hadn't seen for seventeen years, she had to admit he had aged well. He hadn't gained a pound, made sure he wouldn't expand like so many other men did by their early sixties. The advantages of having a personal trainer at your beck and call. The gray streaks in his neatly trimmed hair were even, making Stella wonder if he had a stylist taking care of that as well.

"I thought you said you'd never set foot into this—what were your exact words—oh, 'shithole of a golden cage.'"

Her father threw her own words back at her, catapulting her back into the conversation. She had almost forgotten the words she had used back then, which continued to ring truer and truer with every second she spent in his presence.

"Or have you come to your senses? Are you all grown up now and ready to take your place at the table?" he continued when she didn't bite.

"You don't really believe I'd want that seat?" Stella scoffed and had to smile at his absurd proposal.

As the first-born and only son, her brother Jonathan should have been in line for this grueling honor, but then he had killed himself and the heir to the Empire was gone. Suddenly, Stella had become second best, but she never wanted to be part of this. She never had the hunger for power like her father. The obsession to be the biggest and strongest. The scariest.

Instead of letting him answer her question, to which she did not want to hear his answer, she focused on the only reason she had returned.

"What happened to my mother?"

"I think it's pretty clear. Your mother attempted to end her life but didn't succeed." He sounded like a bored professor who had to explain basic calculus for the hundredth time. Until he spit out the next comment, as if he'd let undercooked chicken enter his mouth and couldn't swallow it. "Now I'm paying for her to recover and explain herself to me."

There was a hint of an emotion. Money and pride would always be reasons for her father to show something resembling feelings.

"We both know she didn't attempt to commit suicide," Stella replied in a tone that was a little more categorical than she felt.

He let out an uninterested sigh and looked up from his papers, rolling his pen between his fingers.

"I don't think you are in any position to say what your mother would and wouldn't do. This weakness runs on her side of the family," he said, referring to her older brother.

"Is that why you haven't bothered visiting her in the hospital? Have you even talked to her doctor?"

"I can assure you, Dr. Abelson is one of the best doctors your mother could have. He'll take good care of her."

Stella couldn't help but notice the similarities in how her father and Dr. Abelson described her mother's caretaker.

"This amazing doctor you are talking about has barely looked at her medical information. He hadn't even examined her. Your favorite doctor doesn't know what he is talking about." Stella deliberately left out the details about her mother's bruising, wanting to get a feel for her father and his current relationship with her mother.

"Oh, and you do?" he interrupted with a patronizing chuckle. "That's rich coming from someone who hasn't bothered seeing her mother in over a decade."

Stella had to admit she hadn't been a model daughter. At first, her mother would ask her to come home but after a few years, she stopped, realizing her oldest daughter wouldn't be returning. She had come home, though. Hopefully, it wasn't too late.

Stella had to live with this every day, the guilt of wanting to live her own life away from the toxicity that came with being part of this family.

"I'm here now, am I not? I've traveled halfway around the world to see her and you sit here in your tower, a ten-minute ride away, and couldn't even bother to show up."

"It's not my fault she's so selfish. She didn't even go through with it. She's looking for attention, that's all. I won't be dragged into that sick game of hers. Or yours, for that matter. I am doing everything I can for her and if she wakes up again, I'll pay for a place where she'll get professional help."

The bitterness of his statement hit Stella like a punch deep in the gut.

If?

"Jesus Christ. You can't just give up on her. She is your wife. She needs you." Stella's hands tingled with anger as she was trying not to shout into her father's face.

"Blame her, or the pharmacist who gave her extra pills or whomever you like, but not me. I'm not responsible for her decisions. But I'll make sure she won't do anything like this again and hurt this family even more."

With that, he signed his name a final time and screwed the cap back on his fountain pen before placing it on its designated wooden pen rest. For him, the matter was settled. But not for Stella.

"Not if I have something to say about that."

"And what is that supposed to mean?" he asked, while leaning back into his chair, making her feel like a child again, always having to fight for her voice to be heard.

"I want to find out what really happened to her. And I don't believe Dr. Abelson has those answers, so I'll get a second opinion," she stated, growing taller in her seat.

"Oh, is this the point where the amateur detective solves the case?" His words dripped with condescension about the career she had chosen. If her pride hadn't been hurt, she would have been surprised he knew or cared about the fact she was a PI.

She got up from her seat and looked down at her father. "Do you really hate me so much that you won't help me?"

For a moment, she had his full attention. He actually looked at her. He must have seen the worry for her mother and the determination to get to the bottom of this, but that moment passed faster than a bullet train. His face turned into a grimace, and he grumbled at her in frustration.

"I gave you everything. I would have even given you a seat on the board and prepared you to take over this company, but you had to bolt off to Hong Kong like some kind of hippy runaway. And where has this gotten you? Look at yourself."

Disgusted, he gestured towards her, and Stella fought the urge to look herself up and down. Instead, she raised her chin while he continued to mock her life.

"Your talents wasted in Hong Kong when you could have been sitting in this chair, continuing the family line."

If Stella were held at gunpoint and forced to say something positive about her father, this would be it. As much as one could accuse him of the cruelest and most selfish disposition, he never discriminated between genders. As he had said before himself, "it doesn't matter if someone has a cock or a pussy, as long as they have balls".

Is that the only thing he is interested in?

Growing his empire, no matter the collateral damage?

Anger bubbled up inside her. She felt it brew in her stomach. Felt the acid burn her throat until she erupted, "What family line? There is no one left. You've chased everyone away, you fool!"

Her father's fist landed loudly on the table, shaking the green desk lamp to its core, its short golden string frantically dangling from side to side. Showing him his own faults was still a surefire way to make him lose his temper, and Stella felt a rush of satisfaction.

"Of all my children, you are the biggest disappointment," he spat.

It shouldn't hurt. Stella was used to it, always had been. But the truth about how her father felt about her, even after all these years, stung more than she thought it should.

She turned without saying another word and left her childhood home once again, wondering if she'd ever be able to escape it for good.

Chapter 3 - The Bar

Stella

THE TWO FINGERS OF golden Jameson burned as they went down Stella's throat. She felt the liquid reach her stomach and turn her anxiety into a warm and cozy feeling. This was exactly what she needed after her encounter with her father. Not that she had expected hugs or an apology from him. But her father knew how to push her buttons and make her feel like the young and naïve kid she used to be.

During her years in China, she found peace from her memories through her work as a PI, helping others. She practiced martial arts to get her heart rate up and even found time for daily breathing exercises.

The quick chat with her father, however, had her on edge in seconds. Breathing exercises wouldn't do the trick, and the nearest punching bag was too far away. So Stella had to turn towards more traditional methods to deal with her emotions. Drown them in something stronger than 80 proof.

Stella had ordered from the grungy-looking bartender who had introduced himself as Pearse. The way he had wiped his hands on the dirty brown towel hanging casually over his shoulder had almost made Stella question if she should order anything in this place at all. But then Ireland's best export would take care of any germs she might contract while spending time in this off-the-main road bar that had seen better days.

Murphy's Irish Pub was the closest to her hotel, though, and Stella had never been picky about where she got drunk. Not even a place like this. Small and dark, with the smell of cold cigarettes clinging to the brown wallpaper that must have once been white, and a floor so sticky she worried it might claim her shoes, forcing her to walk barefoot. She filed all these feelings under *things not to get anxious about* when her second round was dropped right in front of her.

"Anything else, luv?" Pearse sounded as run down as he looked.

Although Stella wasn't fond of terms of endearment from strangers, the dimples in his cheeks gave him a boyish charm that won her over. So instead of biting off his head, she merely shook her own. Taking no offense, Pearse gave Stella time to think about what she should do next while he moved on to his next customer, a sleepy drunk hugging his beer, still managing to lift two fingers to show he wasn't done just yet.

Her father's words rang in her head. Could her mother really have attempted suicide? Mental health issues ran in her family. Her sister Megan had suffered from depression when she was younger. And when she was told to suck it up, Megan had dropped her depression and replaced it with an eating disorder.

Better than what Jonathan had done.

It still hurt to think about her older brother. He was three years older than her and would have turned 39 this year if he hadn't done the one thing he thought he needed to do to escape their father's iron fist.

It would have been easy to blame him for such a selfish act. Like her father had when he denounced his son's cowardice. Despite her loss, though, some part of Stella had felt happy for Jonathan, finally resting in peace.

No matter what her father claimed, she couldn't believe her mother had attempted to commit suicide. Beth Woodworth was cut from a different cloth; old-fashioned and believed in sticking things out through good times and bad. In addition, Grace had been adamant her mother had been happy. It just didn't feel right.

Stella's phone vibrated in her pocket. Hoping to see her sister's name appear on the screen, she took it out of her jacket only to find a message from her assistant with updates from work. Stella checked her emails and texts, but there was still no word from Megan. So she rang her again.

"Hey Megan, it's me again. Can you call me back? Mom is still in intensive care. She seems stable, but the doctors say it's too early to tell. Just call me, okay? Bye."

Stella plopped her phone back into her pocket and grunted at the ceiling. Megan had always been difficult to reach, and the two of them weren't close. They hadn't been for years—since she had moved to Hong Kong, to be precise. The fault wasn't her sister's alone. Their lack of contact was natural and no one's fault in particular. Stella had never felt a connection to her baby sister as strong as it had been with Jonathan. Maybe it was the five-year age gap or their differing interests. Stella used to get in trouble as a child and teenager, whereas Megan was quiet and never acted out. Happy in her room or caring for the strays in the animal shelter, she loved to help. Despite their differences, Stella always made the effort to call her on her birthdays or for Christmas. But this wasn't a missed family call. This was important.

"Can I buy you a drink?" A slurring voice emerged from her right, belonging to a stranger's face with glassy eyes and beer foam clinging to his reddish beard.

"No thanks," she said as politely as possible, which was hard under the circumstances.

"Ah c'mon. You look like you need someone to cheer you up. Let me buy you a drink. I'm sure you'll feel much better once you put a smile on that pretty face of yours."

Why is this happening to me? Stella asked the universe. Neither her posture nor this place gave the impression that she was in the mood to talk to anyone. Aside from Pearse perhaps, and then only to order the next round of her self-prescribed antidepressants.

"She said she doesn't want you to buy her a drink."

A second voice entered the arena of conversations she didn't want to have. Raw and dark, perfectly suited for this place.

On cue, Red Beard continued his slurred speech with stranger number two. "You with her?"

"No, but I know when a woman wants to be left alone, so…"

"How about you shut your mouth then and let me buy her a drink?"

Men.

"How about you follow your own advice regarding your mouth and I take myself off your irrational equation because, if you are honest with yourself, you know this isn't going anywhere but you making a complete fool of yourself?" Stella said, placing a twenty-dollar note on the bar. "So why don't you sit back down, have another drink on me, and call it a night?"

Ready to leave and finish the evening with the miniature bottles from her hotel's mini fridge, Stella grabbed her purse and got up from her stool. She saw stranger number two, a black-haired guy, smile into his glass when she felt a hot and sweaty hand on her arm.

"Why do you have to be such a fucking bitch?"

The smile on stranger number two vanished as quickly as Stella's patience. She felt her anxiety replaced by the all too familiar feeling she would usually deal with in her Kung-Fu class. Having spent a decent amount of time honing her martial arts skills, she also knew there should always be a peaceful way out of an escalating situation.

"Let go of me immediately or you'll regret having left your bed this morning." Those words might not have been the wisest to use confronting a drunk and hurt man. Poking a sleeping misogynistic bear with an overly righteous threat has never led to anything but violence in her experience. Therefore, Stella wasn't surprised when the guy got up and straightened to his impressive grizzly bear-like size. The fading face tattoo on his right side also indicated that this fine specimen of a man had made the acquaintance of the legal system before.

Well done, Stella. You hit the jackpot with this one, she thought, getting mentally ready for what was about to happen.

"Sit down and have a fucking drink with me."

His refusal to let go of her arm did not sway her decision. On the contrary, a charming invitation like this had her questioning why she, and women in general, always had to be de-escalators. Why not give idiots like him a piece of their own medicine?

Stella's right hand curled into a fist. She felt the familiar exhilarating tickle when her heartbeat picked up the pace, like it always did before a fight. Electricity collected in her hand. She took in a deep breath and exhaled loudly, watching her fist rise in slow-motion, gaining speed and going straight for the hairy chin in front of her. Somehow, the Big Guy saw it coming, which surprised Stella and kept her occupied long enough to miss him turning his hip and hence his big torso to which his chin was eventually attached.

Her fist connected with rough skin, colliding with someone's face. Lucky for Big Guy, it wasn't his. Unlucky for Stella, it was the face of the guy behind him. The same guy who had stepped in earlier and whose grin had fully vanished from his face. Or maybe Stella's fist had moved it sideways.

From there, everything progressed quickly. Stella retreated her fist and mumbled curse words to herself while the black-haired guy held his face, shouting curse words even louder. Even Pearse the bartender cursed. The only person not cursing was the Big Guy, who wore a smug smile on his face, proud of himself for having ducked the unexpected powerful right hook from a woman.

In general, people didn't like being laughed at and being laughed at by someone like Big Guy was just another blow to a man's pride. So instead of sitting down or leaving the area, the black-haired guy gave Big Guy a taste of Stella's medicine. This time the fist hit Big Guy straight on his nose. The smile disappeared behind a rush of blood gushing down his face. No one laughed or cursed. Only Pearse let out a grunt, bent down, and slammed a baseball bat he must have kept hidden for special occasions, like nasty drunks, on the bar. The bat hitting the counter sent a shockwave through the glasses, rattling them, until it woke the old drunk snoring loudly in the corner.

"I've fucking had it with you, Sam," Pearse said, bat pointed at the three of them. "Get the fuck out of here. All of you."

And then the night was over for everyone. Big Guy was the first to leave, followed by Stella and the black-haired guy.

Hit by the crisp fall air outside, Stella felt sober immediately, but her anger hadn't fully evaporated yet.

"What the fuck is wrong with you?" She asked the man, who touched his face with two fingers, wincing.

"I thought you needed help," he said, checking his fingers for blood.

"Well, I didn't."

"Yeah, I know this now."

Stella knew her punch would leave a mark and hurt like a bitch in the coming days.

"Stay out of my business. You don't even know me."

"Don't worry. I'm not making that mistake again, crazy lady." He waved two fingers at Stella, straightened his jacket, and walked down Madison Avenue before he vanished into a side street.

The endorphins had left Stella's body, and she felt empty and angry at herself. She hated losing control, but what bothered her even more was how swiftly she succumbed to her old habits upon coming home. She really had to get out of here as soon as possible.

Chapter 4 - The Meeting

Samuel

SAMUEL WONDERED HOW one man could whine so much about his pathetic life. Listening to Jeff drone on about how none of his failings were his fault was giving Samuel a headache. Pain crept in on him slowly, from the front of his forehead to the back of his thick skull. He knew his headache resulted from the fist that had blindsided him two nights ago, but it seemed much more logical to make Jeff the culprit for his pain.

The left side of his face, just around his eye, had turned a series of different colors and would change into a vibrant palette of purple and green soon.

Samuel held on to his paper cup, wishing the dark liquid were rum instead of coffee, when Jeff's mouselike snout opened for another ridiculous excuse why the world was out to get him. It was bad enough that his coffee tasted like water, but being here sober was torture beyond what Samuel deserved. And the meeting hadn't even started yet.

He had just hit his six-month mark. For half a year, he had come to the neighborhood community center at least once a week to talk about the problem everyone thought he had with alcohol. That was 26 weeks of sitting on uncomfortable foldable metal chairs in a circle with too many depressed men, in a windowless room that would even have Winnie the Pooh consider suicide. Samuel didn't want to be here. He didn't belong here, but at this point, it wasn't up to him anymore. If he wanted to keep his job, he had to make it through this nonsense.

It was just before seven in the morning. Most misfits, including himself, were still mingling around the coffee station comprising three thermos cans. One for hot water, one decaf, and one for the black piss he was holding on to. Samuel hated being early to his meetings. He didn't want to have the chance to talk with others, get support from them, make friends. What he wanted was for their group leader Nigel to take control and start the meeting, before he'd die a slow and agonizing death.

He observed Nigel finish setting up the chair circle, chatting with a new guy whose name he couldn't remember. His dark, long hair kept falling into his face, covering half of it and the deep cut above his eyebrow. Red, swollen skin framed the stitches holding the gash together. Samuel assumed the kid couldn't be older than his early twenties and knew what it felt like to get the shit beaten out of him.

Can we please get this show going before someone else feels the urge to do small talk? Samuel wished, checking the big white clock hanging on the wall, his right leg bobbing up and down, making the coffee in his cup slosh from one side to the other.

Almost spilling some on his jeans, Samuel felt Peter's eyes on him. On his face. It was too early for Samuel to deal with his shit, which included an unhealthy appetite for prostitutes.

"What, Peter?" Samuel asked and interrupted yet another of Jeff's monologues over how he couldn't understand why his pregnant wife had left him after he'd drunkenly gambled away their life savings. He had to move back in with his parents, and Samuel felt extremely sorry for the people who were forced to listen to his whining every day. Hadn't they suffered enough by raising such a wimp?

All eyes were on him now. Even the last few men mingling around the coffee station turned their heads.

"What happened to your face?" Peter blurted with a smug smile.

"I got hit."

"I can see that. But how did that happen?"

Even though Samuel had the aura of a man who drew in trouble, he had dodged a fair bit of messy situations in his life. Sitting in his circle of trust with a black eye was, even to Samuel's surprise, a first.

"I tried to help a woman, and she punched me in the face, Peter."

Peter eyes widened. "A woman?"

"Yes, a woman."

"You got this huge black eye from a woman's fist?"

The chuckle in Peter's voice clarified that he came from a prehistoric world in which women were only useful in the kitchen or the bedroom. But Samuel knew that already. Peter's quest to find his manhood in brothels rather than on a proper date was evidence enough he had failed to overcome his personal obstacles.

Where is Nigel when I need him?

Samuel exhaled deeply, the bitter scent of coffee filling the air, before he answered. "Didn't I just say that? Yes, Peter. Women can throw a good punch the same way they can fuck another guy behind your back and take all your money and your house in a messy divorce."

Peter's face turned stony instantly. "Jesus, you are such an asshole."

It was so easy to rile him up. Too easy sometimes. "Right back at you, Petey."

Unexpectedly fast for a man who looked like he hadn't seen the inside of a gym for years, Peter closed the gap between them. He stopped right in front of him, his index finger lifted, angrily pointing at Samuel's bruised face.

"I've told you a million times not to call me that!"

He had. In a very weak moment, which was supposedly called a breakthrough in this group, Peter had shared the painful memory of his wife's lover making a profession out of calling him Petey to his face at garden parties and other social gatherings while fucking his wife behind his back. Usually at the same social gathering.

Maybe he should have felt sorry for picking at him, but Samuel's threshold of being supportive to a bunch of whiny men was near zero.

"Guys, please." Nigel, the group leader, and sober example of ten years, stepped in. "Please, it's seven in the morning. Let's not start the day like this."

"He started it! I only asked him how he's doin," Peter began, with innocence in his voice that didn't translate to his eyes.

"You sure you wanna play it that way?"

"What's that supposed to mean?"

"I think you know just fine, Petey," Samuel said, and Peter took the bait. With hands now curled into fists, Peter growled at Samuel.

"Fuck off, Sam."

"That's enough! You know the rules. No fighting." Nigel tried again, stepping between him and Peter.

As if I'm letting Peter get to me that way!

Part of him was craving it, though. Why not let Peter throw the first punch? Maybe it would bring some visual symmetry back to his face and numb the other pain he felt as well.

Had it really only been a year since he'd fucked up his whole life?

"Why don't we take this to the circle? You can share what's on your mind," Nigel said with a smile on his lips, inviting Samuel to take him up on his honest offer.

Samuel knew Nigel meant well. Sharing his emotions had clearly worked for him, but Samuel was different. His pain was worse than theirs. Samuel's guilt weighed heavier. They wouldn't understand. Even if he tried to explain it to them. Nigel knew the unspeakable thing he had done. Did he really believe this bunch of misfits could help him? By talking about the worst day of his life again and again when coming here for the last six months had done nothing to make him feel better? When had sharing his feelings ever done him any good?

But today was not the day.

"No, thanks."

Nigel's face turned into a quizzical frown, as if from Samuel's polite decline to discuss his feelings or the painful sight around his eye. He wasn't sure. But it didn't matter. Nigel wouldn't let it go.

"Why don't you get seated, Peter? Get the group ready. I'll be over in a second," he said, his hand already on Samuel's elbow, taking him a few steps away from the curious eyes and ears of the others, especially Petey's.

While Peter kept his mouth shut for once, he showed him the finger behind Nigel's back before he rounded up the rest of the men.

What a dickhead.

"What's going on?" Nigel asked in his calm and supportive voice that was carried by kind brown eyes and a soft belly that proved he had exchanged alcohol for the comfort of his second wife's cooking.

Nigel was the perfect example of someone Samuel never wanted to be. A stickler for the rules, understanding to a fault, and so humble about his own perfect sobriety it was sickening. He was too nice for this group.

"Nothing."

"How did you get the shiner?"

"Do we have to go through this again?" Samuel sighed. "I tried to help a woman, and she punched me. Right here," he said, pointing at his eye.

"Ouch. That must have been a shitty day at work."

Samuel hated how well his sponsor saw through him. He wouldn't have mentioned it if he'd actually believed Sam could have gotten this thanks to his line of work as a detective at the NYPD.

"You know I didn't get this at work." Samuel folded his arms in front of him. "I went to a bar. Happy?"

"I'm not judging you, Sam," Nigel said.

Samuel knew he wasn't. Nigel had fought his own battles for many years before controlling the urge.

"You've come so far over the last two months," Nigel kept going.

Samuel felt bad for the charade he had kept up. Two months was a stretch of six weeks. He thought everybody knew that.

He didn't want to lie to Nigel. All he had hoped for upon waking up this morning was to get through the session quietly. But Nigel burst his bubble. Always such a supporter.

"I want to know why you thought you needed to drink?"

You know damn well why I wanted to drink.

"You can always call me when you struggle. You are not alone in this."

Nigel motioned Samuel to open up with a friendly nod. He knew he should. It was part of the deal he had struck. But he really didn't want to open that box.

"Nope. Nothing to tell."

Nigel sighed, but kept his eyes on Samuel, staring into the abyss that was his soul. "I know this time is especially difficult for you. With the anniversary coming up—"

"I said I don't want to talk about it!" Samuel cut in.

The last thing he wanted to talk about, whether it was early in the morning or any other time of the day, was why he had to waste away his time here instead of contributing something meaningful to society. What happened had happened, and talking about it wouldn't make it less real. He wanted to forget, numb his feeling of helplessness and drown himself in alcohol or work. He was a high functioning alcoholic. Why was it so difficult for everyone to see that?

Nigel put his hand on Samuel's trembling arm. The gesture was so innocent, but it cut him deeper than he would ever admit.

"Sam—"

Right on time Samuel's phone rang and saved him. AC/DC blared from his jacket pocket and saved him from going through another round of why he didn't want to talk about it, or worse, actually talking about it.

He fished his phone out of the inside pocket of his black leather jacket and checked the caller ID under the disapproving looks of everyone else. No one liked that he was allowed to keep his phone on during a meeting when everyone else had to abandon it in a bowl at the entrance. When justice called, however, you had to pick up. No one could hold that against him. The perks of being an officer on duty.

He waved his phone at Nigel and relaxed. "Sorry, got to take this. It's work."

Nigel looked at Samuel with disappointment. He took in a loud breath of air but nodded, eventually. Samuel knew Nigel had accepted, once again, his inability to get through to him.

While he walked towards salvation, which came in the form of the exit sign, Nigel moved on to start today's session, calling on the next misfortunate man to share his failure to stay sober and the various ways he had fucked up his life. Samuel doubted that anyone of them had fucked it up as badly as him.

Chapter 5 - The Case

Samuel

THE FROSTED GLASS WINDOW shook when Samuel knocked on his captain's office door. The black paint reading Capt. J. W. Holmes had started to flake, eroding the letters like the tide on a cliff. Holmes' familiar baritone asked him to step inside. Samuel closed the door behind him quietly and strode over to a set of chairs right in front of Holmes' dark desk, waiting for instructions about whether he should sit down.

In front of him, his mentor, a man he had known for a lifetime, busied himself signing papers. His usual friendly face was distorted into a frown, a big fault line running down deep between his eyes. Whatever occupied his mind, it made him look older than he was.

Holmes put his papers aside and leaned back into his chair before looking up at Samuel. He had just celebrated his 60th birthday two weeks ago, with way too much food that must have spiked his cholesterol levels and probably had his wife Gloria add another salad day to his weekly diet. He still had a full mat of hair, but it had turned completely white over the last six months. Right now, he looked like he was ready to retire tomorrow and not in three years.

"Jesus Christ! What happened to your face?" he asked, showing Samuel to sit down as well.

"I helped a woman in need and this was my reward," Samuel replied.

His boss raised his eyebrows. "Is that what you are calling it now?"

Whatever Holmes must have thought had happened, which was probably pretty close to what had actually happened, Samuel didn't want to go into the details of his alcohol-fueled escapades. He sat quietly for a moment, letting his hands rest on his thighs before he broke the silence to move the conversation to the main reason he'd been called in.

"You asked to see me, Sir?"

Holmes tried to read him. His brown eyes focused on Samuel's face. He felt his stare deep in his gut, but he wasn't here to be interrogated about his life choices. At least he hoped not. Eventually, Holmes focused on something else.

"Yes, I did," Holmes said. He opened the drawer on his right side, found what he needed within a second, and handed Samuel a light manila folder. "Look at this and tell me what you think."

Surprised, Samuel took the thin document and read through even less information than he had expected.

"Ever heard of Richard Woodworth?" Holmes asked.

"Heard of? He owns half of the city," Samuel said, skimming through the papers. Richard Woodworth's name was attached to an impressive number of buildings in New York City, because he either built or somehow owned them. No one who wanted to make it in the Big Apple could get around Richard Woodworth, who seemed to have more hands in the New York business game than an octopus. After reading the report, which was received late last night, he closed the file and placed it on Holmes' desk.

"Why are you giving this to me?" Samuel asked, surprised.

"I want you to give me a hand with this one."

"I don't do homicide. I'm missing persons."

"I need someone I know and trust on this. So, I asked to have you transferred over to me for this one."

Samuel had known Holmes for years. He was a mentor to him, from whom he had learned a lot when he started at this precinct. He wasn't surprised Holmes had asked for him to transfer over to Homicide. These transfers happened, but this case seemed straightforward and would be closed in a matter of days. A training officer could do this. Samuel didn't understand why he was needed.

"The case looks straightforward to me. His wife tried to commit suicide, was saved in time, and is now recovering. Well, if that's what you can call her current state. From the hospital report, I don't even know why this is with Homicide. Was there anything unusual when the EMT arrived? Anything stolen or other signs of a break-in, that would suggest mal-intent?"

Holmes shook his head but took in a deep breath before he answered a different question Samuel had on the tip of his tongue.

"Someone called it in."

"Who?"

"His daughter."

Samuel's eyebrows shot up, and Holmes gave him one of his *I know* nods.

"Do we know anything about her? Where was she when this happened?"

Fidgeting with the tie a rookie had given him as a birthday gift, Holmes hesitated before he continued, "Stella Woodworth comes with her own set of issues, I am afraid."

"Sounds ominous," Samuel said, leaning back in his chair.

"She left town over a decade ago. Basically vanished one night. Richard was devastated, not knowing where his daughter went. That was shortly after her brother, Jonathan, committed suicide. I get people deal with trauma in their own ways, but Richard was a mess after his son's death, all while trying to keep the family together."

Samuel was surprised to hear Holmes speak about the city's infamous mogul's personal situation in such detail. Although Woodworth's name was often making headlines, they typically centered on the rapid growth of his empire, rather than his personal life. Also, for as long as he could remember, the media had always tried to portray him as a cartoon bad guy. Insinuating he gathered his wealth unlawfully, or at least unscrupulously. Richard Woodworth, however, remained squeaky clean. Nothing had ever been pinned on him. There didn't seem to be any skeletons hidden in his closet.

Samuel had never heard of the runaway daughter or the suicidal son. But then, he wasn't one to follow the tabloids. He'd take a deeper look into the family later.

It sounded like his captain knew Woodworth, but before he could ask about their relationship, Holmes went on.

"Richard and I, we know each other. Started out in the city around the same time. We keep in touch occasionally. I'd like to keep whatever this is as quiet as possible. Make sure nothing goes wrong. His daughter Stella used to have a bit of a temper and from the way she brought this in last night, it looks like she could do more harm than good."

Samuel wondered what Holmes meant by that when he took the file back. He let his fingers flick through the pages again until he found the details about Stella Woodworth's call. A conversation that was described as loud, harsh, and verging on hysterical.

"I am trying to keep all this extra attention to a complete minimum. And I definitely don't want the press to get wind of this," Holmes concluded.

Keeping the press out of their investigations was something Samuel could agree with. In his experience, any media outlet caused drama. To create a sensational story, most journalists took snippets of information and distorted the truth, benefiting no one except themselves. Considering the machinery of lawyers behind someone like Richard Woodworth, Samuel was taken aback by the importance Holmes ascribed to keeping this case quiet.

"You really think his daughter could cause trouble?"

"I wouldn't put it past her," Holmes sighed. "And I thought you could use this case. Getting a win here would be good for you. Richard Woodworth has a lot of pull around here, as you know."

There it was.

The real reason he'd brought him in. He felt a pang of hurt. *Why couldn't everyone just let it go?* Samuel didn't need to be treated differently. He was fine and just wanted to do his job. If only they'd let him. He hated that the whole precinct continued to look at him differently since last year.

He'd agreed to take some time off right after it happened. Begrudgingly, because he didn't want to stand still and get lost in his nightmares. He'd complied, hoping everything would be back to normal after his return, but nothing was normal since. He was sick of their pity. They gave him the simple cases. The ones where no one would lose too much if he'd fuck it up again. They didn't trust him to do his job. And a part of him understood them. Hell, he'd probably react the same way, but it still hurt. He hated getting special treatment and now even his captain thought he needed a helping hand.

"I know the anniversary is coming up...," Holmes continued, bringing Samuel back to the conversation right in front of him.

"Sir, I'm fine," he interrupted, trying to end the conversation about his state of mind before it went on any further.

"We both know you aren't. The whole precinct knows you haven't dealt with it."

Samuel felt the all too familiar rush of anger pool in his hands, like an electric power surge flashing through his body and finding an outlet in his fingertips.

"I don't need anyone's pity," he said.

"Good, because I am not giving you any. And please never assume I'd use my position and responsibilities in such a way. I am asking you to help me close this case and it is a fortunate coincidence that this is also good for you."

"Anyone can take this case. It's an easy one. Hell, our rookie Derek can do this!" Samuel blurted louder than he wanted to, but he was done with being treated like the poor kid in school.

"I don't want Derek on this. I want you! Someone I can trust and not some kid who is still wet behind the ears and probably hasn't even heard of the Woodworths before. I need someone sensitive to this case, who can close it in a professionally and quietly." Holmes had matched Samuel's tone. His underlying frustration flying across the desk and hitting Samuel right in the face.

He shouldn't be angry at Holmes. He'd had his back in the past more often than he could count, and Samuel knew he meant well. He also wasn't wrong about this approach. This year's new recruits were so very young. No life experience whatsoever. How were they supposed to deal with a tycoon like Richard Woodworth when most of them weren't old enough to shave?

Maybe Holmes was right.

And what did it matter? A job was a job. He had never been too picky. Besides, it would occupy his mind, drown out the noise in his head.

"What happened last year wasn't your fault. You are an outstanding detective. No one could have foreseen what happened," Holmes said, his tone softer now. More understanding.

Samuel had heard this excuse more often than he wanted.

Did people really believe this?

It was his fault. If he had acted faster, she would still be alive. Probably. Maybe.

"There is no shame in accepting help. And this is the only way I know how to offer my help to you," Holmes concluded.

"Thank you, Sir."

Samuel knew there was no saying "no" to him and this case. As long as he worked here, he'd have to take the scraps that were given to him. Like a street animal, he depended on what they were willing to toss his way.

"Are you still going to your meetings?"

"Yes." Samuel's eyes widened as he looked at his superior, who surely sensed the panic building in his subordinate.

"Don't worry, I have told no one."

Samuel swallowed hard, his skin itching all over. As much as Samuel tried to sabotage himself, losing his job right now would make everything worse.

"Thank you, Sir," he said quietly because he was thankful Holmes had kept it to himself.

"Thank me later. Right now I want you to go over to Richard Woodworth and solve this situation for me." Holmes pointed at the thin yellow file Samuel held on to and that suddenly weighed heavy in his hand.

The clock was ticking on this case and on his career.

Chapter 6 - The Tower

Stella

"YOU CAN'T JUST STORM in here," Gladys wheezed, trying to keep up with Stella.

Her father's lifelong secretary was a dinosaur in this office. In fact, she showed an uncanny resemblance to a T-Rex with her beady eyes, short arms, and sharp, claw-like fingernails, which she loved to dig into Stella's shoulders when she was a child. Gladys hadn't changed a bit. One would think age softens a person, but she had clearly ignored that memo.

"Watch me," Stella said.

"He is in an important meeting and cannot be disturbed...," puffed the T-Rex behind Stella.

She must have been well over her retirement age by now, but surprised Stella as she kept up with her. When Stella came to a stop, she almost got squished between Gladys' soft body and the hard door of her father's office.

"What's all this commotion?" Richard Woodworth demanded, opening the door. His eyes fixed on Stella first before they burned into the person behind her.

"I'm sorry, Sir. I tried to stop her," Gladys said, more docile than Stella would have expected from this short but vicious fossil.

In perfect Roman emperor style, Richard Woodworth dismissed her with a silent wave of his hand.

With a swift motion, he faced the men seated around the long conference table in their black suits and ties, and offered an apology for the interruption. Their eyes gaped wide with shock, as if they had never seen someone cause a scene before. Except for one.

The youngest man in this circle of grandfathers was someone Stella would recognize anywhere. Jeremy Evans had been the first and only boyfriend her father had approved of, and once that realization sank in, Stella promptly ended their relationship.

Jeremy looked at her with a slight frown creasing his otherwise smooth forehead. A combination of surprise and confusion.

Right back at you, Jeremy.

Jeremy had always wanted to make a name for himself, to have an illustrious career, and he was willing to do whatever it took to achieve that. Even if that meant dating the daughter of the most important businessman in town. Seeing him here in her father's office tower meant he had gotten what he wanted.

That asshole, Stella thought, commending her younger self for breaking up with someone who prioritized a seat next to her father over her.

"I'll be back in a minute," her father said before he closed the door and ended Stella's staring contest with a man she knew to wear braces and glasses as a teenager.

He was certainly no kid anymore. He fit perfectly into the panel of aging men deciding for others and getting paid exorbitant amounts of money to do so.

Her father gripped her arm, each finger tightening around her flesh. He dragged her to the next available office, swung the door open, and shoved her inside.

"When you are told I am in meetings, I am not available for your fits..."

"What's Jeremy doing here?" Stella cut in and silenced her father for a few beats.

The big white clock hanging on the wall, right above the door frame, ticked for exactly ten seconds before her father let out a breath.

"He works for me."

"Wow, that didn't take him long. Do you make him call you Daddy?" she asked with more resentment in her voice than she wanted.

"Do you really think I am going to discuss my hiring decisions with you?"

Stella wondered how Jeremy had weaseled his way to the top of her father's company. Also, why did this bother her? They had broken up when they were still kids. It shouldn't make her insides churn, but it did. Jeremy had been her first proper boyfriend, and she had really liked him. Maybe more than she wanted to admit to herself. Perhaps she had even loved him.

"Fine, that's not why I am here, anyway," Stella said, waving her hands in defeat. The past was the past.

Pointing to her right hand, her father asked, "What happened to your hand?"

Stella spread her fingers, the pain from punching a stranger still lingering on. Her knuckles had changed from her usual tanned golden brown to an irritated dark red.

Dried blood had crusted on her middle finger, where her skin had opened during her sleep again, leaving a few crimson dots on her pillow this morning.

"Nothing," she said, sliding her hand into her jeans pocket, hiding her injury.

Her father scoffed at her, shaking his head. He moved over to the small metal cart that held a decanter and two crystal glasses. A feature that came with every meeting room in this building. For her father, there was nothing sweeter than sealing a multi-million dollar deal with a good glass of bourbon.

"I see you haven't lost your impulsive behavior," he scolded her, and dropped an ice cube into one of the glasses next to the decanter.

He didn't offer one to her.

It was a fault in her father's eyes. Showing weakness through emotions. Like losing control. As much as she hated being anything like her father, Stella knew her need for control came from him.

"I went to the police," she said, ignoring his comment.

"Why would you do that?" he asked, his attention focused on the glass in front of him. He lifted the bourbon to his nose and smelled it before he took a sip.

"Because that's what you should have done." Her reproach came out louder than she had planned.

Her father turned his head and looked at Stella over his shoulder. "Don't tell me what I should or shouldn't have done. How often do I have to tell you that you are wasting your time? Your mother tried to end her life. That's all."

"We both know that's bullshit. There is more to it, and you will tell me what really happened."

The ice in his drink clinked against the crystal while her demand hung heavy in the air like a summer storm ready to pour down gallons of water.

"You don't know what you are talking about and you better stop this nonsense now."

The darkness in his voice rumbled towards her, and for a moment, words failed her. Something in the back of her skull pulsated. A small red warning light buzzed in her head, questioning her beliefs.

She wouldn't try to kill herself, would she?

With an invisible shake of her head, Stella silenced the shy voice inside her.

"Why? Because you can't stand the fact it was your fault? Again? Even if she did try to kill herself, it would be because of you. Everything you touch turns to shit, and people want to get as far away from you as possible"

His grip tightened around his glass as he threw his head back and finished the rest of his bourbon. When he dropped his glass back onto the cart, he held on to the rim, the tips of his fingers turning white under his firm grasp.

He turned slowly, his eyes as dark as his tone had been. "Keep your voice down. We aren't at a Chinese wet market."

She knew she had him right where she wanted. Cornered inside his world, creating a scene at the place he controlled, where people could see the reality of his imperfect life. Stella assumed each employee knew, though. That they had survived one or many outbursts of her father. But sticking up to Goliath wasn't as easy as David had made it seem. People were afraid of her father, a man who could make or break you and was fully aware of the power he wielded over the peasants in his life.

"C'mon, I can't be the first to tell you the truth," She pushed, closing the short distance between them.

"You are a nuisance."

"If my mother dies, it's on your hands. The same way you have killed Jonathan."

"Enough!" He raised his voice the same time his right hand went up.

Stella knew he was about to slap her with the back of his hand. He had never used his palm when she was younger, and she doubted that this etiquette had changed over the years. This way, he could always say he had never laid a hand on her.

In a reflex, Stella closed her eyes, prepared for the familiar feel of her father's temper. Would it hurt as much as it had when she was younger? Would he break something again, or were her bones stronger now?

"Mr. Woodworth!"

Her father's hand missed Stella by a hair, hitting a void. His eyes moved over her head to the interruption standing in his office door.

Following her father's gaze, Stella turned and her knuckles twitched when she saw the face that belonged to the voice. His dark unruly brown hair, verging on black and the set of steel-blue eyes, wasn't what made her almost choke on her spit. She had seen handsome men, but this one wore a purple ring around his left eye that fit Stella's fist just perfectly.

"Who are you?" Richard Woodworth demanded.

"My name is Detective Green. This is my colleague Detective Bennett—"

"Richard, I'm sorry to disturb you. I thought they had called you before we came over?" the man standing next to Detective Green blurted, going straight towards Stella's father with an outstretched hand and apologetic wrinkles on a forehead that would soon grow further into a receding hairline.

Both men shook hands in a friendly manner. Stella was surprised to see the change on her father's face but not as much as Detective Green, who stood silently behind, gaping at the scenario.

"No, they haven't, Jim."

Detective Jim Bennett glanced an unapproving look at his colleague Detective Green.

"As I was saying, I'm sorry. But don't worry, we'll be out of your hair in no time."

"Good, I have a busy schedule."

"You know each other?" Stella threw into the room, causing all three men to look at her.

A second wave of surprise washed over Detective Green's face when he scanned her face, and put his black eye and her bruised knuckles together. But instead of addressing her, he focused on Richard Woodworth.

"We are following up on a report we received about your wife, Mr. Woodworth."

"Jim, this is ridiculous. Who is this child?" Richard Woodworth asked with an indifferent nod towards

Detective Green, who looked as though he'd just been punched in the other eye.

"Sorry, Richard, but as a formality we need to ask you a few questions," Detective Bennett said.

Detective Green's jaw tensed, and Stella felt a little sorry for him, having to deal with both her and her father. Hopefully, a black eye and a bruised ego would be the only wounds he'd carry away from meeting the Woodworths. Based on her own experience, though, she doubted it.

When Detective Green spoke again, it was clear and strong. "I'm leading this investigation and if you want to get back to your busy schedule, I suggest you focus on answering my questions instead of insulting me. You aren't the only one who needs to get back to his desk, Sir."

Stella couldn't stop the smile from gracing her lips. It was rare for people not to feel intimidated by her father when they first met him.

"And I assume you are Miss Woodworth, the one who reported an assault on her mother, right?" Detective Green continued, now fully focussed on Stella.

"Yes," she replied with a nod. "My mother didn't try to commit suicide."

Her words had barely left her mouth when Detective Bennett rolled his eyes in the same way her father always did. It hit Stella right then that these men would take nothing she said seriously. Perhaps she had made a mistake going to the police. Her father's nails deeply dug into the important circles of society. Convincing anyone to listen to her would be harder than she had thought. Luckily, she was used to fighting against her father's influence. And she'd do it with or without their help.

"Why do you think that?" Detective Green asked while pulling a small notepad from the inside pocket of his weathered brown leather jacket.

"My mother doesn't have any reason to commit suicide—"

"You haven't been home in years. You don't know your mother's state of mind," her father interrupted and directed his next words to Detective Bennett. "Beth hasn't been doing well lately, if you must know. I have been trying to keep all this within the family, but her mind isn't what it used to be. She is depressed, hysterical sometimes, but I had her see a therapist who prescribed her something to calm her episodes. I fear she might not have taken her medication properly and I feel terrible that this happened on my watch."

"Don't say that, Richard. This isn't your fault," Detective Bennett said, reaching out for Richard Woodworth's shoulder, but stopped short as he recoiled.

No one touched Richard Woodworth without his permission.

Stella shook her head in disgust. *What a formidable actor her father was.* He almost had her fooled, and certainly had Detective Bennett on his side. *Pathetic.*

"That's why I am here. To make sure it wasn't anyone's fault, Mr. Woodworth."

A snicker escaped Stella's lips before she could swallow it. She couldn't remember when anyone but her had insulted her father that eloquently.

"Please continue, Miss Woodworth," Detective Green encouraged her.

She cleared her throat, trying to find the right words that would convince someone to trust her without a full range of evidence backing up her theory. Looking into Detective Green's questioning eyes, Stella went for the obvious. A confident half-truth.

"Yes, I've been living abroad for a couple of years, but I have regular contact with my mother. We talk over the phone or video chat and I have never seen her in any state my father is describing. If her health had been on the line in the past, I would know or would have been informed about it by Grace."

The white lie about how much contact she had had with her mother came easy. Stella had convinced herself so many times her mother was fine and that she did enough to stay in touch, it almost felt like the truth.

"Sorry, who is Grace?" Detective Green asked, looking up from his notepad.

"She is my maid."

"Housekeeper of over thirty years, you mean," Stella interrupted her father. "She has been with our family since I was born. Grace was the one who informed me about my mother's hospitalization, unlike my father, who deemed it more important to go to work than to stay with his sick wife." She shot her father an icy stare that ricocheted off his bulletproof ego.

"You don't know what you are talking about, Stella!" Her father stepped in again, but this time Stella continued speaking.

"Being married to my father might have taken its toll on her, but if she had wanted to end her life, she would have done it years ago."

"I will not have you tell lies about how your mother and I lived!"

"Mr. Woodworth! I recommend you let your daughter finish."

Under different circumstances, Stella would buy this man a drink and applaud him for his skill of shutting her father up. Even Detective Bennett looked shell-shocked.

"She had more reasons to kill herself at the beginning of her marriage than now. My mother wasn't depressed. She has actually been quite happy. I don't know why my father would make up a mental struggle."

Detective Green nodded attentively, scribbling down her words on his pad before he turned to her father again.

"Did you and your wife ever argue, Mr. Woodworth? Did it ever get physical?" he asked out of the blue and all hell broke loose.

"Samuel!" Detective Bennett shouted, followed by her father's outrage, "Is this how you train your detectives, Jim? Harassing innocent and hardworking people?"

A smirk formed around Detective Green's mouth and Stella recognized his attempt to poke her father. She had used this strategy herself so many times. How could she not have seen this?

"No one said anything about you not being innocent."

Samuel let the sentence linger in the air, waiting for her father to react. Maybe he had more backbone than she thought? Unfortunately, she couldn't say as much about

Detective Bennett, who shot a silencing glance at the man who had taken on her father.

Her father's stare could have cut through steel, but Detective Green's smile persisted and eventually won the standoff when her father drew back.

"I think we are done here, *Detective*."

"I'm so sorry, Richard," Detective Bennett apologized again, like so many other people did in her father's presence, even though Samuel had done what he was trained to do. His job. And apparently he wasn't done yet because he wouldn't let her father dismiss him like this without having the last word.

"Mr. Woodworth, we are following standard procedures, and we will let you know if we need more information from you. In the meantime, we appreciate your cooperation in uncovering the truth about what happened to your wife."

He held out his hand but took it back when it hung in the air for too long. Richard Woodworth wouldn't lower himself to shaking the hand of the man who got under his skin.

Before Detective Green turned to leave, he addressed Richard Woodworth one last time. "Oh, and I think it would be best if you didn't plan a trip outside the country while the investigation is ongoing."

Stella saw the volcano erupt in her father's head. He fumed, and she half expected him to spit hot magma. But instead of his scalp exploding and a pyroclastic cloud of anger turning Samuel to ash, he took Detective Bennett's hand and shook it.

"Will I see you in the tee-box on Sunday?" he asked.

"Sure, I wouldn't miss it. Marianne and I will keep Beth in our prayers. I hope she'll recover soon."

"Thank you, Jim. I appreciate it."

The two men walked towards the office door that had opened thanks to Gladys' impeccable skill of listening in on conversations through the door. Before Samuel followed, he reached into his inside pocket, the same where he had kept his notepad, and withdrew a white paper card he held out to Stella.

"If there is anything else you remember, please call me."

Stella took the card and put it in her jeans pocket without looking at it.

"Are you sticking around for a bit?" he asked.

Stella was unsure how to answer this question. She had a return ticket to Hong Kong leaving in a week and sticking around was the last thing she wanted, but she couldn't leave her mother behind. She needed to know if there was even a sliver of truth to her father's accusation or if it was just another lie of his. If he was right, however, the truth might be even more harrowing than the fact that another member of her family had wanted to die.

"Yes. I'll be here for a while."

They shook hands, and he winked at her with his black eye before leaving, making Stella wonder how seriously this man would really take her case.

Chapter 7 - The Colleague

Samuel

WASHING HIS HANDS UNDER the cold water from the precinct's bathroom sink, Samuel stared at his face, trying to make sense of what had happened.

How the hell did he end up meeting the woman who was the reason for his black eye and that lingering headache, again? Not in a million years would he have expected to see her after their last encounter, nevermind having to deal with her in a case that could make or break his career.

He'd spent the night doing some research on Stella Woodworth. There wasn't much information available about her, aside from a few paparazzi photos and tabloid articles from her partying days in Manhattan a decade ago. Nothing out of the ordinary for a rebellious teen, though. The sensationalistic headlines had stopped right after she had left the US. Since then, all he could find were snippets on X and WeChat about her career as a PI in Hong Kong. If he wanted to know more, he would need to get one of his colleagues to help him translate Cantonese into something he could understand.

Who was that fucking asshole his captain made him deal with? After the brief encounter with Richard Woodworth, that didn't take more than half an hour, he had quickly and easily made it on a list of people Samuel didn't want to deal with ever again. He had a strong dislike for people who thought they were better than others just because they were born into a family of money and managed not to lose it all. He knew the type of man Stella's father was and Richard Woodworth lived up to his name: he was a dick. Men like him were driven by power, taking everything they wanted and leaving a wasteland in their wake.

He wasn't surprised his wife attempted to commit suicide. And it sure looked that way, even though his daughter had a different opinion. It was always difficult for children to accept that their parents were human, ordinary, and struggling like everyone else.

In the depths of his coffee-filled gut, a feeling started to grow, something he couldn't shake off. Samuel had observed Stella Woodworth when she talked. Her anger and frustration seemed real. In contrast, her father wore this motionless mask that wavered only around his eyes, a millisecond of a nervous tic, whenever his daughter opened her mouth to speak about her family. Richard Woodworth was anxious.

It was the same instinctive feeling he'd had in the past and that made him rise through the ranks at the beginning of his career. Something felt weird about this case.

This brought him to the third, and for the moment, last issue he had. His colleague Jim Bennett had been with the force for decades but who behaved like it was his first day on the job.

Samuel dried his hands with three paper towels and threw them in the trash on his way back to his desk. He couldn't understand why Holmes had sent Jim with him. Jim knew Richard Woodworth. And while Samuel wanted to get this over with quickly, having to work with Jim on this sat badly with him. His colleague wouldn't be able to deal with this situation from an objective point of view. He had made that clear as soon as they had left Richard Woodworth's office, scolding him like a child on Fifth Avenue, expressing his disapproval at his treatment of Richard Woodworth. What the actual fuck! They were supposed to follow a list of simple instructions, get their answers, type up an unimportant report, and be done with it.

Samuel was about to open the Woodworth file on his computer when he saw Jim leave Holmes' office and stroll over to him with a sly smile on his lips.

What now?

"Green! The Captain wants to see you," Jim shouted louder than necessary for the two feet of linoleum flooring that lay between them.

Everyone in the open plan space looked up from their desks, probably wondering what he had fucked up now. The pity in their eyes was worse than their judgment and Samuel's throat cried for the smoothness of a bourbon or whiskey.

Instead of reaching into his locked drawer to take a sip of the flask he had stashed for emergencies, Samuel made his way over to Holmes' office. He expected his boss to ask for an update on his assignment, but when he entered the captain's office, he looked into a grim face.

Fucking Jim!

Samuel knew better than to ask if anything was wrong. He had seen this look on his boss' face plenty of times. The vein on Holmes' forehead pulsated like it was about to burst through his skin. Samuel closed the door behind him, mentally preparing for whatever his captain was about to say to him.

"Sit your ass down and explain to me why Richard Woodworth is threatening to file an official complaint against one of my detectives?"

Word seemed to travel fast in Richard Woodworth's world, with a direct line to the police.

"Well, I—"

"And why am I hearing about your strange behavior from Jim and not from you?" Holmes went on, two fingers on his temple, as if to calm his vein through a pressure point.

Samuel waited for him to add more, but he remained silent, simply staring at him.

"You mean when Jim came running to you to snitch? I am sure this was the fastest he has been in years."

"Don't give me your smug bullshit. You know exactly what I'm talking about and Jim was absolutely within his rights to come to me."

Yes, he had poked the man, but he had done nothing he wouldn't do to any other person of interest.

"What were you thinking?" Holmes sighed. "I asked you to do this quietly, not imply Richard Woodworth had anything to do with his wife's accident." Holmes' tone carried disappointment, and it hit Samuel right in the chest.

"I'm following protocol, like always."

"You made him feel like he tried to kill his wife."

"Everyone is a potential suspect."

"He is not a violent man."

"He was about to hit his daughter before I came in," Samuel said. "I saw him. He had his hand raised."

Holmes interlaced his fingers on his desk and let out another sigh.

"The man might lose his wife, Samuel, and he has been through a rough patch with her mental health. It's understandable that he might be on edge. I am not saying he wouldn't get loud in an argument. He can be an intimidating man, but he is a good man."

How could he be so certain?

"If Jim and I hadn't come in, he would have physically hurt his daughter. He is clearly not as calm as you think."

"Jim told me you walked into a heated argument but that nothing but words were thrown around."

"Since when do you trust *Jim* more than me?" It hurt Samuel to think even Holmes had lost his trust in him. Why would he have given him this case if he didn't trust him?

"Are you sure you are up for this, Samuel? You are feeling ... well enough?"

The way Holmes looked at him, searching his face for anything that could be obviously wrong with him, stunned Samuel. He straightened and cleared his throat.

"I am fully capable of handling this case."

Holmes' head nodded, but he didn't seem sure yet.

"Can I give you some advice?" Holmes asked.

"Of course."

"I know you are a brilliant detective."

Oh boy.

"I've seen you in action for longer than I can remember, and you are more than capable—"

But?

"But I think your usual strategy of going head first won't be as effective this time. Richard responds better to an objective conversation than accusations."

Sure, and I drink a mug of mate before going to bed.

"That's why I picked you."

"And Jim." Samuel snorted.

Holmes' answer came a few seconds delayed and with a small headshake. "You know I don't send officers out alone."

Samuel knew that. It was Holmes' way of making sure no one got hurt.

"Jim is friends with Richard Woodworth," Samuel stated, but Holmes chuckled and waved a hand.

"Everyone thinks they are friends with Richard. Jim plays the same golf course sometimes and they occasionally meet. Richard is aware of Jim, I'm sure, but I wouldn't go as far as thinking they were friends."

For someone who is merely an acquaintance, they surely were friendly and knew a lot about each other, Samuel thought to himself.

Holmes' smile returned. "I have no problem taking Jim off your back, if you are sure you can handle this."

There it was again. Was that why Holmes had paired him with Jim? Because he was afraid he needed help? In case he went off the rails?

As if he had said it straight to his captain's face, Holmes continued, "You follow rules and don't let what others think influence your judgment. You trust evidence. That's why I put you on the case. Nothing else."

Isn't that what I am doing?

"Play nice. It'll get you a long way," Holmes concluded his fatherly advice with a complementary, supportive smile on his lips.

With his eyes fixed on his hands, folded motionless on his lap, Samuel had to admit that Holmes could be on to something. Different characters required different approaches. He could play nice, especially if it meant closing this case sooner rather than later.

"Now, do you have any evidence that is pointing towards anything but attempted suicide?"

Samuel shifted uncomfortably in his seat. He didn't.

"Not yet, but I feel that..."

"Jesus Christ, Samuel. Please don't tell me you have a hunch? Hunches are just that. Nothing else. We need evidence."

"How about he is an arrogant asshole?" Samuel blurted and received a scolding shake of Holmes' head.

"I know he isn't everyone's cup of tea, but it doesn't matter if you like or dislike him. You go by evidence and if everything points to suicide, it probably is."

Samuel knew that, hell, he even believed it himself. Maybe Holmes was right to pair him with someone. Perhaps he had let his feelings for Richard Woodworth take over, against his better judgment.

"According to his daughter, the housekeeper said there were no signs of any mental health issues."

"And you have talked to the housekeeper?"

Samuel's shoulders slumped when he shook his head.

"Did you talk to her doctor?"

Samuel swallowed loudly before his head turned from left to right for the smallest shake possible. He knew exactly what was going through Holmes' head. He really was a fuckup.

Holmes leaned closer, his elbows on his desk. "Listen Sam, I know you went through something unimaginable last year," he whispered. "Something none of us want to go through and only a few can relate to."

Samuel lowered his head, focusing on his shoelaces instead of listening to Holmes. He couldn't bear to hear Holmes pity him again, bringing up the worst day of his life, as an explanation why he had turned into such a loser. Even if it was true.

Once again, the memory manifested in front of his eyes, the faint picture of that wooden trap door, hidden under an expensive rug, and leading into that stuffy basement. He squeezed them shut, hoping to forget the disturbing image of pale gray arms, a filthy white dress, and small red rat bites left on young skin. How could he have let her down so badly?

His hands twitched.

He needed a drink.

"Perhaps I was too quick to give you this assignment. Maybe it's too early for you? I just wanted to help, but I can take you off the case if it makes you uncomfortable," Holmes offered.

Samuel couldn't let another person down. He needed a win and proof to Holmes and to himself that he wasn't useless. He could do this. He wouldn't disappoint Holmes.

"No Sir, I'm fine. And I appreciate your support."

Holmes nodded approvingly. "Good. And Sam, if you need to talk, I am here for you."

Sam swallowed hard. "I know. Thank you."

"Well, then that's settled. I'll take Jim off your back. Now go and finish this. Quietly!" Holmes commanded with a lightness in his voice, Samuel found hard to copy.

"Yes, Sir."

He left Holmes' office and went straight to his desk, where he sat down and fidgeted with his drawer. His hands shook in anticipation, but before he opened the bottom drawer where his temporary salvation lay hidden under a pile of documents, someone knocked on his desk. Samuel turned and stared at Jim, knuckles still on his desk, both eyebrows raised.

"What do you want?" Samuel asked.

Jim's eyes darted to the drawer and back to Samuel. "How did it go in there?"

"What do you think?"

"You know I did this for you? You can't just go around accusing people of crimes. That's not how we do things."

A panicked squeal escaped Jim's throat when Samuel jumped up from his seat and stepped right in front of him, hands twitching at his sides.

He didn't know what he had done to offend Jim. He clearly had an agenda. So while breaking his nose might have done his face a favor, it wouldn't have benefited Samuel's career.

"Fuck you, Jim!" Samuel whispered before he grabbed his jacket from the back of his chair and headed towards the exit, while his flask lay untouched in his drawer.

Chapter 8 - The Promise

Samuel

NURSE CANDACE GAVE Samuel a smile that could brighten up a tornado stricken sky. With her fiery red hair, she looked more like a Viking princess than a healthcare worker. Her Irish lilt made Samuel imagine her standing on cliffs, with her red hair flowing wild like fire, overlooking the rough Atlantic.

"Ah, you know, sometimes my line of work gets physical, but if you want to keep people safe, you need to step up," Samuel said pointing to his eye that had changed color again over night and shone bright purple with specks of emerald green, like Candace's sparkling eyes. "But you should see the other guy."

As intended, his comment made her laugh again, and Samuel wondered if he should ask her for her phone number. She had his business card and could call him, but Samuel was a bit old-fashioned when asking a woman out on a date. It had been a while for him since he last was with a woman. After the accident last year, he couldn't think about anything else but the guilt he felt. Perhaps it was time, and Candace seemed fun and uncomplicated.

He was about to go for it when the sound of raised voices pulled him back to the present, making him shift his focus to the unfolding drama.

"This is ridiculous. I'm her daughter."

Samuel recognized the voice instantly. The edge in it told him Stella Woodworth must have gone through a rough night as well. He wasn't surprised. In the end, it was her mother who lay in an induced coma, possibly never waking from it.

"I'm very sorry Mrs.—" a weakish male voice started.

"Miss!"

"Miss Woodworth. We have clear protocols to follow and we cannot let you in there—"

"Is that hospital policy or a demand from Richard Woodworth?"

"I am sorry, but our hands are tied."

Samuel chuckled at this uneven tug-of-war and felt sorry for the pale doctor. Poor guy didn't know what was in store for him with Stella Woodworth.

"She is my mother. I have a right to see her."

"I understand, but I can't let you into her room. Maybe if you talked to your father. Surely he'll change his mind."

Samuel expected Stella to force her way into her mother's room. Instead, however, he watched her glance at her mother and end the conversation with the doctor by grunting at him rather than giving him a black eye.

After the irritated doctor had stomped past him, grumbling something about it being too early to deal with this shit, a frustrated Stella Woodworth followed. When she recognized him leaning against the nursing station, her face turned even more grim.

This would be fun.

He waved two fingers in a casual greeting while she strode towards him, ready for the next battle. Definitely not a viking princess like Candace. Stella was a warrior, and Samuel had to snicker at the thought of who might be her next victim. Most likely him.

"Miss Woodworth. Sounds like your morning hasn't turned out like you expected."

"Says the man whose face looks like a ripe eggplant," Stella replied.

Touché.

"He had to fight off an attacker. Isn't that heroic?"

Bless you Candace.

Stella crossed her arms over her black v-neck t-shirt and gave her breasts a nice lift. Not that Samuel thought she needed a lift. They seemed absolutely fine to him.

She looked at him with raised eyebrows. "Oh, is that how you got this?"

"Occupational hazard," he replied smugly.

Stella tilted her head and smiled at him. "Looks to me like you pissed off the wrong person."

He nodded at her hand. "I'm sure you know all about a good fight."

Candace's eyes followed. "Oh Miss, are you hurt? Do you need to see a doc—"

"I'm fine, thank you..." Stella interrupted.

Her eyes darted to the nurse's chest, trying to locate the name tag hidden under a braid of thick red hair—something Samuel thought would be fun to pull in certain scenarios. He shook his head and told himself to snap out of it.

"Candace," he answered for her.

"Okay then," Candace said to Stella before her attention went back to Samuel. "Let me know if you want me to take a look at your eye." Candace winked at him and slid over a piece of paper with ten digits written next to her name and a full stop in the shape of a small heart before she left the two of them.

Out of the corner of his eye, Samuel saw Stella roll her eyes when he placed Candace's note in the inside pocket of his jacket.

"Shouldn't you be working instead of flirting with the staff? How is that helping my mother?"

"Don't tell me you have never used your charm to get information?"

"If by *information* you mean someone's bra size, no, I can't say I have."

"Not even to get out of a speeding ticket?" he asked doubtfully.

When she didn't retort immediately, he knew she had.

"I don't need to flirt my way out of speeding tickets."

"Sure sounded like your conversation could have used some."

Her face turned towards her mother's room. "My father told them I cannot see her."

During their first encounter, Richard Woodworth didn't strike him as the father of the year, but barring his daughter from seeing her mother was a powerful message. What was the nature of the family dynamics within the Woodworth household?

"Why would he do that?" Samuel asked.

"Because he is a tyrant who likes to make other people's lives miserable."

There were always two sides to every story. "You weren't awfully nice to him yesterday."

"You've met my father. He is an asshole." Stella said.

While he agreed with her on that one, he didn't say so.

"That doesn't sound like the happy, supportive daughter I expected him to have."

"Well, you can't choose the family you are born into."

He allowed her bitter remark to linger, wondering what had transpired to cause such strong animosity towards her father. Was he the reason she had moved to China?

"You're a private investigator, right?" he asked, wanting to know more about the real Stella Woodworth.

"Yes, but in Hong Kong. I don't have any authority here."

"That's why I'm here. The police. As a family member, you shouldn't get involved, anyway. But as a PI, you know this, so..." He let his unfinished sentence hang in the air, hoping for Stella to bite.

"If you think I had anything to do with this, you are an even worse detective than you seem."

"Ouch, way to make friends," he said with a smile, holding his right hand to his heart as if she had just shot him.

"I don't need you to be my friend. I need you to do your job."

This woman was a piece of work and Samuel knew where she got it from. Richard Woodworth's genes shone through brightly and undeniably. Despite her sharp tongue, there was something about Stella that piqued Samuel's curiosity—perhaps it was the fire in her eyes, or the way she refused to back down.

"Isn't that what I am doing, Miss Woodworth?"

"Your job is to figure out why my father insists on calling this a suicide. He is hiding something. And don't give me this bullshit of everyone being a suspect. If you have done a little work on me, you'll know I just arrived in New York and wasn't even near my mother. I'm not a suspect." Stella retorted, her voice edged with frustration.

Indeed, Samuel knew all of this already. He had spent the evening looking into the family around Richard Woodworth. Stella had been in Hong Kong when her mother attempted to kill herself. The only people near her were her husband, their housekeeper, and a few other staff. But Richard Woodworth had a clean alibi for that night, having spent hours at a charity event his wife had declined to join in writing. Not for the first time, either. In fact, Beth Woodworth's absence from recent events, along with her husband's claims about her declining mental health, supported she may have attempted suicide.

Regardless, he needed to do what he was here for. Get his hands on her medical records. Once Dr. Abelson, the assigned doctor to Beth Woodworth, returned to his office, he'd have a chat with him about her.

Unfortunately, the frustrated woman in front of him wasn't as patient as him. But right now he couldn't get her any answers, which she clearly saw as a character flaw.

"From where I am standing, and with the report from the EMT, everything points towards a suicide attempt. Nevertheless, I'll have a chat with your mother's doctor later and will fill you in afterwards, if that helps."

Her next comment scotched his attempt to extend an olive branch.

"Oh, you mean the same doctor that overlooked signs of strangulation on my mother's neck? Did you see that in your *report*?"

He had not.

The yellow file Holmes had given him was short and did not include this detail. If there was any truth to Stella's statement, though, her mother's hospital file would show it. Right?

"That's what I thought," Stella continued. "My father has pumped a ton of money into this hospital. He has referred all his high value clients to this clinic. My father practically owns this place. Do you really think anything happens here without his knowledge? If this minor fact about my mother is not in your report, then he kept it out. You should ask yourself why my father would want to hide this!"

Samuel didn't have any reason to believe her. Nothing she said was based on facts. For all he knew, this was a daughter trying to find someone to blame for her mother's illness.

"Miss Woodworth, I know you don't believe me, but I guarantee you I'm taking your mother's case seriously. I will do everything I can to find out what happened to her. Trust me," he assured her.

"Sure. The same way your colleague did his job by licking my father's ass squeaky clean?"

"Jim is known to be a good ass-licker," Sam replied with a smirk, but Stella's face stayed hard, clearly not big into jokes. Or perhaps just not his jokes.

"How can I trust anyone when my father controls everyone? Who is going to hold him accountable for his actions when his best friends are high-ranking officials?"

Samuel didn't count Jim as anywhere close to high ranking, but he understood her genuine worry. He thought about Holmes and how important it seemed to him not to put too much pressure on Stella's father. They knew each other better than he had led on and were more than just acquaintances. Samuel, however, knew his captain would never cross certain lines, even for friends, and the law was one of them.

Stella's worry didn't go by unnoticed, though. He knew what fear sounded like, and Stella was afraid for her mother.

"You don't have to trust me, but I'm still giving you my word that I will find out what happened to your mother. If it was attempted suicide or not. And if your father was involved in any way, I will make sure he gets what he deserves. I don't care who he is. No one is above the law."

"Then you really don't know Richard Woodworth," Stella said.

Samuel suddenly shivered. The weight of his promise to Stella hung heavy on Samuel's shoulders. What if she was right and he wouldn't be able to keep his promise again?

Chapter 9 - The Letter

Stella

AFTER HER UNPLEASANT run-in with Detective Green, Stella was convinced she couldn't rely on the police to help her figure out what really happened to her mother. How could a man who was flirting with the nurse instead of asking questions be beneficial to her case?

She'd also gotten a faint whiff of alcohol off him. She used to have a colleague in Hong Kong who started his day with a shot of baijiu and even if he hadn't been drinking for a day or two, that old alcohol smell lingered on—settled in his hair, sweated out through his skin. Detective Green smelled the same way, and while she wasn't against the occasional early morning tipple, she couldn't trust this guy to keep it together. Also, Detective Green's familiarity with the bartender and the bar where they had first met hinted at a certain relationship with alcohol.

This man liked his drink, and she needed someone with a logical mind who could put two and two together.

She'd have to do it herself, as usual.

Hence, Stella had given her assistant in Hong Kong a call to let her know she would be in New York a little while longer and had to hold back on her current clients. She rescheduled meetings and made sure one of her trusted employees was looking after the important clients. She hated letting people down and not following through on her promises, but at least this way, their cases would still be dealt with. An exception Stella hoped to be a one-off.

Then she gave her friend Agnes a call. Blonde, curly-haired surfer girl Agnes lived in San Diego now, but they had met years ago in China when Stella had just arrived and was trying to figure out what to do with her life without having her father's oppressive shadow hanging over her. Finally free to make her own decisions, she had bounced from one job to the next, had learnt Cantonese and had met a colorful bunch of people until she ended up with the police force. That's where she met Agnes and they had been best friends ever since. After it had become difficult for foreigners in the Hong Kong police, they had made the logical choice to join a private investigations team together.

Once Stella had enough confidence and contacts to open her own office, she had offered Agnes to stick together again, but Agnes had always dreamt of returning to the US one day. Their ways parted, but they had stayed in touch ever since. It felt natural to reach out to her to see what possibilities Stella would have to get access to documents in the US and if her friend could help her.

"Let me make a few calls and I'll get back to you in a little while, okay?" Agnes said, and Stella missed her friend more than she thought she would.

"That's great, A. I really appreciate it." The pet name for her friend bounced off her lips easily.

"Sure, anything for you. How long are you gonna be in the big Apple?"

Stella sighed. "Not sure. I hope not for too long, but I also can't just leave her here. I owe it to her after she let me leave all those years ago."

Stella didn't have it easy after she left the US and got started in Hong Kong. When she arrived at Hong Kong International, she couldn't even withdraw money from her own account at the airport. All thanks to her father, who had removed her from the family account and left her without financial support. If it hadn't been for her mother, who had opened an account for her under her own name before she left and transferred a lump sum to her, she might not have been able to get started in the beginning. Stella knew her mother must have paid a high price for doing that. No one went behind her father's back.

"How is your mom?"

Agnes had never met Stella's mother, but she knew about her struggles with her parents and the sacrifices her mother had made. Agnes had a better picture of Beth Woodworth than most people.

"Not good. No one knows if she will wake up again and the people I am dealing with all seem to have something better to do than take care of her."

"I am so sorry, Stel."

"Me, too."

Through the silence on the West Coast side of the line, Stella could hear Agnes think.

"I know you want to say something, so spit it out," she said and got a heartfelt laugh in return.

"You still know me too well. I know you don't want to hear this, but don't do this alone. Yes, you are tough and capable and all that, but you are dealing with your mom and your whole family. You know what we used to tell our clients."

"Personal connections cloud our judgment." Of course, she remembered. She knew that being personally connected to a case made you weak. Somehow, even the strongest people missed the most obvious things when it came to their own family. But Stella was different. She had an unconventional relationship with her family.

"I can't trust these people, A," Stella said.

"At some point, you'll have to let your guard down a little and ask for help. That's how you met me, remember? And that worked out great, didn't it?"

Agnes' positivity had always been infectious and on point. How could someone not smile at the way she lived life to its fullest?

"I still wonder if you drugged me that night at the club. How else could I have agreed to go sing karaoke with you for six hours?" Stella smiled at the memory and moment that paved the way to their beautiful friendship.

"We are where we are and I wouldn't want to change a thing. But honestly, please don't shut people out."

Why couldn't everyone be like her? Then it would be so much easier to deal with people.

"I'll do my best, I promise."

"Anyway, let me know if you want to stop over in California on your way back. Or even better, move to San Diego and let us do our thing here together. You'd love it here. I'll even teach you how to surf."

Stella smiled into the phone. It wasn't the first time Agnes had proposed such a thing and part of her was tempted to accept. Life in Hong Kong had its perks, but it was a tough place to be at the same time. Hong Kong bureaucracy was hard to adapt to, and it took on more Chinese characteristics with every passing year. But she wasn't ready to return to the country her father lived in. She was glad to have an ocean between them.

"I might be able to stop by for a quick visit."

Stella held the phone off her ear when a loud and excited squeal reverberated through it.

"Great. You'll always have a place here." Euphoria dripped off Agnes and sank into Stella.

"Thanks. I love you."

"Love you, too, Stel. Talk to you soon. Bye."

"Bye."

Stella hung up and pocketed her phone in her jacket. She straightened herself and took a deep breath, getting mentally ready for the next thing on her list. Her watch showed two in the afternoon. If her father's schedule was still the same as it had been, he'd be at Ferrypoint right now. While others went to church on a Sunday morning, the golf course was his temple, where he could meet his buddies and make business deals. At least this should give her enough time to look around her childhood home. Her father was hiding something and she would find it.

The elevator pinged before the doors opened right into the hallway. She was surprised the doorman had let her up that easily. He must have been new because, a mere glance of her family name on her passport, had been sufficent to grant her entry with no further questions. This would most likely be his last day. Once her father figured out he let her up without as much as calling him, he'd get rid of the potential security threat. Stella felt sorry for the young guy, not knowing what was coming for him.

She entered quietly. There was no other sound than her beating heart filling the empty space. She didn't expect to be welcomed by Grace. Her father had fired Grace right after her meeting with him and the two police officers. After all these years, this was where he drew the line? Getting rid of Grace because she had told her that her own mother was in the hospital. He had fired people in the past, more often than Stella could remember, but Grace had been there since her mother had been pregnant with Jonathan. It was strange that he'd cut ties with her now, unless he was afraid Grace knew something about her mother.

But why not keep her close then instead? Stella wondered. She'd checked on Grace, and offered to help her in any way she could. Grace had been quiet and quick on the phone, already looking for a new job. She'd give Grace a few days to come to terms with what had happened before picking her brain again about her mother.

Unsure what to look for exactly, she started walking around in what should have been a happy and warm place for children to grow up. Where was everyone else? Her father might have hired no one new yet, but he used to have a daily cleaner scrubbing the floors and surfaces until they sparkled. His driver was with him, but what about the handyman? The fewer people, the better. However, this also meant that she had to act fast. One of his minions could just be on an errand run for him and return any second.

She stopped in front of a closed, dark brown door. Her fingers curled around the shiny golden doorknob and turned it. When she entered her old bedroom, she was catapulted back into her childhood. She stood in the doorway and looked right at the *KISS* poster she had put up just to annoy her father. Everything was exactly the same as on the day she had left New York almost two decades ago.

Slowly, she moved over to her bed, that was half covered by the yellow quilt her mother had made for her sixteenth birthday. She lay down, the wooden frame sighed under her weight, and rested her head on the freshly washed white pillow that smelled of lavender. Did her mother really have this washed regularly, just in case?

When she let her fingers run over the soft fabric, a wave of anger rushed through Stella. That her childhood had been so hard, that her brother had died, that she had to run away, that she left her baby sister behind. She clenched her fists, seething with anger at her mother's refusal to move on.

The air suddenly felt thin. A mixture of memories and guilt took her breath. Stella got up, rubbed her tired eyes and left her bedroom without looking back. She went right to where the other bedrooms were, and while the mansion seemed unchanged, one important thing was not how she remembered it. She stood in the quiet hallway, looking at her sister's bedroom to her left. Jonathan's was next to that. Both doors were closed, like they always used to be.

But to her right, the door to the guest bedroom was slightly ajar, allowing Stella a look inside. And right there, in the middle of the floor, lay clothes that belonged to her mother. She knew immediately that at some point in the past, her parents had started to sleep in separate bedrooms.

It might sound trivial, but it was a big deal in the Woodworth house. Back in school, Stella had a friend whose parents couldn't share the same bed because of a snoring issue. But her own parents were old-fashioned. They sucked it up and played pretend for the entire world. Even themselves.

That her mother had moved bedrooms meant she had revolted against her father, even if it was in the small space of a bedroom. Stella wondered what else might have changed in her parent's marriage. What wasn't she aware of, and did she know her parents, or had she been gone for too long?

She reached out her hand and pushed the door open. Stella frowned when instead of looking at meticulously folded pants and sweaters or neatly hanging dresses and blouses in the closet, she stared at a few pairs of pants and blouses carelessly dropped on the gray carpet floor. One of her mother's drawers lay open, exposing a chaotic mix of underwear and socks. And while Beth Woodworth would have never left a room looking like this, her mother had always lived life in the Marie Kondo style. Grace had probably grabbed the first things she could find and thrown them into an overnight bag before going to the hospital.

Instead of firing Grace, Stella's father should have hired a new cleaner because this one had clearly not done her job in the last couple of days.

Checking the squeaky clean and tidy en-suite, she found the usuals. Like her mother's toothbrush or the comb she must have used the day she was admitted to the hospital because it still had some of her shoulder long hair dangling from it. She also found her mother's collection of creams and perfumes neatly displayed in a glass cabinet between the sink and her dressing table. She took the round pink flacon with the black bow tied around it and sprayed once on her wrist. The smell of her mother soothed her soul. In all the years, she had never changed perfumes.

Knowing that there was a cabinet behind the mirror, she touched the small metal clutch and opened it, but wasn't prepared to find an abundance of orange pill bottles that had her mother's name written on them. She touched each bottle, turning them to read the labels. The first ones comprised pain killers and something for the migraine she had always struggled with, but the second row contained a multitude of prescribed pills. Sleeping pills, more painkillers and mood enhancers.

Detective Green's words echoed in her head about the simplest answer often being the correct one.

Stella didn't find it particularly shocking her mother needed antidepressants. Surely living with her father was the direct way to the pharmacy, but these pills were strong. They'd knock you out for days. Was her father right? Could her mother have developed some mental health issues? Maybe she had been confused and took too many pills? Could she have attempted to end her life?

As much as everything around her screamed potential suicide into her face, Stella didn't want to accept that her personal hatred might lead her the wrong way or cloud her judgment. In order to incriminate her father, she needed evidence.

Just as she was about to go back to the bedroom, her gaze landed on the drawer of her mother's dressing table, where a small white triangle was peeking out. Leaning closer, she sat down on the stool in front of it and proceeded to slowly open the drawer. Inside it were small velvety boxes holding earrings and necklaces, as well as a row of stacked makeup brushes of different sizes. But there was also an item that didn't fit the rest of the contents.

A white piece of paper, folded three times, sat on top of one jewelry box. Unease crept over Stella. One she had felt many times before and that had never led to anything good. With the hint of a shake in her fingers, she retrieved the paper and opened it.

Her breath caught in her throat when she read what was printed in big capital letters.

YOU DON'T DESERVE THIS, WHORE!

The exclamation mark loomed over Stella, sending shivers down her spine. She swallowed hard. This was meant to intimidate her mother. Someone had tried to scare her mother. Why else would she have hidden this letter inside her dresser? But who could have written this?

Stella turned over the letter, then peeked inside the dresser. With her left hand, she tried to feel for a second page or an envelope that could reveal a sender, but her fingers touched nothing but brushes and tubes.

Damn!

She shut the drawer and stared at the words again. Who sent this to her? And why would her mother hide this? If someone tried to threaten her, why didn't she go to the police? Did her father know about this or— Stella stumbled over the thought for a moment— or, could he have been the one who sent it to her?

On cue, a loud and dark voice rumbled through the empty halls of the thirty-million-dollar mansion on the Upper East Side.

"STELLA!"

The master of the house had returned.

Chapter 10 - The Journalist

Stella

SAYING STELLA'S FATHER was unhappy to hear his daughter had returned to his den without his knowledge was an understatement. He was furious to hear from the doorman that she had entered the premises.

On the one hand, Stella gave the doorman kudos for trusting his gut and informing the hand who fed him. On the other hand, what the fuck was that kid thinking? Not only had he told on her, he also blamed her for sneaking past him, when, in reality, he had let her up with no resistance. Seeing him pack his things on her way out felt like a cherry on top of ice cream, though. Karma was a bitch.

He must have called her father a few minutes after she had arrived. His favorite golf course wasn't far and traffic on a Sunday afternoon was as good as it gets in the city. Hence, it hadn't taken her father long to return to his home and shout his daughter's name in a manner that chilled her to her very core.

Had Stella not been so distracted by the discovery of this letter, she would have instantly seen her father's fury rage much further this time. She would have seen the vein on his forehead, too prominent for someone who regularly took an elevator to the penthouse floor. She would have also seen the back of his palm coming for her face. But she didn't. And that hurt her more than the actual slap.

His order to her came loud and clear. "Get out of my house and never come back!"

For once, she didn't want to stand up to him or give him a snarky reply. With the piece of paper hidden in her jacket's inside pocket, Stella left her childhood home with her heart racing. Had she been more focused, she would have emparted a few last words of wisdom to the kid packing up his stuff: that's what you get for working for Richard Woodworth. Instead, she rushed past him, finding a moment to breathe once she was outside the suffocating mansion.

She inhaled the warm fall air in an attempt to calm herself and zone out the surrounding noise. Silence was hard to come by. She heard everything. The honking of impatient New Yorkers, the ambulances rushing through the streets with their sirens blaring, and the voice of a man calling her name.

She turned to see a person she had never met before. The man approaching her while repeating her last name was tall, lean, and sleek. He had a tightly shaved angular jaw that culminated in a deep dimple in his chin and bright brown eyes that were half covered by glasses with a thick black rim. From his looks, she placed him somewhere in his forties, perhaps younger, but the wrinkles around his eyes were solid proof he wasn't in his twenties anymore, even though he tried to dress that way. His jeans were just a bit too tight, and his coat was just a bit too vintage.

Did she know this man?

But more importantly, how did he know her? She hadn't been in Manhattan in ages.

Then she saw the silver Leica slung around his chest, bouncing off his side and the phone he was holding out towards her.

This guy was press.

"Miss Woodworth."

Stella's eyes darted to the black SUV in front of her and to the driver she had hired to get her around the city for the time she was here. She didn't want to spend precious time scheduling Ubers or hailing smelly taxis that rattled with the dangerous prospect of breaking down at any second. That she might need it as an escape vehicle to rid herself of persistent journalists had not been on her mind then, but it sure came in handy now.

"You are Stella Woodworth, right?" he enquired, his footsteps getting closer.

In a situation like this, Stella usually found it best to stay quiet. She had seen other people get lured in by journalists just because they acknowledged them. By pretending not to hear him, she could, maybe, convince him she wasn't a Woodworth and make him leave her alone. Just a few more steps and she'd be out of here and away from this guy.

"I just have a few questions, Miss Woodworth."

Gee, why was this guy here, anyway? Probably because of another business deal by her father. But how did he know her name? Her driver Giovanni had stepped out of the car, moved around it, and held the backdoor open for her to make that quick escape.

She thanked him before she stepped inside, but stopped short.

"I heard your mother had an overdose?" the reporter yelled across Fifth Avenue.

Frozen in place, Stella held on to the top of the door, unable to swing herself inside the car and drive off.

"What did you say?" she asked, with her back to the man behind her.

"Your mother is Beth Woodworth, right?"

He was now right behind her. She could feel his negative aura and when she turned slowly to face him, fueled by anger, she was glad Giovanni was a barrier between them.

"I just want a brief statement," he offered, as if there was any way she'd give him anything.

"You must be out of your mind thinking I'd talk to you about my family."

"Don't you want to give us your side of this story?"

"There is no story. Now leave me alone."

"There is always a story when your father is involved!" he said it with such vigor Stella was speechless for a second.

She glanced at the skyscraper behind this man invading her personal space and racked her brain for ways to escape.

"I am Mark Fullerton from the New York Times," the persistent hack said, holding out a small card. "I cover the business news and have written about your father before." His card still swayed in his hand.

"Great. You have a lot to write about then. Stick to business and leave my family out of it," Stella hissed.

But Mark didn't let it go. Instead, he took another step towards her, causing Giovanni to tense up.

"I've been following your father for a long time. Everything he does, everything he touches, is for his business. And I've met your mother many times over the years. Do you really think she tried to commit suicide?"

His questions hung heavy in the air.

The details of her mother's situation had been tightly guarded. How did this guy find out? And why was he suspicious? Of course, she didn't believe her mother tried to kill herself, but why did he think that?

"These don't sound like the questions of a business journalist."

"As I said, I've followed your father *closely* for years. Something feels wrong here, Miss Woodworth. Help me understand what's going on." He reached out and pushed his business card towards her. His insinuation wasn't lost on Stella and she wondered if this guy could help her uncover the truth?

"Will you leave me alone if I take your card?" Stella feigned disinterest in a man she was not sure she could ever trust.

"I can help you tell your side. You can trust me."

There was this word again people seemed to be so willing to throw around. Didn't they know it took time to build trust and even then, it wouldn't always be the right thing to do? She would reach out to him, but right now she wanted him off her back to figure things out, including who this journalist really was.

"Fine," she said, taking his card. "I have your contact information. Now leave me alone."

"My cell number is on the back. You can call me anytime," he said with a victorious smile on his face.

She slid his card inside her pocket and was surprised when he kept his word, turned and left.

"You okay?" Giovanni asked in a thick Brooklyn accent.

"Yeah, I am fine."

He handed her a tissue and pointed at her face. "Got something on your cheek."

Her hand went up and when her middle finger touched her flesh, she could feel the heat from her father's blow radiate off her skin. Her finger was dotted red and Stella realized her father had cut her with his alumni ring when he hit her. She took the tissue from her driver and dabbed at her cheek.

"Thanks."

Giovanni nodded and moved back to the front seat, giving Stella a moment to catch her breath. With her eyes closed, she tried to calm both herself and her mind. How did she feel? She wasn't so sure. Ever since she had returned, she felt like she was playing catch up. Always too slow, always one step behind. Or a few.

"Having a bad day?"

Her eyes suddenly sprang open and to her shock, she found Detective Green outside her father's pompous entrance walking towards her.

What was he doing here?

"Detective Green, what a lovely surprise." She didn't even attempt to hide her sarcasm. "Out for a stroll?"

Detective Green chuckled at her remark and closed the distance between them in a few small strides.

"I was in the neighborhood, thought I would drop by. What happened to your face? Another friendly encounter in a bar?" he teased, but Stella wasn't in the mood to jump on it.

"It's nothing, I just cut myself," she said instead. "If I didn't know better, I'd say you are following me."

Detective Green studied her face, especially her now burning cheek. He didn't believe her, but she didn't blame him. How often must he have heard women telling him they were clumsy, that they accidentally bumped into a corner? Her father's backhand probably showed already. But whatever he thought about how she had gotten that cut, he didn't press her for more information and let her off easy.

"Sorry to disappoint but you are not the Woodworth I am trying to get a hold of," he said with a wink.

"Hm, and how is that going?" Stella asked with a glance towards the entrance to her father's building.

Detective Green let out a sigh and put his hands on his hip. "Well, I had better days. Your father is making it a challenge to see him. Any chance you could...?" he asked with a nod to the front door.

"Do you have a warrant?"

"No, I just want to talk to him."

Stella let out a laugh. "Good luck with that. I just made it on his list of people banned from entering that place, so I can't help you with that."

"You and your father have a run in? Anything you want to tell me about?"

Stella considered not answering his questions when Agnes' words echoed in her head unexpectedly. *Don't do this alone.* Harried by her best friend's suggestion, Stella had to admit to herself that Agnes wasn't wrong, which Stella would never tell Agnes to her face.

Frustration dripped off Detective Green like sweat after a long run. Maybe he had found something out and wanted to talk to her father? Maybe she could get him to talk. Extract some information from him. She wouldn't exactly work with him, but use everything and everyone to get to the bottom of this mystery. From what she knew about him, she guessed that a drink or two would relax him and make him more talkative.

"And what happened with that guy just now? Looked like a heated exchange," Detective Green said.

Stella wanted to leave him, drive off, and find another way to get more information, but her inner Agnes made her stay.

"Ah, nothing really. Just some journalist trying to make a living by stirring up some dust."

"Hm, yeah, I know how nasty those can be," he said with a smile on his lips that seemed genuinely supportive and understanding.

Ask him for help. Sometimes, her inner Agnes was a real pain in the ass. She sighed and pinched the bridge of her nose before she blurted out her next words.

"You look like your day has been as fucked up as mine." The phrase rushed out louder than she had planned—much to the disapproval of an elderly white-haired woman with a stick in one hand and a teacup dog looking out from the pink Chanel bag hanging around her right arm. The woman gave her a disgusted look and shook her head.

When had her beloved tough New Yorkers turned so soft over a few fucks?

Samuel looked at her, scanning her demeanor for her true intentions. Like x-ray vision, she thought he looked right through her and at the tight knot in her chest, but instead of brushing her off, he simply nodded in agreement. "I've had better days."

Open up a little.

"How about I buy you a drink, then?" Stella asked.

Chapter 11 - The Agreement

Samuel

SAMUEL WATCHED STELLA down her shot glass the same way he had done hundreds of times. Without so much as blinking an eye. She was obviously used to drinking and could keep up with him, which impressed him on the one hand but also worried him. He knew what numbing pain looked like. What had happened to her in the past that made her think she needed to numb hers?

The question was on the tip of his tongue, but they were only a few drinks in and she wasn't ready to talk yet. Same as him. He knew what she was up to. He had used this method on others before and even though Stella had figured out at this point that he liked his drink, he wasn't the talkative drunk she hoped he would be.

He held up two fingers to the bartender, who was dressed in flannel and ink, both of which suited his beard and nose ring in the typical hipster way that most Manhattan bartenders wore nowadays. In his eyes, this Upper East Side Bar didn't represent the real New York at all. It was clean, modern and awful. Despite his longing for the familiar wooden stool at his local bar, where the sticky counter and potent drinks were the norm, he begrudgingly had to admit that the hipster in front of him knew how to pour a proper drink.

Feeling the spirit of this place—and maybe the drink a little—Samuel reached for the bowl of nuts the bartender had placed between him and Stella with their first order. He wasn't the biggest fan of nuts, but he had a weakness for salted macadamias, so he went for it, anyway.

"Why did you go to see my father?" Stella asked.

"I just wanted to talk to him. Ask him a few more questions," Samuel said, his hand going for another nut.

Stella eyed him. He could feel her doubting his motive. Samuel weighed his options, but he gave nothing away by letting her in a bit. It would also ease her into opening up herself. He believed Stella Woodworth had more information about her mother's situation than she revealed. Perhaps this way, he could get it out of her. Make her trust him just enough.

"I thought we got off to a bad start and wanted to see him again." Sam was glad that his captain had agreed to send him out again without Jim in tow. If he wanted to have a more pleasant conversation with Richard Woodworth, he didn't need Jim constantly talking him down.

"If you want to speak to him again, make an appointment. He won't see you if you just show up."

"But where is the fun in that?" Sam said, wiggling his eyebrows playfully.

"Suit yourself. I am just trying to give you friendly advice."

Samuel washed the macadamia nut down with another swig of his drink, considering his options, or rather what Holmes would want him to do.

"Okay, so how do I get to see him quickly?"

With an enormous sigh, Stella turned towards him, her eyes meeting his.

"My father likes to be in control. If you show up unannounced, he won't even consider seeing you. Never mind talk to you anytime soon. You can easily avoid this if you follow his rules."

"Do I want to know what those rules are?" he asked jokingly, but dreaded her answer when he saw the shadow falling over her face.

Her voice turned darker when she explained, "You schedule an appointment through his assistant, Gladys, and you take whatever time she gives you. When you get to his office, don't barge in. Don't act like a detective. Wait until he decides to see you. Take something to read. The less he thinks of you as important to him, the longer he will make you wait. At least that was my experience as his daughter." She dropped her gaze to her hands and the small piece of skin she was tearing at on her left index finger. When she realized what her hands were doing, she stopped, wiped her palms against her pants, and continued with a fake lightness in her voice. "Well, and then you basically kiss his ass until he tells you to stop. Simple as that."

Maybe he should bring Jim—ass-licker par excellence—with him, he considered, but thought the better of it immediately.

"Simple as that? Gee, you sound like my boss," he said instead.

"Apparently, your boss knows how to deal with my father," Stella said with the hint of a smile on her face.

Samuel took another nut and rolled it carefully between his finger and thumb, as if inspecting it. "Well, your father made it very clear to my boss that I was overstepping and that a different approach was necessary." Then he ate the round white nut.

"He called your boss?" Stella gave him a quizzical look and Samuel explained after he had swallowed the rich and buttery contents in his mouth.

"Yup. Right after our first meeting. Looks like he didn't like the way I talked to him."

"That's my father for you," Stella mocked, shaking her head in disbelief.

"My boss believes that if I want to keep going, I should *adjust* my strategy."

"Ouch. That must have been a real kick in the ego." With the lift of her index finger, that had a slim and simple golden ring around it, she emphasized her statement by pointing as much at his ego as at his black eye.

Somehow, taking her right hook felt less painful than the task his captain had given him.

"It was, because when I do my job, I do it a thousand percent right and that includes following protocol."

"And your boss doesn't let you follow protocol when it comes to my father?"

Her question hung in the air while Samuel thought about an answer. He didn't have any proof her father was involved in her mother's suicide attempt. The idea of murder was pure speculation, a vague possibility, created by the person sitting in front of him. But if he didn't rule that option out, he also couldn't take it off the table. He didn't understand why Holmes was so eager to brush it under the carpet. If Stella's father had nothing to hide, it would quickly become clear. But right now, in the depths of his macadamia nut-filled gut, another feeling grew. One that suddenly had him wonder. What if?

Samuel glanced at Stella. Their eyes met, and she looked at him with no judgment. Something that hadn't happened to him in a while. Someone always judged him or had pity for him. Not her, though, and he felt a strong sense of gratitude and something resembling a connection between them. He knew she didn't have it easy in her life, either. There was a weird bond between broken people like them. An invisible force, forged in dark times, connected them.

He had looked her up, gotten all the details about her life before she left for Asia, and even got an insight into the life she had built for herself in Hong Kong. Which was quite impressive. Especially since she had done it abroad and without her father's support, as he expected. She struck him as someone who got what she wanted if she set her mind to it. They had that in common, as well.

"What made you decide to become a private investigator?" he asked, changing the topic.

"I see you did your homework."

"What sort of detective would I be if I didn't know that?" he quipped with a wink.

She took a long sip from the bottle of lager in front of her, taking her time before she started. "When I arrived in Hong Kong, I didn't know what I wanted to do with my life. I just wanted to disappear for a while. I hung around, worked in a pub, drank and partied. There were always a few regular foreigners that came in wearing a uniform. So I asked, and they told me they were the Hong Kong Police. They raved about the life they had, helping people and all the crazy stuff they have been working on. It got me interested. Back in the days, foreigners could still join the Hong Kong Police force and it sounded fun."

"So you are police?"

"No!" Her answer came as quick as a bullet. "I don't trust the police." She added a sorry towards Samuel at the end that he waved off so she could continue. "The police are too easily corrupted. Give them enough money or power and they'll do your bidding. That's why I left the force after my training. I wanted to get away from men with too much power, telling me what I could and couldn't do, as long as it played in their favor."

His face didn't show the shock he felt about her feelings towards the police. It explained why it was so difficult for her to trust him. She had made it abundantly clear she had no faith in him.

"Maybe you just met some rotten apples?" he asked, hoping to restore some amount of faith in the system.

The small shot glass scraped off the bar when Stella moved it around in circles, eyes fixed on a few leftover drops of whiskey in it. "Maybe," she replied and double tapped the bar for a refill.

"What happened that you don't trust the law?"

"It's not the law I don't trust," she started, pausing before she continued. "It is the people enforcing that law."

"What do you mean?"

"I had a pretty good time in the force at the beginning. But one night, after my classmates and I went out for some drinks, one of them had a bit too much. He got touchy. I didn't like him that way, so I told him off, but he was pretty persistent. I tried talking to him, pushed him away and when all this didn't work, I slapped him."

Samuel rubbed the slightly less sore area under his eye, where her fist had met his skin just a few days ago.

"He was not happy and punched me. Knocked me out. When I fell, I hit a table with my head. Had to go to the hospital, got stitches and all that." She turned her left side towards him, lifted her hair and pointed at an almost invisible scar two fingers above her ear.

"Shit!" Samuel said, leaning closer to get a better look.

"Yeah, but when I got back to work and complained to my boss, he didn't believe me. He told me I must have given Jeff the wrong impression. He asked how much I had to drink. If I was sure, I didn't just trip in my high heels and fell," Stella scoffed.

"I'm sorry," Samuel said. "But not all of us are bad," he insisted, but even he knew that there were a bunch of assholes out there who'd ruin it for everyone. Even in his own department, he had heard plenty of inappropriate comments and seen too many complaints go untouched because the word of a man or the word of a more powerful individual often still counted more. The system wasn't perfect, that was certain, but he strongly felt that it was better to change it from the inside.

"What happened then? After your talk with your boss?"

"I left. Went back to the pub trying to figure out what to do. During my time training, I had practiced Kung Fu and Taekwondo. My trainer had a client who worked for a private investigator. When I looked into them, they were the right combination of what I wanted to do."

"And what's that?"

"I want to help people who can't help themselves."

Samuel wondered if she really meant that or if this was only part of her strategy to get him talking. He couldn't pinpoint anything on her, for she was as cool and smooth as the over-the-top big ice cube in his glass. If she was genuine though, she could give him inside knowledge that would surely help him close this case quickly and hopefully regain some sort of status at work and with Holmes.

"What made you choose this line of work?" she suddenly asked, taking him by surprise.

Opening up to others didn't come easy to Samuel, and he struggled with letting people see the real him. Another thing he expected him and Stella to have in common.

Gain her trust.

She told you about her experience.

"My dad was killed in a car accident," he blurted before he could stop himself. "Seventeen-year-old kid was on the phone when he missed the red light and drove right into him. He was from a wealthy family, had a 3.6 GPA and a football scholarship. His dad's lawyer and the judge decided it wouldn't help to ruin his life with a long sentence. He got off easy. Only had to do some community service, picking up trash while I buried my father. That's when I decided I would make people like him get what they deserve."

He hadn't thought about this moment in his life for a long time. How tough it had been for his mom to work three jobs to keep him and his two sisters fed. She had sacrificed so much for them. He was glad he could support his family and be useful. Joining the police was the reason he had been able to help them and so many others.

But one.

He leaned in closer, his mind sharp. "Listen, I think you could help me solve this case. I know you don't trust the police and I get it. Believe me, I do. We can be a bunch of assholes sometimes. But we are not all like that. Some of us really want to make a difference. Like you."

"You are a drunk." She threw the fact at him like it was the most normal thing to do. Catching him off guard.

"You want me to trust you, but how can I?" she asked, looking at the next round of drinks she had ordered for them.

She wouldn't agree on working together if he didn't give her something else but his word. She needed proof that she could trust him. He felt shy suddenly. His heart hammering in his chest. His lips were dry, and he ran his tongue over them.

"There was an incident at work last year which I can't seem to shake off. It was one of those that keep you awake at night, replaying in your head whenever your mind goes quiet. I found bourbon helps me drown out the quiet like white noise." He looked at her, waiting for an answer.

"Yeah, I know about those healing powers."

With that, she downed her shot in front of him. Sharing time was officially over.

He reached into his inside pocket and handed her a small batch of folded papers to reel her in.

"I got this in the morning. That's why I wanted to talk to your father."

Stella understood immediately. She grabbed the copies of her mother's hospital file, clung to them, like her mother's life depended on it, before rustling through the papers, searching for the ultimate answer.

"There's nothing in it and I mean nothing. Nothing strange or out of the ordinary," he said.

She looked at him with more questions in her eyes.

"If your mother had mental health issues, like your father claims, something should be in there. And I am not talking about those prescribed pills they found in her stomach."

"This is her hospital file. Wouldn't her GP have more information about that?"

"Which the hospital requested. That's normal procedure. Now look at the date the hospital states as the date for her prescribed pills."

Stella's eyebrows shot up, and Samuel knew she was as surprised as he had been about the fact that Beth Woodworth had only started taking pills two months ago. There was no sign she had been on pills before that, which meant that Richard Woodworth had lied about the fact that his wife had been seriously ill and medicated for some time.

"Something must have happened two months ago that got your mother to take pills."

Stella looked up from the medical records. He knew what she was thinking. This raised the likelihood that her mother had attempted to commit suicide. The question was just over what?

"When did you last talk to her?"

"I talk regularly with her. I think we talked a month ago."

"Did you notice any changes in her?"

"No, nothing."

Talking to her mother once a month might be regular enough for her, but in his experience, people could talk to their families daily and not fully know them. He believed Stella Woodworth didn't have a clue what her mother was doing. Or she wasn't telling him the full truth.

Only one way to find out.

"Help me figure this out." Deep down, he knew something was off about this case, but he also knew he needed help. He wasn't sure how helpful Holmes would be and, worse, he wasn't sure how much he could trust his gut anymore. It had failed him before and he wasn't willing to pay the same price he had paid last year again. He couldn't let Stella's mother down, and more importantly, he couldn't fail himself again.

"If I agree to help you, I want access to everything you find out. Even the smallest, unimportant piece of information, I want to know about it."

Samuel smiled at her, knowing he had won. He held out his hand. Stella took it and they shook on their agreement, but before he released her from his grip, he added, "These terms go both ways."

Stella's nod came immediately, but her soft and warm hand trembled just for a split second. Too short for anyone else to really notice, but long enough for Samuel to know that she wasn't fully on board. She would decide how much she was willing to share with him. And right now, this was enough for him.

They let go of each other's hands, and Stella waved at the bartender for the next round.

"I hope you know what you are getting yourself into with my father."

"I can handle a bully." Samuel chuckled.

Something in Stella's eyes changed, and a darkness set over them that almost had Samuel choke on his laugh.

"My father is way worse than any bully you might know. A bully you can get away from, but if my father thinks you have something against him, he bites. Like an alligator, his teeth are sharp and once he sinks them into you, he won't let go until he has destroyed you."

"Is that why you left and moved halfway across the globe?"

Stella leaned back in her high chair and sighed. "Families are a tricky thing, Detective. You get born into one you might not have chosen for yourself, but you are stuck with them. Everything you do reflects on your family and if you were born into a family like mine, appearance is more important than anything else. Happiness is for fairy tales. My father lusts for power and he isn't worried about doing anything to keep this power, even if it involves hurting his family. I couldn't bear the thought of possibly turning into a soulless son of a bitch like him. That's why I left."

Samuel had his own experience growing up in a less than perfect family. Looking after his mother and his two sisters had not been easy. They hadn't done too badly. He was one of the lucky ones. Not every kid would have that chance though. He had learnt that the hard way.

"Do you regret leaving?"

Her answer came like rapid fire. "No. I had to leave. There was no other option for me if I wanted to live. And

I had to get as far away from him as possible. But I regret I left my sister behind. We were never as close as other siblings but in our own fucked-up way, we cared for each other, stood up against the tyrant together. But once you literally put an ocean between you, it gets so easy to forget. *This* world was so far away, and I loved it. But my mother and sister definitely paid for it instead of me."

It was hard to believe that Richard Woodworth had that much power, that he was such a monster, but Samuel knew Stella was speaking her truth. Throughout his career, he had seen the worst in people, what they were capable of. How bad some family structures were. There was no such thing as a perfect family.

Chapter 12 - The Second Chance

Samuel

EVEN THOUGH HE'D HAD a day to recover, Samuel woke up with a slight headache. Nothing he hadn't experienced before, but enough that he started his morning with black coffee and two aspirins. The pulsing in his head was a lingering reminder he might be too old for daytime drinking. And while he preferred to drink in the night's darkness, his Sunday afternoon excursion had proven to be quite successful. He shouldn't have done shots of whiskey and bottles of beer with her at all, but if that was what it took for her to open up to him, he was up for the challenge. And it had worked.

Once he and Stella had agreed to work together, the conversation had turned less formal and stiff. He actually found it easy to talk to her. She was smart and witty and even had a sense of humor. That she could hold her liquor was just a bonus. A few hours in, and a few drinks later, they had even agreed on being comfortable on a first-name basis.

On his way to work this morning, while standing in a crowded subway line with his mind returning to their conversation, he realized he liked her. She was tough as nails but also had a soft core inside her seemingly stony heart. He knew this because she wore her worry like a millstone around her neck whenever she talked about her mother or sister. That was something he could relate to. Growing up without a father, he had quickly become a caregiver of sorts himself. He saw a lot of himself in her.

He had also followed her advice and called the office of Richard Woodworth first thing Monday morning to officially request an appointment. And while he didn't expect to see Richard Woodworth the same day, to his own surprise, Gladys, the woman on the other end of the line, with a voice as raspy as a grinder, had told him to come in the next day.

Maybe Stella and the Captain were right. Sometimes it was easier to swallow the urge to demand answers immediately if it got you to the finishing line quicker.

This theory went out the window around two hours ago. At that point, Samuel sat comfortably enough in an armchair in the waiting area of Richard Woodworth's office, and it had dawned on him that Gladys' remarking 'Mr. Woodworth will see you as soon as possible' didn't carry any weight. Samuel was taught a lesson. If you want to play with Richard Woodworth, you play by his rules.

A few times, he had seen him leave his office, always followed by his shadow, Gladys, who was quicker on her short legs than Samuel had thought possible. Usually someone else kept running after them, scribbling notes on iPads they carried around and a look on their face that wasn't just work stress but fear.

Each time Samuel stood up, took a step towards Richard Woodworth, even called him out, only to be reprimanded by Gladys that Mr. Woodworth would get to him in due time.

After four hours, six surprisingly excellent coffees from the waiting area and two calls from Holmes asking where the heck he was, a tiny figure appeared in front of him and finally addressed him.

"Mr. Woodworth will see you now. If you'd follow me, Detective Green," Gladys said, tapping her foot on the gray carpet and taking a long look at the silver watch on her wrist.

Samuel got up, grabbed his jacket, and followed the short woman to Richard Woodworth's office door. There she stopped, knocked twice and waited for her boss to ask her to come in.

After she introduced Samuel as the next visitor, she left him in the dragon's pit from which he hoped to get out alive, or at least with all his limbs still attached.

He hated that he couldn't deny that Richard Woodworth's strategy worked on him as well, at least to some extent. He had never felt this uncomfortable speaking to a suspect in an ongoing police investigation.

"Ah, Detective Green. Please, sit down," Richard Woodworth said, his open palm waving to the chair in front of his desk. Samuel followed his gesture, placed his jacket over the back, and sat down.

"Thank you for seeing me on such short notice." It hurt Samuel to be so gracious to a man who was clearly playing with him, but he had promised Holmes to play it nice and he knew from Stella that this was the way to deal with her father.

"I hope you didn't have to wait too long." Richard Woodworth barely hid his mockery. He leaned back into his chair, let his fingertips touch in a triangle in front of him, and openly cocked a smile at Samuel.

The motherfucker.

But Samuel wouldn't bite. He wouldn't give Richard Woodworth the satisfaction.

"I know you are a busy man. I appreciate you made time to see me," Samuel replied through gritted teeth, hoping to sound somewhat convincing.

Richard Woodworth studied him for a few seconds before he got up, ambled to the front of his desk, leaned against it, and looked down at Samuel.

"Nice to see that your captain could talk some sense into you." The smile was still on Richard Woodworth's face. He clearly felt in control of this situation. His sinister undertone snaked its way down to Samuel and caused him to grip his thighs tightly.

If Samuel wanted to get out of here without causing another scene, he would have to occupy his hands as much as he needed to muzzle the pit bull inside him, who wanted to go straight for Richard Woodworth's throat.

Instead, Samuel pressed his lips together and nodded.

"Well, how can I help you, Detective?"

Let's get this over with as quickly as possible.

"I was hoping you could help me fill in some blanks and answer a few more follow-up questions?" Samuel said.

Richard Woodworth sighed dramatically. "So you are still hung up on this nonsense?"

"It is an open investigation into your wife's—"

"Detective," Richard Woodworth interrupted. "I've given you a statement and if you remember correctly, I wasn't even at home when my wife committed suicide."

"Tried to commit."

"What is that?"

116

"Your wife is still alive. So she *tried* to commit suicide," Samuel emphasized, wondering what it meant that the man in front of him considered his comatose wife already dead. Something heavy moved in Samuel's gut. He strongly disliked Richard Woodworth, but that still didn't make him a murderer. It just made him an asshole, and he had dealt with plenty of those over the years.

"What do you want?" Richard Woodworth asked, the mocking smile on his face fading.

"Can you tell me more about your wife's state of mind the evening before she was admitted to the hospital?" Samuel asked while opening his little notepad, ready to write down whatever Richard Woodworth would give him.

"I already told you in my statement."

Samuel lifted his head and focused on Holmes' voice in his head when he offered the menace in front of him the friendliest smile he could give.

"Well, please tell me again. In case you forgot something the first time."

"I did not, but since you are asking so nicely. Nothing was out of the ordinary."

"Okay, how about the days building up to the event?" Samuel poked, suddenly feeling the urge to throw his pen at Richard Woodworth.

"You are wasting your time, Detective. Beth did not seem any different. She had acted the same way she had all the other evenings and no, nothing was out of the ordinary. I assure you, everything has been the same. Is that what you wanted to hear?"

The condescending tone in his question, carried by a chuckle and head shake, catapulted Samuel back in time to tenth grade. His English lit teacher had made it clear in front of the entire class how little he thought of Samuel's analysis on Shakespeare's growth as a writer, comparing his first tragic love story *Romeo and Juliet* to his later piece *Anthony and Cleopatra*. English literature had been ruined, but he wouldn't let Richard Woodworth make him feel like an idiot, as well.

"Mr. Woodworth. I am not your enemy here. I am merely trying to help you. So how about you make both of our lives easier by cooperating now and answering a few simple questions? Alternatively, I can take you down to the station right now, but I guess that would really break your schedule. Since you are so busy, I mean."

In hindsight, he could have probably just brushed this and any other nasty comment off, but he had had it with this man who clearly thought he was above everyone and everything. Including a police investigation.

Screw Holmes' kid-glove approach to this guy.

"I think you are forgetting who you are talking to," Richard Woodworth said with an icy tone that sent a shiver through Samuel.

No wonder people feared this man.

A rush of adrenaline surged through Samuel as he got up slowly to face Richard Woodworth.

"You know, something just doesn't add up. I mean, when people want to commit suicide, in my experience, they leave a suicide note. But there was nothing your wife left, right? No letter, no text message?" His question hung in the air for a few seconds while Richard Woodworth searched for an answer in front of him.

"My wife had issues and was on a mix of prescribed medications—"

"About that," Samuel interrupted. "That's the other really strange thing." Samuel retrieved the copy of Beth Woodworth's hospital file and handed it over to her husband. "Last time we spoke, you stated your wife had a history of mental health issues and that she had been on strong medication for a while," he said calmly, waiting for a reaction from the man in front of him, but Richard Woodworth didn't even look at the papers he had been handed.

"According to her hospital file, she did not start taking any medication before mid September. That's roughly seven weeks ago."

"Your point?"

"Seven weeks can hardly be described as a history of mental health issues, wouldn't you agree?"

There was still nothing coming from Richard Woodworth but an annoying silence. Why wouldn't this man answer a few simple questions? He could have already been out of here. This shouldn't take longer than a few minutes, unless...unless Richard Woodworth wanted to keep something from Samuel. But what?

"I can assure you, Detective, that I know my wife's medical history. I assume this file isn't complete," Richard Woodworth eventually answered with a nonchalant shrug.

"Well, it's nice that you *assure* me of all these things, but I need a bit more than that. Which is why I also included the file of your family's GP, who had sent over a more detailed list of prescriptions your wife has been on," Samuel said and pointed at the paper in Richard Woodworth's hand, who finally examined it himself.

With each passing second, his smile faded from his face.

"Same answer," Samuel concluded before Richard Woodworth's bitter expression hit him hard. He wasn't sure what Richard Woodworth was more angry about, that he had gotten personal information from his GP or that he had caught him lying to the police.

"Why did you lie about this?" Samuel finished, taking a step back to give Richard Woodworth room to digest this turn of events and also to prepare himself for whatever outburst might come his way. But Richard Woodworth remained calm.

"I think it is time for you to leave."

"Excuse me?" Samuel asked, watching Richard Woodworth as he walked back around his desk and pressed his finger on a number on his phone. Gladys' voice echoed back instantly.

"Yes, Sir?"

"Gladys, prepare my next appointment. The Detective is leaving now."

"Right away," she chirped.

"Mr. Woodworth," Samuel cut in. "We are not finished here."

"Detective, do I need to call security?"

"You are kidding, right?" Samuel asked, almost dumbfounded.

"I don't need some trainee to come to my place—"

"Detective," Samuel interrupted.

"Disrupt my working schedule and call me a liar," Richard Woodworth continued, as if he hadn't heard Samuel. "I am too—"

"Yeah, yeah. You are too busy to care about what really happened to your wife."

That shut him up, but only for a few seconds.

"You should have listened to your boss."

Samuel was dumbstruck by Richard Woodworth's remarks for the second time in under two minutes. How much of Holmes' suggestions were his and how much was Richard Woodworth behind it. But more importantly, why would he let a man who was involved in an open investigation dictate the way they were doing their work?

What was going on here?

The door to the big office opened and Gladys entered, followed by a hunk of a man dressed in black.

"Sir, your next appointment is ready."

This giant man was clearly not Richard Woodworth's next appointment; he was an obvious attempt at intimidation. He folded his hands in his lap, awaiting instructions.

"Thank you, Gladys. Please show Detective Green out," Richard Woodworth said with a wave of his hand.

"Are you serious?" Samuel asked when the giant cleared his throat and waved Samuel to follow him. Not wanting this situation to escalate even further, Samuel let him lead. "This is ridiculous, but okay. I'm going," he said, lifting his hands in a gesture of surrender before following his escort. Right at the door, Samuel turned and looked at Richard

Woodworth. "I do not know what is pissing you off so much, but I will find out why you don't want to cooperate with me and if you had anything to do with your wife's hospitalization. This is not over."

"Oh, you are so done, *Detective!*" Richard Woodworth stated, that sly, maleficent smile back on his lips and when he lifted the phone again, Samuel knew exactly who he was calling this time.

Chapter 13 - The Instruction

Samuel

SITTING AT HIS DESK, which looked like the copy machine had exploded and dumped its contents of 200 pages on his workspace, Samuel shuffled through his notes. His encounter with Stella's father still had him on edge.

What a dick.

Samuel knew it was merely a matter of time until Holmes would realize he was in the office. So far, his captain's door had remained closed, though, which had given Samuel time to think.

That Stella's mother tried to commit suicide remained the most logical explanation. Everything he had so far pointed at it and it made the most sense. Especially after he had heard more about Stella's brother. Maybe it was the last shot of bourbon that had loosened Stella's tongue two days ago but she felt free enough to talk about her brother, whom she had looked up to until he took his own life, leaving her with the burden of being the oldest in the family.

Samuel leaned back in his chair, lifted his hands above his head for a stretch, and closed his tired eyes for a moment. Maybe her mother just hadn't been able to cope in the end. Maybe a memory had triggered something in her.

But he didn't believe it. He had dealt with plenty of suicides in his life. Fuck, the thought had even crossed his mind when the noise in his head grew too loud and the physical pain of his failure became unbearable. He wasn't proud of those dark nights, and though he no longer seriously considered it, he still understood the comforting in believing death could end all pain. But one thing he knew for sure was that those intent on committing suicide usually leave a goodbye letter or something to explain why they were ending their life or leaving someone behind.

"Green, in my office, now!"

There it was. Samuel jumped at the sound of his captain's hard voice. He was angry. Samuel had hoped to be wrong. That Richard Woodworth did not call his captain right before he was thrown out of his office. But of course he had. That man had it out for him, and the easiest way to shut him up was to talk to his boss. He followed his captain's instructions and entered his office, preparing himself for the shit he was about to get, once again.

The door hadn't properly closed when the shouting began. Samuel saw his colleagues in the adjacent room look up at him through the small slot of the closing door before it shut them out completely. Some of them seemed worried for him while a few others, including Jim, smirked at the possibility that Samuel would leave the Captain's office with his tail between his legs.

"I gave you a simple instruction. And what do you do? You go straight to Richard and accuse him of lying? Of being responsible for his wife's hospitalization? And you make a scene by needing to be escorted outside like you are some sort of lunatic? This isn't what I asked you to do." His captain's head was red from fury and Samuel worried for his flailing heart, knowing he had a few stents that helped his blood reach the most important muscle in his body.

"Can I sit down?" Samuel asked, pointing to the chair in front of him.

"Spare me your attitude. You are in trouble, son, and you should lose that fucking smug smile if you know what's good for you."

It wasn't the first time someone had compared his resting face to having a cocky attitude. But it was a first for Holmes to make a big deal out of his facial expression. However, he wasn't at fault here and he really wanted to clear this up with his captain, explain what had really happened, so he kept a comment that *this was the only face he got* to himself.

Instead, Samuel sat without as much as making a peep, which was difficult enough on a chair that looked like it had lived through the Declaration of Independence.

"I don't know what has gotten into you that you cannot follow a simple instruction. But the way you have acted and treated Richard is unacceptable. He is a decent man with a lot to lose if word gets out that his own daughter is trying to pin a terrible accident on him. Her accusations are preposterous and could damage him and his company. You are playing with someone's life."

He had heard his boss say those exact words before and still couldn't quite figure out why it was so important that the rules were bent for this man. Based on all the encounters he had with Richard Woodworth, he couldn't understand how anyone would describe Stella's father as a decent man. And the worst was that his captain seemed to see a completely different man. There it was again. That nagging feeling that something was off.

How was he supposed to change how Holmes saw Richard Woodworth?

"I assume you are talking about the life of his wife who is in hospital while her beloved husband tries to block me out and stop me from finding out what really happened to her?" Now that would surely not ease his captain into calmer waters.

"Richard is not a very emotional man, but I guarantee you, he cares for his wife very much. I've known the two for longer than you've been nagging my ass."

From what Samuel had learnt about Stella's father last night, he didn't care about anyone else but himself. And it had nothing to do with caring but only with controlling. How his boss couldn't see that went far beyond him.

"If you don't get your shit together, I don't see any other option than to..."

"To what?" Samuel interrupted, realizing in which direction this conversation was spinning.

"Take you off this case."

The chair under Samuel creaked with relief when he got up. "What? You want to take me off because I am doing my job?"

"Don't be ridiculous. Of course, you are supposed to do your job. You are about to lose this case because you cannot follow orders. Coming at him like a tank isn't going do it. That's why I instructed you to follow protocols quietly and that includes not invading this man's personal space, but working with him."

Samuel opened his mouth to respond, but his captain wouldn't have it.

"Don't you dare interrupt me again while I'm speaking." He waited for any response from Samuel and got a disgusted grunt before he sat back down in his chair.

"I thought I'd be doing you a favor, but it's clear now that giving you this case was too early. I should have seen that, and I take full responsibility."

Holmes' words ricocheted in Samuel's head. He didn't think Samuel could do it. Fuck it, Samuel often had a tiny voice inside himself telling him the same thing. But deep down in his bones, he knew this time was different. He was ready and he could solve this if they'd let him.

"You can't take me off the case."

Holmes sighed, a sound heavy with defeat. "Samuel, you said it yourself. You are missing persons, not homicide. This might not be the right thing for you."

Anger bubbled up in Samuel for the way he was bouncing off Holmes' decisions. One day, being the right guy and now being the wrong one.

"You don't even believe it's homicide," Samuel spit out, and Holmes looked at him in disbelief.

"What's that supposed to mean?"

"You put me on this case and expect me to do my work, but you are not letting me. All I've been doing is following protocol. You were the one who told me over and over that no matter what, you always follow protocol. How am I supposed to do that if you don't want me to look into the husband? Everyone is a suspect until proven differently. Everything points to suicide, but in order to prove that, I have to talk to Stella's father."

"Stella? You mean Miss Woodworth?" his captain scoffed at him and shook his head. "Jesus, son. Is that what this is all about? What weird ideas has she planted in your head?"

"She has put nothing in my head. And if you heard what she has to say about her father, you'd cringe..."

"Stella has always had a way with men. She knows how to wrap them around her finger and squeeze them for what she needs."

The insinuation that Samuel would let Stella, or anyone for that matter, interfere with his investigation infuriated him more than the possibility that she used him. The Captain had known him for years, watched him work and grow under his wing. The fact that Holmes even considered the possibility that he'd drop it all for a pretty face pissed him off.

Could he be right, though? He felt a connection to Stella, but maybe she was playing with him? Trying to manipulate him? It didn't feel like it, but she was Richard Woodworth's daughter in the end.

Whatever Holmes saw on his face, it made a difference because eventually Holmes grunted in defeat and banged his fists on his desk. "Fine. You can stay on the case. I know you mean well, but you are not doing anything without my prior permission, or you are off the case. Are we clear?"

"Crystal clear." The two words were out of Samuel's mouth just before someone knocked sharply on the door behind him. Holmes didn't have time to say anything when the door opened and Virginia, the receptionist on day duty, popped in. Clearly unimpressed by the destructive energy in the room, she continued to chew her gum with an open mouth while addressing Holmes.

"Boss, you have a caller on line five who insists on talking to you now or he'll have your head. I'll put him through in a second."

Holmes rolled his eyes at Virginia, who was already halfway back to her desk. Samuel felt sorry for his captain when he realized he had people chopping at him the same way, probably making him regret his decision to postpone retirement for a few years.

Holmes' hand went up and pointed straight to the door that Samuel was more than willing to go through. He didn't need a verbal instruction to leave. Once outside, he closed the door to give Holmes privacy for his call and turned back into a bullpen full of dumbstruck police officers.

His colleagues had never heard him and the Captain get into a fight before. At least nothing cutting this deep and even Samuel was irritated by this recent development in their relationship. It made little sense that his boss, the maddest stickler for rules, would suddenly go beyond his way to help his friend.

He needed to find out who was working with him or against him, if he could still rely on his instincts and if he could trust Stella.

Samuel grabbed his phone off the desk and dialed the number she had given him two days ago. She picked up after two rings, her voice soft and melodic and with a hint of sass when she called him *Detective*.

Concentrate.

"Hey, listen, I think we need to talk. Where are you?" He waited for her response and asked her to stay and meet him at the hospital, while he grabbed his jacket from the back of his chair. He needed to get Stella to talk to him, see if there might be any truth to Holmes' suspicion.

Before he left, he glanced at his captain. Through the window with the blinds pulled, he saw his boss rubbing his forehead like he was hoping for answers to flake off it. He looked at an aged man who desperately needed a solution and wondered why his boss relied on this friendship with Richard Woodworth so badly that he'd keep him sheltered no matter what.

Chapter 14 - The Ghost

Stella

HAD STELLA BEEN SURPRISED when Samuel called? Yes. Even though she had insisted on them agreeing to share information with each other, she hadn't been sure if he'd keep that promise. Their arrangement had not been mutual. At least not from her side. Yes, she had shaken his hand on it, but obviously she couldn't give him all the details. She needed more information about him before she could even consider trusting him.

He had even received a medal for a case he had closed a year ago. How could someone like him, an alcoholic, receive such a reward? No wonder the police were in such a disordered state. There was no way Samuel had a squeaky clean background. Surely a man like him was hiding something and until she knew what dark secret he hid, she was probably better off not trusting him.

Looking down at the black iPhone in her hand, she had to admit, though, that so far he had kept his part of their agreement. He had talked with her mother's doctor and even arranged to see her father earlier this morning. And whatever it was he wanted to talk with her about, it sounded important. She tapped her screen; the time popping up on it in sleek white metallic letters. Almost half an hour had passed since his call, and she couldn't suppress her curiosity about what he might want to share with her. Did he actually get her father to confess his involvement?

"Miss Woodworth. Can I help you with something?"

Stella rolled her eyes, not bothering to look up. She knew immediately it was her mother's incompetent doctor. Abelson wasn't supposed to be on call today. Thanks to a few calls to the hospital and innocent sweet-talk, a nurse on night shift duty had been tired enough to rant about the fact that Dr. Abelson wouldn't be in today. He was supposed to spend a long weekend with his wife. Apparently something the nurse could have used as well, but in a position like hers, she couldn't just take time off whenever it suited her.

Stella had hoped to use this opportunity to sneak past the reception and see her mother, but here he was.

"Well, I thought I'd stop by to see how my mother is doing."

Dr. Abelson handed his tablet over to the nurse at the station and frowned at Stella. "I thought I was clear last time we spoke. We can't give you any information on your mother's condition, and we can't let you into her room."

Since her last strategy of being open with him about his stupidity didn't benefit her, maybe this time she should try a sweeter approach.

"I know we got off on the wrong foot last time, so I wanted to apologize. You know best how to deal with your patients. I know how busy you are and don't want to take too much of your precious time. I was just hoping you could give me something. I am so worried about my mother and I'd really appreciate it." Who knew that buttering up a grown man could feel so disgusting? But his features softened, and he looked genuinely torn.

"I know you want to look out for your mother, but your father was very clear in his instructions."

Ouch, so much for catching flies with honey.

"Is there nothing you can do, Doc?" Stella asked, batting her eyes.

"Not if you don't change your father's mind."

Well, that's unlikely to happen.

"You don't think it's strange that he doesn't let his own daughter see her mother?" Stella asked, nodding towards the room her mother lay in, attached to machines and tubes, providing her weak body with vital support.

"Even if I were to agree with that, it would still violate HIPAA laws. Both your father and the government could take legal action against me, the hospital, or even the nurse who is currently attending to your mother, and who has two beautiful daughters eagerly awaiting her return every evening."

Dr. Abelson sighed, and for the first time, she really understood his position. He had to hold up his side of this forced agreement or he himself would suffer. Even worse, Dr. Abelson knew Stella's father well. Knew that he could destroy the life of every person who had been in contact with her mother, just to get his way. Dr. Abelson was a hostage with no chance of release unless his kidnapper decided to free him.

Behind Abelson's head, movement had Stella focus on her mother's room, which a doctor in a flawlessly white coat and surgical mask exited. For a split second, she glimpsed her mother lying in bed. What if her mother didn't make it?

What if she'd never get the chance to talk to her again? All because her father's vindictiveness.

She needed to change her father's mind. Surely there was something she could offer him, but what would it cost her and how much was she willing to pay?

She felt a warm palm on her shoulder.

"I am sorry and if the circumstances were different, I'd be the first to show you to her room. Believe me," Dr. Abelson said before an announcement cut through and had Dr. Abelson frown.

"Code blue. ICU North room 1176. Code Blue."

He turned and looked towards her mother's room, while several nurses went in and out.

"If you'll excuse me," Dr. Abelson said, moving away from Stella while the announcement repeated over the internal hospital speaker system.

"Is everything alright, Doc?" Stella asked, but Dr. Abelson was already out of earshot.

What was going on?

Drawn to her mother's room, Stella approached the door behind which Dr. Abelson had vanished a second ago. The man who would have let her see her mother if circumstances were different. Was this different? Would Dr. Abelson let her see her mother now, in case it was the last time?

Her heart beat loudly and fast in her heaving chest, and the surrounding noise stopped. How could everyone be so calm when a storm was raging inside Stella?

What was happening to her mother?

Was she okay?

Through the numbing fear that this might be the last time Stella could see her mother, she opened the door. She prepared herself for a nurse or Dr. Abelson to throw the door shut, but no one did. Reeled in like a fish on a hook, Stella stopped in the doorframe and stared helplessly at the traumatizing scene in front of her.

Hands pressed down rhythmically on her mother's chest, while another person in blue scrubs pumped air into her mother with a resuscitator bag. Her mother's torso lay bare in front of her when white pads were attached to her skin. One on the left side of her chest and the other under her right breast. Then, all hands were off while electricity surged through her mother's body. This must have felt normal enough to the surrounding staff, Stella thought. Hardened by experience, they were probably immune to yet another person knocking on heaven's door.

Snippets of a conversation wafted towards her.

"What happened?" Dr. Abelson asked.

"She was stable. Her vitals were good, getting better. She shouldn't be getting worse," A nurse replied.

"Who was the last to check on her?"

"You, Doctor."

But the last person leaving her mother's room had not been Dr. Abelson. She had seen the other *male* doctor. Clearly he had been the last one, but of all the people in this room, he was nowhere to be found.

Where did he go?

At the same time as a shocking idea formed in Stella's mind, another alarm went off, only louder this time and encompassing the whole hospital. A fire alarm.

Stella had never believed in coincidences. It was awfully suspicious timing that her mother's body would fail right before a fire alarm demanded evacuating her entire hospital floor.

Against her instinct to stay with her mother, Stella ran for the emergency exit in pursuit of the mysterious missing doctor. She tried not to consider that this might have been the last image of her mother when she pushed through the door. The words *I love you* on her mind.

Her sweaty hands gripped the cool metallic railing, and she looked up and down the stairway. He had just left her room. He couldn't be far. She ran down the stairs, taking two at a time until people started flooding the emergency stairway. Bumping into people telling her to be careful and not to panic, she eventually slowed down in the mass of strangers, making it impossible to figure out if any of them were the man she was looking for.

And then, right at the bottom of the stairs, a figure caught Stella's eye. Something about him was off. As others scuttled quickly but calmly to the exit, this man walked erratically. She couldn't make out a face under the blue baseball cap, but something about his build seemed familiar. Could this be the man she was looking for? Pushing her way down, Stella ignored the rude words of the people she shoved aside in order to get down. Three stories below, she found a white coat on the floor, trampled on and shoved into the corner. The name tag read Christine Johnson, a woman. Stella was sure now, whoever had left her mother's room was not supposed to be there.

When she finally reached the bottom floor and exited the building, she was surrounded by people gathering outside, wondering what was going on. Three FDNY trucks had arrived with a group of fully geared up firefighters making their way inside the building while one of them stayed behind talking to a doctor who looked like someone who might know what's going on.

Through all the chaos and turbulence of irritated people, there was no way for Stella to determine who might have been in her mother's room. The person could have been long gone or standing right next to her. She wouldn't know.

What she did know, however, was the familiar voice that, out of nowhere, started calling her name. When she turned, it was Samuel who emerged through the crowd.

"What happened?" he asked, his eyes questioning the scene in front of him.

She told him, convinced he wouldn't believe her. Even to her own ears, she sounded like she had imagined a ghost. But if he thought she was crazy, his face didn't show. He listened intently, nodded understandingly, and when she was done, he paused, probably trying to make sense of what he had heard and what he was seeing.

His eyes scanned the area and latched onto a small camera attached to the outside of the building facing the emergency door.

"Security camera!" they exclaimed in unison.

"They have cameras on each floor as well," Stella added.

"Follow me," he said and then they were running along the building and into the main entrance of the hospital.

Samuel went for the elevator, pushing the up button a few times more than necessary. But the building was still running in emergency mode, so up the stairs it was. During their ascent Stella felt a strong admiration for those firefighters who always made it look so easy running up buildings in heavy clothing.

When they reached the eleventh floor, they were both breathing raggedly. Stella's lungs ached with every inhale. But she didn't have time to catch her breath. Dr. Abelson was right in front of them.

"What happened?" she asked, holding her side where a sudden stitch was trying to keep her from speaking.

"I am sorry, it was a false alarm—" Dr. Abelson started.

"Not the fire alarm. My mother!"

What's wrong with this man?

"Miss Woodworth, I told you. I'm sorry but I can't—"

"Fine," she said, frustration seeping into her voice, and shoved Samuel in front of her. "How about you talk to this man, then?"

Slightly startled, Samuel took out his shiny silver badge and held it up to Dr. Abelson. "Detective Green. NYPD. I'm investigating the attempted suicide of Mrs. Woodworth. I know you can't talk to Miss Woodworth, but surely *we* can figure this out?"

Dr. Abelson still hesitated, one eye on the badge and the other on Stella, as if he was waiting for her to explain that he was too afraid of her father to even talk to the police.

"We can do this the easy way and you tell me what happened to Mrs. Woodworth, or we try the hard way. Which would be an obstruction of an open investigation and I don't have to tell you how nasty that paperwork can be if I bring you down to the station for that. I could even escort you myself. However, I believe you've had enough excitement for one day. Your choice Doc."

At that moment, and for a brief second, when Dr. Abelson essentially crumbled in front of her, Stella had to reluctantly admit to herself that she liked Samuel and the way he worked.

"Your mother went into cardiac arrest. Her heart stopped for reasons we don't know yet, but we were able to resuscitate her. She is stable for now and we are monitoring her."

How the fuck was that possible?

"How could this happen?" Stella asked.

"I don't know. We are trying to find that out."

Even though she understood they needed to look into what had happened, it wasn't the answer Stella wanted to hear. She was on edge. Why did she always have to fight for even the smallest piece of information?

"Why don't you start by telling me who the male doctor was that left my mother's room before all this happened?" she asked as calmly as she could muster.

He looked at her, a big question mark hanging over his head.

He doesn't know about the other person.

"I-I don't know what you mean."

Stella wanted to shake him. How could they not know a stranger had entered the ICU and her mother's room seconds before she collapsed?

"Yeah, I figured as much," she spat disappointedly. "We need to see your surveillance footage," she demanded, pointing at the camera hanging over the reception desk.

"I'm sorry, but I can't just give you—"

"Let me make this easier for you." Samuel stepped in again and at last, Dr. Abelson stammered his cooperation, "I'll see what I can do."

He left hastily down the hallway, like the grim reaper was out to get him, a long sickle in hand, ready to chop off his head, and take his soul. Or maybe it was just the effect Stella had on him.

She was glad he had left. With the adrenaline ebbing, she felt exhausted and slumped onto a bench in the waiting area. She closed her eyes for a few seconds or maybe more, for when she opened them again, feeling a bit more relaxed, Samuel sat next to her, holding out a plastic cup.

The ice cold water felt good going down, extinguishing the last embers of her fury.

"Feeling better?" Samuel asked.

"Yeah, thanks."

"Can you remember anything about the man?"

"No, not really. I only saw him for a second when he left her room and I thought nothing of it." She let her head fall back and rested it against the white hospital wall, when she noticed Samuel's hand moving to her knee, where it hovered for a few beats before he retracted his hand and instead of touching her, ran it through his hair.

"Don't worry. Let's see what the surveillance camera taped."

"No matter what this camera taped, one thing is sure."

"And what is that?" he asked.

She turned her head and looked him dead in the eye. "That this wasn't a coincidence. Someone is trying to kill my mother."

Chapter 15 - The Video

Stella

TWO DAYS.

It has been two days since Stella's mother almost died a second time. Two days since Stella rained fire on the hospital staff for not knowing who went in and out of her mother's room. Two days since Stella had given Samuel's boss a talking-to. Focusing on his failure to treat her situation with the importance it and she deserved, she almost sounded like her father. The Captain had not taken it easily. Men in his position rarely did.

She had tried to explain to him that the possibility of someone trying to hurt her mother was not simply her imagination and that suicide was not the only answer. She had also expected more support from the police.

What she got in return was radio silence.

Instead of taking her calls or answering her questions by email, he instructed his assistant, a woman with the voice of a century-old tractor, to inform her he was indisposed but would call her back. Captain Holmes never did. If it hadn't been for Samuel, who was still working on her case, Stella would have lost all access to information. She was grateful Samuel was still on her team. And while she wasn't afraid of dealing with this herself, she had come to accept and even appreciate having someone in her corner.

She was excited when Samuel called her a short while ago with news he wanted to share in person. He sounded animated and tired at the same time as he asked her to meet him. And now she was staring at her silver smart watch, wondering what was taking him so long to meet her in her hotel bar.

She had just ordered a second coffee when she saw him enter the lobby. He wore black denim, a beige sweater, and a brown leather jacket that was clearly vintage. His five o'clock shadow was gone and his hair was still damp. He looked like an actor on NCIS and wore it with confidence, which people noticed. When he talked to the hostess and the girl blushed, laughing at something he said to her, Stella rolled her eyes.

This fucking guy.

"What can I get you?" the girl behind the bar asked the second Samuel sat down next to Stella.

"I'll take a Coke, no ice."

Samuel waited for his soft drink to arrive, thanked the bartender, and turned to Stella. "How's your mom?"

Appreciating his concern, she relayed what the doctor had told her. That they were lucky to help her so quickly, but that she still wasn't out of the woods and that the next few days would be crucial for her recovery. Samuel told her he was sorry, and she believed him.

"At least the hospital is letting me see her now."

Apparently, Dr. Abelson still had some backbone left.

"I have something I want to show you." Samuel pressed the play button on his phone and a silent video started showing a fuzzy person emerging from a hospital room and making their way out of the building.

"What is this?" Stella asked incredulously, taking the phone from him.

"This is the man who tried to kill your mother."

"How did you get this?" Still transfixed on the small screen, Stella couldn't believe what she was seeing. She had tried everything and everyone she knew in order to get some footage. But nothing had worked, except for Samuel's promise that he'd get this done. Although it felt impossible, she was now looking at a male figure with almost no hair left, walking calmly but resolutely from her mother's room to the emergency stairway, where he slipped on a blue baseball cap before pushing the fire alarm button and vanishing. This was it!

"Remember when you thought charming the nurse wouldn't get me anywhere?" Samuel asked with a glint in his eye.

Stella remembered, but instead of acknowledging that his charm offensive had clearly worked, she found herself wondering if charming was code for sex. Why that thought suddenly popped up in her head, she didn't know, but the sudden unexpected churn somewhere deep in her gut made her extremely uneasy.

"It worked on Dr. Abelson as well. He was very cooperative in the end and more than willing to share a copy of the video footage with a detective in an active investigation," Samuel said with a big smile on his face.

He deserved to be proud. As a PI with no jurisdiction in New York, let alone the US, she couldn't have gotten this on her own. She also wouldn't have gotten a chance to see this if it had been any other police officer. She owed him big time.

"I know, it's not great quality and the camera on the outside of the building didn't capture much more. He knew exactly how to hide from the security cameras. But at least this proves you were right and I have something to work with."

There she had it in front of her. Proof that she wasn't imagining things, that her mother did not try to kill herself. Someone was after her, and Stella needed to know who and why. She felt the powerful urge to hug Samuel, but resisted.

"Any chance forensics found something on the coat he ditched?" she asked instead.

"They are still checking it for prints, but so far there's no match."

Who was this man who wanted to kill her mother?

"I'm sorry I don't have more yet, but the good news is that with this, I can get the Captain on board. Get more people involved."

Stella stopped herself from telling Samuel that he was probably expecting too much of his boss. When she looked at Samuel, there was a spark in his eyes she hadn't seen before. Something inside him had come alive. He looked sharp and focused and, if she wasn't imagining things, there was the hint of a genuine smile on his lips. She could burst his bubble another time.

"Thank you!" she said instead.

Genuinely shocked at her gratitude, he asked, "What for?"

"For holding up your part of our deal?"

"I told you I would. You can count on me. We're a team now," Samuel said, and Stella's intestines tightened.

145

Fuck.

With a grunt, she opened her purse and slid a piece of paper across the bar and over to Samuel.

"What's this?" he asked.

"I found this at my father's place." Stella nodded at the paper, asking Samuel to open it and waited for him to read the words written on it while she took another sip of her coffee.

Samuel's eyes widened.

"My mother had it hidden in her bathroom. At least I think she hid it."

"Any idea who could have written it?" he asked, turning the paper over, probably hoping for more words.

Stella shook her head.

"And there was no envelope?"

"No, nothing that would show the origin."

"This could be the same guy who was at the hospital two days ago. Can I take this?"

Stella nodded and let him fold the paper and put it in his inside pocket. She didn't know what he thought he could find. There were no fingerprints or handwriting to detect. This was a printed sentence on an otherwise clueless sheet of paper.

"Maybe Larry in our lab can find something. Are you the only one who touched it?"

Stella nodded.

"Okay. Might be good to come down to the precinct and leave your prints for comparison. That okay?"

"Sure."

"How long have you had it?" Samuel asked after a moment of silence.

She hesitated to tell him the truth. Guilt crawled up inside her again.

"A few days," Stella said, looking at him counting in his head.

Samuel wasn't an idiot. He knew she had kept this a secret from him. Would he be furious that she hadn't been straight with him? Might he hold it against her and shut her out of his investigation? Would he leave?

"Thanks for telling me," he said a few silent moments later, catching her by surprise. "Does your father know?"

"I doubt it."

An awkward silence crept in while Stella finished her coffee and Samuel played with the condensation on his glass.

"Any idea who else might know about this letter?" he pressed again and Stella knew immediately that he was thinking about a specific person. The same one she had thought about herself. Someone who knew the Woodworths better than anyone else and might have seen or heard something that could help them find out who wrote this letter and probably who was trying to kill her mother.

"I've already reached out to Grace," Stella said and Samuel nodded at her with wide eyes and anticipation on his face.

Of course she had. She wanted to talk to Grace and ask her more questions now that they'd found additional clues. But she also wanted to apologize to Grace in person. Guilt over her father firing Grace had gnawed at her.Wwhile Grace insisted it wasn't her fault, Stella needed to tell her in person how sorry she was. If she hadn't come back, Grace would still have a job.

"And?" Samuel cut through her thoughts in anticipation.

"And I am seeing her on Saturday to ask her some questions."

"Great! Yeah, I think that is a solid idea." He shifted on his chair, slurping the last drops of his Coke through a plastic straw. He was waiting for more, expecting her to offer it now that he had given her so much.

Dammit, he was good.

"Do you want to join me?" The words hadn't left her mouth fully yet when his answer washed over her.

"Yes! Thanks for asking."

Stella rolled her eyes at him, wiggling his eyebrows, but she could barely keep it up. She drank the last sip of her now-cold coffee and asked the bartender to put his Coke on her tab as well. They walked into the lobby, where she gave him the details of when she'd meet with Grace. Stalling, Samuel thanked Stella again before saying what he really wanted to get off his chest.

"Why didn't you tell me?" he asked eventually, his eyes boring into her like he could see right through the shield she kept up.

Because I always had to fight for myself?

Because I've been fucked over more than I dare to admit?

"Because I find it hard to trust people," was the answer she settled on.

"What changed your mind?"

Stella shrugged because she wasn't sure herself. It wasn't just the fact they had an agreement, or that she felt guilty she hadn't been as committed to it as he had. Perhaps it was still her inner Agnes pushing her to work together with someone, or maybe he just genuinely seemed to care.

"I think you are not as bad to work with as I thought."

Samuel's eyebrows shot up and Stella braced herself for one of his cocky answers, but he only smiled at her and nodded. "Okay. I can work with that." Then he started walking towards the revolving doors of her hotel and winked at her before he pressed through them and onto Madison Avenue.

Chapter 16 - The Call

Stella

PATIENCE WASN'T ONE of Stella's strong suits. It was one thing to wait for paternity or DNA test results to give to one of her clients but waiting to talk to Grace with the hopes of shedding some light on who could have written this cryptic message to her mother was almost more than Stella could handle.

Grace had suggested to meet Stella at her local church in Astoria. She was nervous and didn't want anyone close to where she worked asking questions. Which was fine with Stella. After getting fired from the Woodworth household, Grace didn't need someone showing up at her new job asking questions. They had agreed to meet during her lunch break around two, and Giovanni had gotten her to her destination on time again. Early actually. A quality she appreciated in a driver. With his silent and calm nature and no history of accidents on the road, Giovanni was the perfect quiet man for her needs—which reminded her of the other man she needed and who would meet her in a few minutes.

There was still no sign of Samuel. At first, she had thought the dark Suburban behind her was him, but when Giovanni had parked the car in front of the church ten minutes ago, the Suburban passed them. Afraid Grace wouldn't have agreed to meet her if she had known Samuel would be there, too, Stella had kept that detail from both Grace and Samuel.

Trying to kill some time and calm her nerves, Stella picked up her iPhone that lay silent on the black leather seat next to her. She grabbed it and dialed her sister's number again. It had always been a challenge to reach Megan. She was a popular girl and liked to party. And when Megan had started classes at Columbia University, Stella often only received a reply from her sister days later.

Stella was about to hang up again when someone answered.

"Meg?"

"Yeah?" Megan's familiar voice replied.

"It's me, Stella."

"I know. I have caller ID."

"Of course," Stella began, startled by the coldness in her younger sister's voice. Maybe she had reached her at an inconvenient time? Stella checked her watch again but knew what it would show. Almost two in the afternoon.

"I'm glad I finally got you. Have you heard my messages?"

"Yes, I did."

Silence.

"Well, I wanted to keep you updated on mom and everything—"

"How is she?" Megan cut in.

Playing with the button of her blouse, Stella let her eyes wander to the window and to the people outside passing her car. This wasn't a question to answer easily.

"She is still in the hospital," Stella started, pictures of her mother's limp body appearing in front of her. "There was an incident a few days ago and I-I. Meg, I'm not sure mom tried to commit suicide." The last words Stella pushed out through a tightening throat.

Silence again. If it hadn't been for the increased breathing on the other line, Stella would have thought her sister had hung up on her. She must think her crazy like everyone else, throwing this accusation around.

Meg's voice softened, but curiosity laced her words. "What do you mean?"

"Someone went to her hospital room and tried to kill her. She almost died."

"Do you know who it was?" Megan's voice trembled with worry and Stella felt an urge to be close to her sister. To hug her and to find comfort in her embrace as much as she wanted to support her baby sister right now.

"No, I've got nothing so far. The only thing I know is that it was a man, but that's it."

Stella could only imagine what must be going through her sister's head. Especially upon hearing someone tried to kill their mother.

"W-will she...?" Megan asked, a quiver in her voice.

"She is stable for the moment, but the next few days will be crucial. Do you want to come and see her?"

"No!" Megan's answer came like a bullet, and Stella didn't blame her sister.

She didn't want to be here either. But this was their mother. She wanted to tell Megan she might not get another chance to see their mother, but she didn't want to scare her even more. "You know our father isn't here. He hasn't come to visit her since she was hospitalized."

"I'm not going near him. I'm done with him."

Stella wished the same, but this was a situation she couldn't turn her back on. What she wouldn't give for the anonymity of her beloved Hong Kong skyscrapers right now. But chances were high it would soon only be her and her sister. Stella needed to make it clear to Megan that she had her back.

"You know I am here for you, right? We can get through this together."

"I should have done what you did." Megan's answer crashed through the phone like a shockwave.

"What do you mean?"

"You did the right thing by leaving everyone behind. Just drop everything, leave, and never come back."

Stella knew her sister was referring to the day she had packed her things and left home to free herself from her father's tyranny, but the words she used stung. They hit that spot where she kept her guilt locked in over turning her back on her mother and sister, cracking the wall she had built around it slowly but steadily with every day she spent in New York.

"You left this hell of a home and started your own life," Megan continued, and for the first time, Stella heard more than hurt in her baby sister's voice. She felt the anger that had built up in Megan. The same anger she had felt when Jonathan had left her behind.

Tears collected in her eyes, but Stella wouldn't let herself cry over the choice she made to save herself. Crying had never helped anything or anyone. She had to look forward and make sure that when this was over, she would have a better relationship with her sister. Maybe even offer her to come over to China. Spend some time together.

Stella sniffed away the dampness in her sinuses and concentrated on the next step in front of her.

"Did mom behave strangely lately? You know, more than the usual?" she asked with a sisterly smile on her lips, hoping that Megan could shed some light on the personal developments her mother had gone through recently.

"I wouldn't know. We haven't really been in touch the last few months."

Megan sighed, and Stella's heart sank. She had hoped her sister might have been able to give her something, but everyone she tried was a dead end. How could it be so difficult to know more about her own mother?

"You know mom," Megan continued. "She has changed after Jonathan and then after you—"

Stella knew. Stella had first witnessed the change in her mother when they carried her only son out on a stretcher and then on the rainy day when they laid him to rest deep into the wet grounds of the family graveyard. Not only had Jonathan died, a piece of her mother had died with him.

"I don't know, Stel. Maybe she tried to kill herself."

It would have been so easy to accept that. But a man had entered her mother's hospital room intending to kill her. Was her father involved? Maybe. Did he know more? Most likely. Deep in her gut, Stella knew her father wasn't telling her the truth and while he might not have walked into that hospital himself, he knew why her mother was in there, fighting for her life.

"I promise you, I will find out what happened. Even if our father is trying everything to stop me."

There was a moment of silence on the other line and then, with a faint but worried voice, Megan asked, "Are you sure you want to get in our father's way? You know what he is like. What he is capable of."

"I'm not scared of him, Meg."

"Maybe you should be," Megan whispered, her voice heavy with concern. Stella's stomach churned. It hit her again at this moment that when she had left New York, she had gained her freedom, but her baby sister had lost another sibling. Living on the other side of the world, Stella could have also been dead, only reaching out to her sister once every six months.

"You remember the summer we went to Greece and stole our father's car?" Meg suddenly asked, jolting a memory back into Stella's mind that she had almost forgotten.

"You mean the night you bribed me into driving you to a nightclub an hour away so you could meet this cute Greek guy you ran into earlier that morning?" Stella replied with a smile on her face.

"Not the guy, but the dancing on the beach under the stars, surrounded by strangers who didn't know or care who we were."

Stella remembered. They had danced the entire night, and when the first morning light had hit the beach, neither of them wanted to return to the luxury villa their family had rented. It had been one of those few nights they'd gone out together. Megan was four years younger than Stella and way too young to party, but she took her anyway and it had become one of the best nights of her life with her sister. Both of them knew what the consequences of their nightly adventure would be. Still, that night had made the shouting, the beating, and being grounded under the same roof as their father for the rest of the summer worth it. That was the last time she spent a carefree night with her sister. Four months later, Jonathan took his life. Five months later, Stella boarded a plane to Hong Kong.

"That was a pretty great night," Meg sighed into the phone.

"Yeah, it was."

Stella smiled. God, she really missed her sister. No matter what happened to her mother, she'd make sure to be there for her baby sister more. Out of the corner of her eyes, she saw Samuel's familiar cocky stride as he approached the church steps, then quickly ascended them two at a time before disappearing through the large wooden doors.

Time to go.

"I'm sorry Meg, but I've got to go. I am meeting Grace to ask her a few more questions. Maybe she knows more," Stella said and just before she ended the call with her sister, she heard Megan again.

"Stella?"

"Yes?"

"Let me know if mom gets worse and...you know."

"Of course. I love you."

"Ditto."

Then the line went silent. Stella was alone again. She hadn't talked to her sister in over a year, but she hoped it wouldn't take them another year. She wanted to hear her sister's laugh that made everyone around her smile. She wanted to get to know her again, to rebuild their relationship, see her sister, and hopefully find her happy in the place she had made her own home.

Chapter 17 - The Church

Samuel

THE DARKNESS AND THE smell of incense soothed Samuel's senses. He hadn't been to a church to worship since he was little, but even he had to admit the quietness was comforting.

Whenever he went to church, he wondered what the people kneeling on the creaking old wooden benches were praying for. Was it as trivial as money or health, or was it something darker, like forgiveness?

Standing in the votive area of this local church in Queens, he held the stem of the long white candlestick between his thumb and index finger. Using one of the already ignited candles as a match, he tilted the wick of his into the flame until it caught fire.

Looking into the flames dancing in front of him, he thought about the person who had made him step foot in a church again. Melanie. What he would do to get her back? But she wouldn't come back. She was dead, and no matter how much he begged, cursed, or prayed to an invisible entity, it would never change that fact. How could people think that words directed to the heavens would change that?

Even though he didn't believe that lighting a candle would would bring her back, he did it every time he visited a church, which was happening more often than he had expected. It started a month after he had found her. He went to her funeral. He hid from the judging eyes of her parents in the shadow of an oak tree, watching as they lowered her coffin into the ground.

This started an addiction that was almost as strong as his thirst for alcohol. Since then, he had gone to Melanie's grave weekly. He wasn't sure what he was hoping for. Maybe absolution from a dead girl. Maybe he wanted her parents to scream at him. He had never given them the chance to do that. He always hid when he saw them approaching their daughter's grave or moved towards the candle section where they would light one for their lost child. Afterwards, he'd go over and light a candle on their flame, wishing for a chance to turn back time.

"I didn't take you for the believing-kind-of-guy."

He jumped, his eyes sprang open and the picture of blonde hair, white lace, and red turned into the familiar black framed face of Stella.

"Jesus, you almost gave me a heart attack," he said, one hand going to his chest while the other still held the candle.

"What are you doing?" Stella asked, her eyes transfixed on the candle in his hand.

"Nothing," he replied and pressed the candle into an empty holder. When he was finished, he rubbed his hands together and looked at Stella.

"Is she here yet?"

He hoped Stella would drop whatever thought sat on the tip of her tongue. He didn't want to answer questions about—well, whatever she thought was happening here. The intensity of her stare got him sweating, but she let him off the hook.

"No, but Grace and I agreed to meet at two. So she should be here any minute."

"Great," he replied with a dry mouth.

"Listen, I think it might be best if I speak to her alone."

"Yeah, that's not gonna happen." The chuckle came out loud in the otherwise quiet church, and the old man sitting next to them in the back row of the seating area shushed at him. Samuel mouthed a silent sorry to him before he focused on the perplexed woman in front of him.

"Why not?" Stella asked with a frown on her forehead.

"This is an official police investigation, and I'm the lead detective. Of course, I will talk to her."

"I don't want Grace to freak out."

"Does she have something to hide?"

"No. Of course not."

"Well, why wouldn't she want to talk to me then?"

Stella looked at him with the same face his younger sister Rebekka used to wear whenever she couldn't understand why she was supposed to tell him where she was going and with whom. That he was just a year older than her but almost a head shorter hadn't helped him explain to her he had to look after her. Since their father had died a few years ago in a car accident, he had seen himself as the only man in the house needing to protect his family.

But this situation was different. He wasn't a teenager anymore. He actually had every right to talk to this person, and her reluctance to answer his questions put her high on his list of potential suspects.

160

"You remember she just got fired for letting me enter my childhood home? If my father finds out she is talking to the police, who knows what he'll do," Stella said.

She made a good point. Samuel could already see Richard Woodworth calling Grace's employer, planting distrust. Why else would someone as famous as him have to fire a housekeeper of over twenty years when that person had done nothing to deserve it? He wouldn't even need to say she had stolen something or misbehaved. Just the hint would weigh strong enough for most people. He could destroy Grace with a single call.

"And if I let you, the police, talk to her, she will know that it'll go straight to him. Your boss is going to tell him faster than you can type the report. You know I am right."

Damn it, she had a point, again.

But what was he supposed to do? Sit back, let her take the lead and wait for Stella to give him information?

"I will not let you go alone. But—" he added when he saw Stella's frown cut even deeper. "If it makes you feel better, you can introduce me as your partner. Another PI you brought on and I promise I won't take notes about this meeting. You are in charge, but I need to talk to her as well."

"What?"

"I'm not going as Detective Samuel Green, but as your partner, I don't know...call me Tony."

"Tony?"

"Yeah."

"You don't look like a Tony at all," Stella said, her head cocked to one side. "You look more like a Simon or a Roger."

"Simon? Seriously? Do I look like a Simon to you?" Samuel stared at her, playful offense dancing in his eyes. He sighed in defeat when she shrugged her shoulders. "Call me what you want but don't make it Roger. I hate that name. My lab partner in high school was called Roger, and he loved to singe my stuff when the teacher wasn't looking."

Pretending to assess his offer, she let out a sigh. "Fine, Tony it is, but don't start talking with a fake Italian accent or any other stupid kink you want to give your fake persona."

He crossed his fingers over his heart and tipped his head to signal to her that someone was approaching them. Samuel had never seen the housekeeper before. In fact, he had never set foot in Richard Woodworth's mansion. The woman strolling down the aisle was short and round. Looking around the church, she clasped her handbag as if fearing someone would tear it from her.

When her eyes found Stella, they lit up. Gone was the confusion, replaced by relief, but she was still on edge. Her fingers were glued to her handbag, and she eyed every person warily on her way towards them. Once she had reached the safety of their corner and submerged into the shadows, she eased a little.

Stella was right. This woman was scared to be seen with anyone who could jeopardize her job. She was afraid Richard Woodworth would ruin her life, but why would he? Did he really have something to hide and was his housekeeper a witness to something that could compromise him? Would Grace be able to lift the secret her former employer seemed desperate to hide?

Grace took Stella into an embrace that lasted longer than Samuel expected. Under the motherly hug, Stella softened and for the first time he saw a glimpse of the real Stella. Not the tough and demanding one yelling at doormen or journalists and not the cold and distant one that could drink him under the table. This version of her was raw and vulnerable. She was comfortable to be her true self with a woman who must have meant more to her than someone who cleaned after her or prepared food for her.

Samuel suddenly felt out of place, as if he was a perv with a kink sneaking up on an intimate moment he wasn't supposed to see. And for the first time, he really understood why Stella didn't want him here. She was afraid for her friend and he was the reason she felt so protective of her.

He took a step back and lowered his gaze, giving them time and room for Stella to decide when she was ready to continue.

"Thank you for coming, Grace," Stella said and then directed her attention towards him.

Samuel lifted his head in time for her introduction.

"This is a friend of mine who is helping me try to figure out what is going on," she continued, but Grace was hesitant.

She eyed him like a hawk, looked him up and down. It reminded him of himself whenever his sister had brought a boy home for the first time. Like Grace, he'd make them sweat by staring at them in silence until they cracked and either said something ridiculous or genuinely acceptable. Only a few had returned a second time, and this moment felt exactly the same. Grace tried to decipher his intentions on both the case they were working on and the relationship he had with Stella. Would he stand Grace's test?

Introduce yourself.

Tell her why you are here.

That you want to help.

He glanced at Stella, whose stance had changed again. Apprehension covered her like a second skin. Why he decided to ease the tension in their little corner by winking at her in exactly that moment would be one of those unsolved mysteries he'd try to figure out when he was alone. She didn't smile, but her face softened slightly.

"You can trust him, Grace," Stella's eyes met his, surprise grew in him about her statement he felt to be true. And then she added, "He is here to help, isn't that right...Roger?"

Samuel's eyes widened and this time there was a smile on Stella's lips. He opened his mouth to retort, but Grace went for his hand and he found himself shaking her warm and soft hand, stealing his moment of payback.

"Nice to meet you, Roger," Grace said and Samuel clenched his teeth while Stella stifled a laugh in the background.

Turning to Stella, Grace opened the conversation in a whisper. "I don't have a lot of time, but there is something about your mother you need to know."

"Is it true, Grace? Did she try to kill herself?" Stella's voice quivered.

"I don't know. I don't think so."

"You are not surprised that Mrs. Woodworth took pills regularly?" Samuel interjected.

Grace faced him and shook her head.

"No. She took pills, but she would never end her life."

How could she be so sure about that?

The detective in him studied Grace's face, listened for an underlying tone that could compromise her integrity and give him a clue about her role in this whole situation. After over twenty years in the Woodworth household, she was clearly more involved in the family than other housekeepers. She probably knew them better than anyone and had seen more than she'd ever admit.

"Do you know who could have harmed her?" Samuel pushed and this time he saw a twitch in Grace's face. Right under her left eye. A nervous tic or maybe something more.

"Stella, I can't talk about your father."

"Of course you can," Stella said, but Samuel had a feeling it wasn't about Grace's willingness to talk.

"He made you sign an NDA, didn't he?" Samuel let out. He observed Grace getting paler and then, with the slightest move of her head, she nodded. Almost embarrassed by her confession, she lowered her eyes, unable to face Stella.

Stella threw her arms in the air. "Fuck!" Which got her an angry "shhh" from the same guy who had pierced Samuel with his disapproving stare. But she was right. Grace couldn't tell them anything without risking more than she probably could.

But Stella wasn't ready to let it go yet.

"Grace, please. If you know anything, tell me," she pleaded when Grace stayed silent, fidgeting with her handbag.

What was it she struggled so much to share?

"Remember when I told you she had been happy?" Grace started, her voice as quiet as it could be, making it difficult to hear the words pouring out of her.

Samuel leaned in closer.

"It is true she is taking pills. She has migraines and trouble sleeping. Always had."

A quick glance towards Stella who, with the nod of her head, confirmed the statement, had him concentrate on the woman in front of him again.

"She was fine until a few weeks ago. Your father had called Dr. Finkelstein because your mother wouldn't get out of bed and—"

Stella needed Grace to go on. "Why did he see her, Grace?"

Samuel assumed Beth Woodworth had suffered some form of breakdown. It happened, and he knew the feeling of lying in bed, being unable to get up. Or never wanting to get up. The bigger question, however, was what had caused her to be in such a state?

"I think it was too much for her. She had been so happy, and then, when she didn't see him anymore, she couldn't handle it. I tried to tell her that everything would be okay. I really did, Stella, but she was heartbroken. And Dr. Finkelstein only gave her pills, but she needed someone to talk to, but there was no one—"

"What are you talking about?" Stella asked, confused.

Samuel's gut twisted. He knew what Grace was talking about. He knew what message she was trying to deliver to Stella.

With a heavy sigh, Grace opened her handbag and retrieved a small bundle of envelopes that she passed to Stella. Unsure of what she was looking at, Stella took them, turned the bundle in her hand and stared at the name that was clearly written on top of them. *Bettie.* Slowly, the penny dropped and Stella's expression changed from confusion to dread.

With the hint of a shake in her fingers, she pulled at the brown cord and opened the little bow that held the package of letters together. He watched her read every word and every line of the first one, her eyes flying over the contents she held. She then skimmed over the others with big eyes. Whatever she was reading had her speechless and bewildered.

When she was done, she passed the opened bundle to him and stepped aside. Her hand reached for the stone wall of the church. Grace moved over to her, a hand gently stroking her arm, soothing her, and Samuel imagined the two of them sharing such an intimate moment in the past.

Eventually, Samuel tore his eyes from her. He read the letters the same way Stella had. Although he had expected them to contain very personal information, he was still surprised to find that these were love letters. Heartfelt and honest love letters to Beth Woodworth from some man called Paul. A man Stella's mother had apparently started seeing months ago and with whom she had a romantic relationship. Quite a steamy one if the letters were to be believed.

Why did Stella have such a intense reaction to this? Was it a surprise? She had told him she talked with her mother regularly. Surely Beth Woodworth had mentioned something. But the Stella he looked at right now had been clueless.

What other secrets had her mother kept hidden from her? And more importantly, did Richard Woodworth know about his wife's affair and could it be a reason for him to harm her?

"How did you get those?" Samuel asked.

"Mrs. Woodworth gave them to me. She was afraid her husband would find them."

It was a simple answer that made sense to him, especially after knowing that Stella had found another letter in her mother's bathroom. One that sounded nothing like the lovey-dovey words written here. Had her lover turned angry? Jealousy could transform the sweetest labrador into a vicious bloodhound.

"Do you know why they broke up?"

Grace shook her head, still holding on to Stella.

"I am so sorry I never told you, Stella. She made me swear not to tell a soul, but now that she is in the hospital, I couldn't keep it to myself anymore. Someone is trying to hurt her and maybe those letters are the reason."

The accusation hung heavy in the air. Was she referring to Beth Woodworth's lover or to her husband?

"Does my father know?" Stella's voice was weak and strained.

"I don't think so. He called the doctor. Why would he do that if he wanted to harm your mother?"

Why indeed? If Richard Woodworth really wasn't more than a dick, who else could have tried to kill Stella's mother?

Paul could have reason enough and they'd only get to the bottom of this if they spoke with him directly.

Feeling the urge to get going, to pay this man a visit, Samuel let Stella have a few more minutes to come to terms with all this new information. He waited patiently when she moved into the last row of seats and even when Grace left to return to the job she depended on, he sat quietly next to Stella for another fifteen minutes.

"How are you doing?" he asked, genuinely concerned.

"How did I not know this, Sam?" she muffled through the fingers covering her mouth. "How did I not know that my mother had an affair and was seeing this guy?"

Was she upset about her mother's affair or that she didn't know her mother as well as she was trying to prove to everyone?

He squeezed her arm, unsure how to answer that question.

"I am such an idiot." She grunted, leaning back into her seat. "I thought I knew what was going on in her life. But I was just telling myself what I wanted to believe."

"Don't be so hard on yourself."

She turned to face him, her eyes raw. "She is my mother, Sam. What does this say about me as her daughter that I didn't even know what was going on with her?"

"It means your mother did a good job of keeping her affair a secret. She didn't want you to know, and that's on her, not you."

Shifting her head from one side to the other, Stella seemed to contemplate his answer and tried to make sense of what had been dumped on her.

"Jeez, she actually did it. I didn't think she had the guts." She chuckled in defeat and the chaos in her head seemed gone.

"Come on," he said, nudging her shoulder with a smile. "Let's find this guy and have a chat with your mother's lover." He got up from the shrieking wooden bench and held out a hand towards a cringing Stella.

"Oh, you mean as in now?"

"Of course now, or do you have anything better to do?"

With a big sigh, she took his hand and let him help her up. Then they walked silently side by side out of the church and into the afternoon light.

Chapter 18 - The Lover

Samuel

PAUL WAS NOTHING LIKE Samuel had imagined him to be. From the disturbed expression on Stella's face, she felt the same about the man in front of them.

Apparently, Stella's mother had a type: men with little to no hair and a protruding belly, a testament to their love for good food and drink. Samuel liked Paul immediately. Everything about him shouted soft and loving and even Stella smirked at the man who wore a blue down vest over a checkered shirt that was neatly tucked into his slightly oversized pair of dark denim while serving them homegrown peppermint tea on a wooden tray.

It didn't take them long to find Paul, since one letter was neatly labeled with his address, featuring a red fox. The same red fox they passed as a ceramic version on Paul's front porch. Paul's house exuded the same warmth and coziness that he did. He fit perfectly into this small suburban town in Upstate New York where Samuel expected people to know their neighbors' names and go apple picking in fall.

"I still can't believe that she would do something like this," Paul repeated himself while nestling down in his worn-out dark brown leather chair, passing over a plate with homemade ginger cookies, his hands trembling, suggesting early stage Parkinson's. The news of Stella's mother being in the hospital and the possibility that she had tried to end her life had shocked Paul.

Aside from Paul having an alibi for both occasions when Stella's mother almost died, his shaky hands could barely carry a glass of water without spilling. That and the recent knee operation he had gone through was enough proof for Sam to rule him out. There was no way Paul could have descended multiple flights of stairs in a hospital and attempting to kill Beth Woodworth. He wasn't their guy.

"How long have you known Mrs. Woodworth?" Samuel asked before taking a ginger cookie that complemented the contents of the steaming cup in front of him.

Paul glanced over at Stella, who sat silently on the velvet sofa next to Samuel. She had said nothing since they'd arrived, strangely transfixed on the man her mother used to have an affair with. He wondered if this was what she did as a PI. Observing every move of the person of interest, looking for clues in the way they talked and moved. If what they said matched their expression. He used the same method in his job.

"We met at a fundraiser in the city almost a year ago. You know at my age, you don't meet people easily you click with immediately. I was smitten by her the second I saw her. She looked so confident and strong, but also sad, so I introduced myself. It's very easy to talk to Bettie, you must know. We talked for hours and when the evening ended, I knew I didn't want to let her go."

Next to Samuel, Stella flinched at the mention of Paul's nickname for her mother.

"You were not aware that she was married?"

Suddenly nervous, Paul held on to his cup of tea tightly, making the flower-ornamented ceramic shake even more. A few drops of tea landed on his thighs, creating dark spots on his jeans.

"Well, I did. Everyone knows her, her family. Her husband," he added in a darker tone. "But when you meet someone with whom you have such a strong connection, like we did, you don't let them go."

"What did you do?"

"Before the night was over, I told her I wanted to see her again." Paul chuckled at Samuel's surprise. "She turned me down, though. Said she was married and didn't think this was a good idea."

"When did you see her again?" Samuel asked while writing the word *Stalker?* in his little notebook.

"I made sure to go to every meeting, function, gala, wherever I thought she might attend. To be completely honest, I'm not sure what got into me. I am never this impulsive, but I wanted to be with her and if we could only be friends, then that would have been enough."

"But you weren't just friends."

"No, even though we really tried. I respected her decision, and I didn't want to make it harder on her than it already was. And it was hard. I saw the circles under her eyes, the sadness. I wanted to be there for her, be someone she could rely on, because I didn't think she had anyone to turn to. And then it just happened."

Samuel saw the tension in Stella, her rigid posture, her white knuckles, and the predator-like eyes fixated on Paul, ready to tear him to shreds. He could only imagine what it must feel like for her to sit opposite a man who claimed to be the love of her mother's life—if his words were to be believed.

"Do you know if she has behaved any differently or strange lately?"

Paul thought for a second and then shook his head. "No, Bettie was happy. We were happy. We had planned to make it official and be together." Paul paused and looked at Stella. "She wanted to leave your father and move in with me. We had made plans for her to move up here, but she needed to straighten out a few things at home first."

Stella's eyes widened. She took in a deep breath, almost too quiet to hear. Samuel could see her having a hard time listening to all of this, to hear the truth about her mother's life from a stranger.

"I'm sorry," Paul offered Stella. "I never wanted you to find out like this, but your mother insisted on keeping this a secret until she had left your father."

Stella's eyes met Paul's. "Do you have children, Mr. Fox?"

"Yes, I have two sons. Andrew and Daniel," Paul replied, his eyes going to a photo frame on a side table that showed him and his sons on a vacation in Yellowstone National Park with Old Faithful erupting behind them.

"And they are okay with you having an affair with a married woman?" Stella spat.

Samuel's hand twitched with the want to show her his support with a gentle touch. But he kept his hands to himself, concentrating on writing down every detail, hoping to find clues that would lead them to the attacker.

"As I said, it's not that we didn't try, but being with your mother feels like I've finally come home."

"I wonder if your wife sees it that way."

Paul let out a sigh before he got up to grab something from the bookshelf behind him. He slid his fingers gently over a silver frame and handed it to Stella and Samuel. "I don't know what she would have thought because she died ten years ago. But I hope she'd want me to be with someone who makes me happy."

Samuel could almost hear the big lump being swallowed by Paul. His eyes were glassy, but it wasn't hurt or sadness he saw in Paul's eyes. It was the same look Samuel's brother-in-law had worn on the day of his sister's wedding and the birth of his niece. Paul was grateful for the time he had spent with his wife.

"Leaving someone with whom you have spent half of your life isn't easy. Even if you aren't happy, there is comfort in knowing what to expect. That's why I believed your mother when she wrote me she couldn't go through with it." Heartache had crept into Paul's voice.

"What do you mean?" Stella asked before Samuel had a chance.

"Your mother left me a letter two weeks ago. Wait a second, I'll get it." He straightened his vest and left the living room, giving Samuel the opportunity to turn to Stella.

"Are you okay?" Samuel asked.

"I can't believe I didn't know about this?"

"The affair?"

"Everything! I've been so occupied with getting as far away as possible from all of this," Stella said, quietly staring at her hands. A small drop of blood appeared on her thumb, just beneath her nail, where she had peeled off some skin.

"I should have been there for her. I might have been able to help her. Leave my father. Be with Paul. Save her."

Samuel knew the feeling of guilt all too well. The nagging question of "what if" had kept him awake at night more often than he could count. He hated to see the pain those two words caused on Stella's face. If he could, he'd take the burden off her, but for the moment, he could only help her find out what happened to her mother. He put his hand on hers and gently squeezed it.

"It's not your fault. You are not responsible for other people's actions. You can't change the past, but we can keep working and looking at every angle until we find out what really happened."

Stella turned to face him and smiled at him weakly, squeezing his hand back when Paul returned with a letter in his hand.

"You didn't think I'd just let the love of my life go like this, right?"

Stella's eyes ran over the lines that explained that her mother had decided not to leave her father. That she would not destroy a life she had built so carefully over the years and that he should respect her decision and let her go.

She handed the letter to Samuel, who read the two brief paragraphs quickly, then placed the letter on the table in front of them.

"I tried to get in touch with her. Wrote to her, called her and even went to her house. God, I stood there like a heartbroken teenager for hours, hoping she'd just walk out of the lobby, but nothing. I was worried her husband had found out and would give her a hard time. I'm so mad at myself that I didn't insist on her staying with me the last time I saw her, but she wanted to tell your father in person. It looked like he had successfully convinced her to stay. So, I decided to give her some time and hopefully talk to her at one of the functions she'd be at at some point. But she never showed up to any."

"You sound like you think her husband could have had something to do with her hospitalization," Samuel threw in, testing Paul's reaction.

"Bettie didn't talk about her husband often. Don't get me wrong, I also didn't need to hear about the husband of the woman I was having an affair with, but sometimes she'd be lost in thought or extremely sad. I never saw bruises on her, but violence comes in plenty of forms and doesn't always leave visible scars."

"Do you really want to make me believe Mr. Woodworth would risk his freedom over a broken heart?" Sam asked.

"No!" Paul exclaimed. "But he would go a long way to save his reputation."

"What do you mean?"

"A few days before I received this letter from her, Bettie had arranged a meeting with her lawyer. The family lawyer."

"Why?" Samuel asked when Paul hesitated to continue.

"She needed money," Stella interjected.

"Yes, Bettie wanted to make sure she wouldn't be a burden to me. She wanted to take her share of money out of the family account."

Money. It was always money or ego in Samuel's experience.

"That would have been a nice little cushion for you, then."

Paul laughed at Sam's remark. "Thanks, but I really don't need the money. I am doing pretty well, always have and I assure you I wasn't with Bettie for her money. I love her."

Samuel had to agree that Paul didn't seem like your typical gold digger. He lived in a nice house, in a friendly neighborhood and everything he had seen of him shouted comfortable retiree. Still, he struggled to believe that a man like Richard Woodworth would risk everything over some alimony he might have to pay, which would probably barely leave a dent in his pockets. But men like him also had other ways of getting their way without making their own hands dirty.

A bitter chuckle escaped Stella. "My mother didn't write this letter," she said suddenly and with such certainty in her voice, Samuel was convinced she'd cracked the case.

Both men looked at her, letter in hand, eyes transfixed by the words on it.

"What do you mean? Are you sure?" Samuel asked.

She sighed and dropped the letter on the coffee table for them to read. "This sounds a lot like my mom and I can see how someone could mistake those words for hers. But my mom didn't sign her name like this." Stella pointed to her mother's last name and the T with two almost straight lines going through its middle.

"There is only one person I know who writes a T like this," Stella said.

"Who?" Paul asked, but Samuel knew the answer already.

A shadow fell over Stella's face. She swallowed hard before she answered, "This letter, Paul, was written by my father."

Chapter 19 - The Kiss

Samuel

SPRAWLED OUT IN FRONT of them on the beige carpet floor of the hotel room, Stella and Samuel looked at the evidence they had collected. Stella sat cross-legged next to the paper chaos of her mother's case. With a gigantic yawn she didn't hide behind a hand, she stretched her arms above her, tilted her head from side to side and eased the tension in her neck with loud cracks. After hours of hunching over documents on the floor, his spine felt the same, but he never cracked his neck like that.

Stella sighed. "This is ridiculous. How can we not have anything?"

A sheet of paper came flying across the coffee table Samuel was sitting at. He leaned back into the soft gray fabric of the sofa with an annoyed grunt and closed his eyes for a few seconds. She was right. After days of looking at every single angle, they still had nothing. No one wanted to talk to them. Either they genuinely knew nothing or they were too scared of the wrath of the all-too-powerful Richard Woodworth.

When Paul had told them about Stella's mother intending to bring her financial affairs in order before leaving her father, Stella immediately reached out to Bob, the lifelong family lawyer. Her mother must have tried to move money into her own account. According to Stella, growing up and living in the Woodworth household meant financial affairs were something her father dealt with. They never had to worry about money or about being unable to pay for anything with their Platinum American Express credit cards, but Stella could never own her own bank account. Everything went through her father, including her mother's finances. The fact that Beth Woodworth took out money to put it in her own account would have made her father furious, and maybe that's how he found out about the affair. But would it be motive enough for him to try killing her? Would he really go that far?

As expected, Bob didn't give them anything, but it had been worth a shot.

There was another option that seemed more likely now that they looked at all the information they had collected. Maybe Richard Woodworth didn't do it. Maybe he was just a dick. A terrible person, the worst, but not involved at all in this mess in front of them.

He heard Stella get up and move towards the opposite side of the room.

"I need a drink. Want one?"

"Sure, I'll take a beer—" Samuel said, stopping himself immediately. "Actually, can you grab me a Coke?"

The mini fridge door opened and Sam watched Stella rustle through its contents of miniature bottles, searching for the right remedy. She settled for a mini-bottle of Smirnoff and grabbed a can of Coke before closing the fridge door with her foot.

She had changed into a pair of black lounge pants and a gray sweater that looked expensively soft—cashmere probably. Her dark hair fell loosely onto her shoulders. Barefoot, she moved over to him, studying the can intently.

"You really shouldn't drink this. I know it says no calories, but what the fuck is aspartame?"

Samuel blinked his concentration back and scratched the stubble on his chin. He took the can offered to him and thanked Stella.

"Says the one who is about to down her vodka," he deadpanned in her direction when she twisted the lid open.

"Vodka is basically water and potatoes. And both of them are good for you." She tipped her bottle towards Samuel in a mock toast before taking a drink.

His gaze was glued to her sleek neck while she swallowed the contents of the mini bottle. His mouth felt suddenly dry. The can fizzed open, and he poured the dark brown, almost caramelized liquid into his system.

His phone rang next to him. Staring at the number on the screen, he eventually pressed the decline button and took another sip. Still holding the phone in his hand, another call broke through the silence. Samuel put the can down on the coffee table, right on the light cherry wood, ignoring the coasters staged in the middle. He declined the call again and turned off the sound before he slid it strategically under his jacket that lay crunched up on the sofa next to him.

Stella looked at his jacket and back at him, questions on her face she didn't ask. The muffled vibration of yet another call had her break the silence.

"You should take that. It might be important."

Samuel followed Stella's index finger, pointing at his jacket. "It's fine," he sighed. "I can call back."

"Are you sure? Whoever is calling seems determined to reach you."

Samuel knew he should answer the call from Nigel, his sponsor. He hadn't been to a meeting since he started working on the case almost two weeks ago. He hadn't even checked in by phone. No wonder Nigel was worried. But he didn't want to do this now. In front of Stella. He averted his eyes, staring at his hands in front of him instead of the sharp green eyes that were fixated on him, slicing through him like he was soft butter.

Stella picked up her empty vodka bottle and strolled towards the white door opposite her bed. "Take the call. I have to use the bathroom, anyway." She closed the door quietly. He heard her dump the bottle in the trash with a metallic clatter.

He ran his hands through his hair and glanced over to his jacket, where the vibrations had started again. He took in a deep breath before he fished out his phone. Sliding his right thumb across the screen, he unlocked the screen and answered the call as cheerily as possible.

"Hey Nigel. What's up?"

But Nigel didn't fall for his unusual gaiety. "Jesus, Samuel. Where are you? Are you okay? I've tried to reach you for ages. Why haven't you called back or texted?"

While his sponsor continued to list all the possibilities of returning a message, Samuel got up and trotted over to the window. Moving the curtain aside with one finger, he listened half-heartedly to him go on about the urgency to check in regularly with his sponsor, dropping the occasional "uh huh" or "yep" to prove he was paying attention.

"I'm sorry, but you really don't need to worry. I'm fine."

"That's the worst line a sponsor can hear, you know that."

Samuel closed the curtain, turned around, and tucked his hand under his arm. "I actually mean it."

The momentary silence on the other line told Samuel that Nigel was at least considering this to be honest.

"Have you been drinking?" Nigel sounded worried.

"No." It came as a reflex, like saying his name, but for the first time Samuel realized it was true. He had been so occupied with this case that he hadn't felt the urge that always creeped up in the evenings. Or mornings. Or afternoons, if he was really honest with himself. His brows furrowed when he saw the half-empty can of Coke sitting triumphantly on the table.

"I haven't felt the urge to drink in a little while." He chuckled into the phone, surprised by the fact himself.

"That's great, Samuel."

It was. He had been sober before. For a time, but that nagging voice in the back of his head had always been there with him, questioning his strength. Luring him into his old habit, eventually. Not this time. That voice had been quieted by another voice he always heard. One that would always stand up for the right thing. One that would honor the promise he had given when he joined the police force. *Fidelis ad Mortem*; faithful unto death. He felt strongly about this case. Protective over Stella. And he would do everything in his power to solve this.

Through his epiphany, he saw the bathroom door open and Stella emerged quietly. Checking for him and if he was still on the phone, he nodded at her to enter.

"Are you still there?" Nigel's faint voice broke through to him.

Samuel cleared his throat before he spoke. "Yeah, I'm still here."

"Why don't you come down to a meeting tomorrow? It would be great to hear about your achievement."

"Yeah, sure. I'll do that. I promise." Time to get Nigel off his back.

"Oh, and Sam."

"Yeah?"

"You should be proud of yourself. This is a big deal. Stick to whatever you are doing. It sure seems to work."

They exchanged their goodbyes and Stella sat down next to him on the sofa.

"Everything okay?" Stella asked and the protectiveness he felt for her came rushing over him with another sensation. One that was way more dangerous than the possibility of getting shot.

"I'm an alcoholic, Stella," he pushed out before he changed his mind. She had called him out on it before, but he had never told anyone so bluntly outside his support group. Not even Holmes. He braced himself for the reaction of either disgust, disappointment, or pity. He hated pity the most. But he couldn't find any trace of it on her face. Her eyes darted to the can on the table. A droplet of condensation running down the black-coloured tin. She tilted her head and squinted her eyes at him, questioning his statement in her mind.

"I haven't seen you drink for a while now," she stated as a matter of fact.

Samuel smirked. "I could be drinking when we don't see each other."

Stella suddenly leaned into him, taking him by surprise when she took an audible sniff at him. His smirk vanished, replaced by a confused gape.

"I don't smell any alcohol on you."

Her statement took his breath. Or maybe the fact that she was close enough to him he caught a sniff of her scent. A mixture of heavy earthiness and light flowers filled his nose. He swallowed hard.

"I brushed my teeth this morning," he replied.

Stella tilted her head and squinted at him. "Yeah, but the smell lingers. On your skin, in your clothes."

"You seem to know your drunks."

"I've made acquaintances with some," she replied, and for a split second, her eyes shot to his lips. Or so he thought. He wasn't fully sure. What to make of this, her in front of him, his heartbeat increasing slightly. He wanted to blame whatever boiled inside him on the alcohol he hadn't had. Maybe it was a rush from the Coke. Or simple imagination, coming from tiredness. Stella hadn't given him any sign that she was interested in him other than solving this case. He wasn't interested in more, right?

"Have you?" she asked, but he looked at her, confused. "Have you been drinking when you aren't with me?"

He shook his head in response.

"Why not?"

For a moment, he hesitated, contemplating how much he should open up to someone he basically just met.

Someone he was working with. Someone who made him feel less like the loser he was.

"I started drinking just over a year ago. My drink-versary was two days ago," he started with a chuckle and a gaze into the emptiness of the room. "I had been working on this really nerve-racking case of a sixteen-year-old girl gone missing. Her parents had contacted us about the disappearance, crying the whole time. The dad, in particular, was shaken to the core. Melanie, their daughter, had never done anything like this before. She'd always tell them where she was and with whom. They trusted her completely, their perfect daughter."

Stella scoffed at the phrase but said nothing, so he continued.

"For months I wrecked my head, contacted everyone who knew her, spoke to every family member. I followed all the rules to make sure we'd find her quickly." He shook his head uncomfortably, like a nerve was stuck in his neck, causing him constant pain.

"What happened then?"

"I don't know why, but I had this feeling. Deep in my stomach, just underneath my last rib, whenever I saw a photo of her with her uncle or spoke to her uncle. He had this look that hit a nerve or something. He was so friendly and supportive, worried to death. A really nice guy, but his eyes were stone cold. Like he was a puppet, attached to strings that made him move, but his eyes didn't show any emotion. They were lifeless."

A shiver ran through him as he rubbed his arms, trying to fend off the chill of his memories. Stella placed a reassuring hand on his arm, encouraging him to continue.

"But he was clean. Had an alibi and witnesses. I couldn't find anything on him. When I told my boss I wanted to go back to his place, check it again, he shut me down."

"Why?"

"I think after months of nothing, they'd become tired. Or they thought she must have run away. Nothing hinted at something more sinister. So my boss told me to sit tight. To follow the rules and trust in the evidence. He laughed at me when I told him about my gut feeling," Samuel scoffed.

"But you didn't sit tight."

Samuel smiled at Stella. She knew him better than some of his colleagues did.

"No. I went back anyway. Sat in my car for hours, waiting for her uncle to leave his house and once he had driven off to work or wherever he had to go, I stepped inside. I looked everywhere. Took the whole place apart. It was a mess, and I knew I would have to pay hard for this. Suspension probably."

It was still hard for him to think about the frenzy he had worked himself into. The ease with which he had cut through the sofa cushions, or how he ripped each cereal box apart, little round honey Cheerios rolling around the floor, crunching loudly under his step.

"I knelt on the living room floor, crying like a baby and threw a glass of water he had forgotten on his coffee table across the room. Water drenched the hardwood floor. And then I saw it. The small crack in the floor where the water pooled and vanished."

Stella let out a quiet gasp at the discovery and suspension of what was to come.

"Once I had ripped that one floor board off the ground, the others lifted easily." Samuel wiped his forehead like he was sweating under the effort of opening the floor right here, right now, and not over a year ago.

"The round metal grip to a hidden door was just there, inches away, and it led into a separate basement he must have dug himself over the years. Raw walls, miner's lamps hanging off the ceiling. I knew he had her down there before I saw the provisionary bathroom he had installed with something that looked like a toilet and a sink. Seeing the dirty pink drape covering a mattress was the proof I didn't want to see."

His hands shook the same way they had before he'd pushed that damned curtain aside. Stella took his hand and squeezed it gently.

"Melanie was behind that curtain, right?"

He nodded and swallowed hard. "She lay there, covered in a white linen dress. She looked like a fucking bride. But instead of a hopeful smile for the future on her face, I stared at the pale shell of a young and vibrant girl that was supposed to go on dates, have her first kiss, and decide which colleges to apply for."

He remembered turning around and vomiting whatever was left in his stomach right onto the ground. That was also when he saw the scratches on the door, which she must have left trying to claw her way out of her chamber of horror.

"I'm so sorry Samuel."

"If only I had listened to my gut feeling earlier. If I had looked into her sick uncle earlier, I might have been able to save her. But I was a coward. I obeyed the rules people in the office had written who had never been out there doing the job. Sometimes you need to bend the rules because the bad guys don't play by rules either. I should have been there earlier. I should have saved her." He stopped to press his hands into his eyes and rubbed them until he saw stars.

Stella's fingers drew circles on his arm, gently numbing his anxiety with her warm touch.

"Jesus, Sam. You don't know that. Maybe you would have been there earlier. But maybe you wouldn't have found that hidden door trap. No one could have known that her own uncle was such a pervert and kept his niece as a bride to be under his living room."

He believed Stella meant well, and he had heard those exact words before, but he knew it was his fault. The same way Melanie's parents knew it when he had to tell them that her uncle had raped her repeatedly over months before strangling her while he was following the wrong leads. In that moment, when he looked Melanie's mother in her eyes, he saw her rage break free. And her fury over losing her daughter manifested in him. She had slapped him hard across his face before smashing her fists into his chest. He had hoped her father would do the same, but the man just sat on the steps of his front porch, rocking back and forth, mumbling that this cannot have happened to his baby girl.

"When I came home that night, I went straight to the liquor cabinet and emptied two bottles of Jim Beam. I didn't even take a shower to wash off all the dirt. I've basically been drinking since then." While he had talked about every detail of finding Melanie's body with his colleagues, he had never shared this last piece of information about the night that destroyed him. He didn't know why it felt okay to tell Stella. Maybe because he had always been drawn to broken souls like him who had seen the devil before.

"What happened to her uncle?"

"The fucker got what he deserved. At least what the law sees as the right punishment," Samuel spat through his teeth. "I know I should be happy we got him, but Melanie was still dead. Her family was so devastated. I couldn't bear looking at them. If I had just trusted my gut. Maybe—" The tightness in his chest blocked the words from coming out.

"You did everything you could," Stella offered, but Samuel shook his head, unable to believe what he knew not to be true. Her hand palmed his cheek, and she turned his face towards her. "Look at me!"

Her understanding and encouraging eyes burnt into his soul, hurting him deep within.

"You gave them closure. Thanks to you, they could bury their girl. You got a crazy, sadistic perv off the streets. You should be proud of yourself!"

They locked eyes for a few moments, Samuel's heart pounding in his chest. He felt Stella's warmth radiate through her hand into him until she dropped it. The warmth was gone, yet she still smiled at him.

"You know what's really insane? I never talked to them. That night or at Melanie's funeral. I never mustered the strength to speak to them."

"You should. I am sure they'd like to thank you."

It seemed so easy coming from her, as if it wasn't the hardest thing to do.

"Hm, maybe."

Stella shifted her attention back to the pile of paper in front of her, swallowing hard under Samuel's gaze.

"Why is this case so important to you?"

"I don't want anything to happen to your mother," he said. "Or to you."

He didn't add that he couldn't let this go unsolved, the fear of failure looming over him since the discovery of Melanie's fragile body. He also didn't add that he needed to figure this out for his own wellbeing, and what he thought made him a good detective. And he definitely didn't add that he couldn't bear the thought of losing Stella to yet another psychopath who might be running through the streets of Manhattan.

Her eyes darted back to his.

Her hand was still on his arm when he covered it with his, his thumb softly stroking her wrist, just above the golden bracelet with a half moon pendant dangling off it. He felt the hair on her arm stand up and it sent waves of heat through him. He should stop this right now. He was jeopardizing his job, this case, the friendship that had developed between them. Any sane person would get up and leave, but Samuel was far from thinking rationally. When she opened her palm to his touch, Samuel eagerly traced the skin of her palm with his forefinger.

He hadn't expected this urge to feel her close to him, and he wasn't prepared for her leaning into him and brushing her lips over his. Her lips felt warm and soft. He knew better than to give into this, but his body craved the comforting embrace of another person.

His attempt to resist lasted only a few seconds. Then something carnal took over. Samuel's heart almost jumped out of his chest when he slid his hand up to Stella's face and cupped her head. He didn't stop her when she parted her lips, inviting his tongue in. He didn't stop when she moaned loudly as he held her tight against him. And he didn't stop her when her fingers fidgeted with the buttons of his light blue shirt, opening each one until his chest was fully exposed to the touch of her hands and lips.

Instead, he let her lead him to the king-sized bed in the adjacent room where he drowned himself in her touch and quieted the voices in his head for a short while.

Chapter 20 - The Talk

Stella

STELLA HADN'T INTENDED to sleep with Samuel for two reasons. First, she didn't want him to think she had initiated the kiss because she felt sorry for him and the story he had shared with her. Second, she didn't want him to think there was more to them. She wasn't the relationship type. Men rarely stayed with her, or at least not for long. She had emotional baggage she couldn't shake off, like Chen had pointed out to her so kindly a few years back. Chen and she had dated only a few months, casually, when he had told her he wouldn't be seeing her again. And she had been okay with that. He could have said it with less relief in his voice, but she generally agreed with him. It's not that she had wanted a husband and a family, anyway. Not with her terrifying gene pool.

Exhaustion had gotten the best of her, and knowing Samuel was equally broken had just led to the inevitable. It had been an urge she needed to get out of her system.

Nothing more than a fuck to release tension. She assumed Samuel knew that. But when she woke early this morning, trapped in his warm bear hug, one of his legs draped over her and an expression of peace and bliss on his sleeping face, she wasn't so sure anymore. That's why she wriggled her way out from under his touch. Why she grabbed her clothes and shoes off the carpet, her bra dangling off the side of the armrest. And why she tiptoed out of her hotel room like a cheap hooker without leaving so much as a note for Samuel to explain what she was doing or where she was going.

It was somewhat strange and comforting at the same time to work with a person who was so much like her and thought the same way as her. If she hadn't known better, she would have been convinced they'd been partners for years. And it's not that she hadn't enjoyed it. Despite his inclination for alcohol and his often wild appearance, he knew how to please a woman. Which was very unexpected. Stella shook off the memory of a loud moan escaping her mouth.

She needed to clear her mind, which was why she currently exited her hotel in search of fresh air and a coffee shop. Making out with the lead detective on her case wouldn't get her the answers she was looking for.

A black Suburban slowed beside her but continued to match her pace. It wasn't her driver, Giovanni, because she had told him she wouldn't need him today. With black tinted windows, Stella couldn't look inside the car. There was no way for her to make out the driver or the occupants in the back. Her stomach twisted. Was this the same car she had seen when she met Grace? Was she imagining things? A black Suburban in Manhattan was as common as Mustangs on the Florida Keys Highway. They were everywhere.

There was only one way to find out who was following her.

She stopped and turned to face the vehicle, which had slowed to a standstill. Her eyes burned into the car's body while she took step after step towards it until she was almost certain she could see a man's silhouette behind the wheel. But before she reached the door and knocked on the window with her knuckle, the car sped up and drove off.

What the fuck was that?

A sudden idea appeared in Stella's head. Maybe it was paranoia, but after everything she had heard and seen in the last few days, it wouldn't be too far-fetched. Had her father put someone on her to follow her? Was he trying to scare her?

This had to stop.

Her encounter with Grace was stuck in her head like an old LP. It had been so obvious that her father knew more and had hidden information from her. Which was why Stella hailed the next Yellow Cab and told the driver to get her downtown as quickly as possible.

Twenty minutes later, she stood in front of her father's office building, waiting for him to come out. Since she had been banned from the building, she couldn't just go up. He'd have security tackle her and throw her on the ground faster than she could say her name. So she had to do the next best thing: lurk next to his office building, waiting for him to exit.

She checked her watch. Almost two hours had passed since her arrival and she'd had no sighting of her father yet. At least there was also no sign of the Suburban that had followed her. When she was ready to admit that this had been a terribly childish and unorganized idea, he finally emerged through the revolving doors of his building. Stella threw the cup of coffee she had gotten half an hour ago in the trash and readied herself to walk over to him when she stopped in her steps. Right behind him, a tall man followed him outside. She would have recognized this man anywhere.

Jeremy.

Her ex-boyfriend carried a portfolio from which he retrieved documents that he then handed over to her father. They exchanged words, probably further instruction, before her father patted Jeremy on the arm. While Jeremy turned to go back inside, she watched her father walk over to the black SUV that was parked in front of him.

A man in black stepped out and walked around the car to open the door for her father. When he closed the door and made his way back to the front, Stella jumped on the opportunity. With just a few fast strides, she reached the car herself, opened the back door, and slid into the luxurious leather seat next to her father.

To her relief, the car keys were on the front console, just as she had hoped. Before her father could react to the sudden intruder, she grabbed the keys and locked the two of them inside.

The newspaper her father had opened rustled loudly when he scrunched it together and placed on the middle seat.

"What the hell…" he grunted, and Stella wondered if he hadn't had his morning coffee yet.

"Hi, Dad. I was just in the area when I saw you. You don't mind if I catch a ride with you, do you?"

Both of them could hear the driver's frustrated cursing as he struggled in vain to unlock the car. When he banged against the blacked-out windows, Stella's father lowered the window down on his side.

"It's fine, John. It'll just be a minute."

John immediately complied, and in a moment of confusion about what to do with himself, he leaned against the car, probably waiting for his next instruction.

Stella's father closed the window again and turned to her.

"I told you never to come back here and you still have the audacity to show your face like this."

"Since when did you know?"

His eyes narrowed, but he didn't ask her what she was talking about, so she repeated her question, adding Paul's name. A spiteful grin washed over her father's face.

"You mean that pathetic little fling?" He snickered before he folded the newspaper neatly, which he had thrown around like a spoiled child.

Stella crossed her arms over her chest. "Clearly not that pathetic if she planned on leaving you."

Glancing over at her, he almost rolled his eyes at her. "Please. Your mother would never leave me. She knows quite well where her place is and what is best for her."

The way he talked complacently about her mother had Stella wanting to take the newspaper and whip him with it.

"Because she is too scared to leave. Like everyone else, they have always been too scared to leave the prison you have created for them."

"You clearly weren't."

He was right. Of all the members in his family, she was the only one who had broken the circle and stepped into a new life. If one didn't count Jonathan, who killed himself to escape.

"That's because I'm not scared of you."

The look he sent her had her doubting her words for a second. The tinted windows dimmed the harsh morning light, covering half of his face in dark shadows and sending a shiver down her spine. It would play tricks on the bravest men. Was there really ever a way to escape this devil?

"Is there anything else you want to tell me or are we done?" He broke the spell with his usual annoyed voice that meant he wanted to get on with the important things in life. If she didn't push further now, he would simply dismiss her without providing any new information.

"I know it was you who wrote the letter to Paul. I recognized your handwriting."

He sighed loudly and reached for the bottle of Pellegrino that was neatly stacked in the console between the two of them. Twisting the cap open, he poured water into a glass and took a long sip, not even acknowledging her remark.

"Detective Green and I met him," she said.

A few seconds passed before her father let out a smug chuckle. "I see where this nonsense is going. You've been spending too much time with this failure of a police officer."

"That man has shown more professionalism in this case than any of your buddies."

He didn't react at first. He just looked at her, scanning her face for something. When he leaned into her, she instinctively retreated. "He is a drunk and a disappointment to law enforcement."

"Sometimes people drink to rid themselves of the horrors of their life."

"And I assume one of those is me?" he asked, pointing at himself. "Is that why you are sleeping with him?"

Stella's mouth dropped to the floor. Her silence was the assurance to his statement, and he nodded proudly. She tried to form a question. How did he know? Why would he ask this? Or what did it matter? It wasn't officially against the rules. She wasn't a person of interest in this case, but she also knew that they walked in a very shady gray area and that her sleeping with Samuel would look more than strange if it ever came out. That her father knew verified her suspicion that he had someone following her. How else would he have known? Someone must have seen Samuel meet her in her hotel on several occasions and not leave last night.

"You must be very desperate if you let someone like him touch—"

"Who I sleep with is none of your concern. I'm not the person who should be judged. You are. And I will show everyone who you really are."

Threatening his status and his power has always been the key to the stone of a heart he had beating in his chest. And it worked this time as well.

"Threatening me will have consequences you can't even conceive."

"Is that what happened to my mother? Did she put up a fight? Did she tell you she'd take half your money? Money that also belongs to her? Or did she threaten you otherwise?"

A muscle in his jaw twitched and Stella's eyebrows shot up like tents.

"She did, didn't she? She threatened to make her leaving you public and you wouldn't have that." Confidence drove her forward, closer to him, trapping him between her and the door of the car.

"You are as insane as her," he spat.

"Is that why you want her gone?"

The force of his backhand hit her unexpectedly hard. Her hand shot up to her cheek where the heat of the impact radiated. For a few beats, there was silence around her, just a faint ringing in her ears. It felt exactly like that time when she was a teenager and some trash reporter photographed her coming out of a club wearing nothing but a black bra and tight black leather pants. He'd hit her not because she was risking rape or murder. He'd hit her because the journalist threatened to publish a negative piece about him if he didn't pay him a decent amount of money. The payment was never made. Instead, her father had gone after the journalist, digging up dirt about him and his family until he was fired and the police sent over to his private residence. That's the efficiency with which her father worked.

"You can also call off your sniffer dog," Stella added as a side note.

"I don't know what you are talking about."

"The guy you have following me?"

He looked at her, perplexed. "I expect a lot of insanity from you, but this is even too much for you."

"Jesus Christ. Even now, you can't be honest." She waved her hands in front of her.

"You know what? Don't. I don't care if you have someone following me. I care about my mother. I know you have something to do with it and I swear to you I'll find

201

out what it is and finally bring you to admit the horrendous things you do to people."

If he hadn't slapped her already, he would have done it now. Stella saw his hand twitch again, primed to release the pressure of his pent-up anger on her body. When he lifted his hand, she braced herself for the next one, but instead, he clicked the button on his side to open the door and got out. In a few unusual quick steps around the back of the car, Stella's side opened and his big hand reached for her arm and dragged her out of his car.

"I will not listen to any more of your ludicrous accusations."

His fingers dug painfully into her skin. When he finally released her, blood returned in pulsating waves to the spot just under her armpit where her father had clawed at her. She turned to face him, massaging the area that would soon show five small roundish bruises, and stared at a forefinger pointing at her.

His nostrils flared, but his voice was low and sharp. "Never come back here. You are not welcome and if you ever show your face again, I'll have the police drag you out and dump you where you belong. On the streets."

"Don't worry, *Dad*. Next time we'll meet, it'll be before a judge," Stella hissed.

He turned and let John help him in the car again. The SUV drove off quietly, like nothing had happened. She had spent less than fifteen minutes in the car with him, but to her, it felt as if she had lost a year of her life.

In order to stop her furious hands from trembling, she grabbed her shoulders. She wouldn't let him get away with this. Not again. For once in his life, he would have to deal with the consequences of his actions.

"Having a bad day?" a familiar voice asked next to her, a voice she hadn't heard in years, but that still sent butterflies through her as if she were a teenager.

She turned and there he was, the boy that had taken her virginity. The only one she had ever felt something resembling love for. Only that he wasn't a boy anymore. Jeremy had grown into a tall, handsome man who knew how to dress and who hadn't lost the boyish grin that had always made her knees go soft.

He was still one of the most handsome men she had ever seen. Streaks of gray adorned the sides of his head, but they didn't make him look old. They gave him character and a feeling of knowledge on an otherwise boyish face.

"I never expected to see you again," he said with a friendly chuckle, one hand casually resting in his navy blue pants pocket.

"Well, I could say the same, but then, I always knew you had a fond feeling towards my father." It came out harsher than she had expected. Who knew a broken teenager's heart could do that twenty years later?

Jeremy frowned, and his smile changed into disappointment. Or was it sadness?

"Listen, I know it's been years but I am actually happy I ran into you," he said, but Stella wasn't that easily convinced.

"Oh, really?"

"Yeah. The way things ended between us—"

Digging up that part of her past was not an option. "Please, that was a lifetime ago." There really was no need to open an old wound, in her opinion.

"But it still bothers me. I think you misunderstood what had happened—"

"Oh, I think I got it just fine. You wanted a seat at the big table and you didn't mind getting there through me. Don't worry. I'm not insulted or angry. Anyway, it worked out for you, didn't it?"

"That's not—" he started searching for words. "Yes, your father's company is one of the biggest in the city, in the US even, and I'm very lucky that I got to be part of this company—"

She already knew that part.

"My father has bought this city with dirty lawsuits and threats and he is using every single one of his employees to keep it that way and to make himself richer and stronger. So, I'm glad you are so happy to be part of his entourage."

Jeremy's mouth dropped, and Stella felt a pang of satisfaction. Maybe it was a good idea to discuss some unresolved issues and let off some steam.

"I am sorry you see it that way."

And when Stella thought the encounter from her past was officially over, Jeremy added a question she was not prepared to answer honestly. "Is that why you broke up with me? Because your father liked me?"

"I knew your priorities, and that you didn't mind going for the daughter of the biggest hit in town to reach your goals and get what you want. Actually, now that I think of it. You are the perfect fit for his company."

There was no denying that she had not gotten over how their relationship had ended. Although Stella had been the one to call it quits, she felt cornered into making an impossible decision. Accept that she would only ever be second best and stay with the boy she had loved or end it before her father's control drew her in even further.

"Wow! Is that what you think?" Jeremy scoffed.

She had clearly upset him, but she didn't understand why he made such a big deal out of it. They were adults now. He didn't have to tell her what he felt he needed to do in order to make it to the top.

"You'd have broken up with me soon, anyway. Why prolong it!" she explained, but Jeremy shook his head and she felt an uncomfortable tingle in her stomach.

"I was never with you because of your father. If you had asked me to drop my internship, I would have done it. For you."

They paused for a second and Stella let his statement sink in.

No way, she told herself, feeling her stomach twist.

"Ah c'mon, Jeremy. This is all water under the bridge. I am not angry at you. You did what you had to."

Who was she trying to convince?

With an unexpected step toward her, Jeremy closed the small distance between them. She felt the heat of his body, smelled a hint of cologne, and a memory exploded in her head. Him, right in front of her on the stairs of the private school both of them went to. She, standing just a little taller thanks to the steps leading up to their school building. She didn't intend to tower over him, but she needed to put some distance between them. Make sure she'd say what she had to say. The look on his face when she gave him the news. They were over. Yesterday they had spent the day together as a couple, holding hands, kissing, and tomorrow they wouldn't even greet each other in school. Jeremy didn't understand why she was doing it. She barely understood it herself. Almost didn't go through with it. But she had to, no matter how much he asked her to sleep on it. She had made up her mind and needed to see it through. She had done the right thing. It had been the right choice.

Then why did it hurt so much and keep her up night after night for weeks?

"I didn't understand what you were working through back then," he was referring to the problems at home she had told him about when they smoked joints and she didn't care if he knew. About the shouting, the rules, the occasional smack. "You were my first love," he continued, with nostalgia in his voice. "And I would have been there for you if I hadn't been such a dumb teenager." He smiled at her like he used to. Warm, honest, and absolutely adoring.

Unsure how to react and afraid to say something stupid like *I loved you, too*, she just nodded at him.

"How long are you staying? Maybe we can catch up over dinner—"

Oh no! That is a terrible idea.

"I won't be here long. I'm just here to check in on my mom, make sure she is okay, you know. So, there really isn't much time and then I'll be heading straight back home. You know, work and all—"

God, stop babbling.

"I don't think I'll have the time."

Jeremy nodded understandingly. "Of course. How is your mom, anyway? Any news? I sent her flowers, wishing for a speedy recovery."

God, the guy was perfect in every way. Where did he learn all that? The school for good boys?

"Thanks for asking, but I don't know yet. The doctors are doing their best." Stella didn't want to go into details about her mother's state. Hell, she didn't even know what to say. Nobody knew anything.

"I'm really sorry. I know how much you care for her and how tough this must be for you, too."

"Thanks."

"And your sister?" he asked out of nowhere, breaking the silence that had embraced them.

"Megan? Why do you ask?"

"Oh, the last time I saw her, she looked rough. As if she was going through a tough time."

"When was that?"

"Uhm, I'm not sure. A few months ago, I think. Your father had asked me to drop off some documents, and when I was at your place, your mother and Megan had a bit of an argument. I didn't want to intrude, so I dropped the files off and left. I don't think they even noticed me."

"She is fine," Stella replied on command, but didn't even know if that was true. She had been wrong about a lot lately. She also didn't want to get even more into her family with him. With his understanding eyes and encouraging voice, the risk of her doing something stupid again was too high.

He shrugged and gestured to the files stacked under his arm. "I should head back up. It was great seeing you. You look great."

Too late, she stopped herself from saying. "Thanks, you too."

God, you are such an embarrassment.

But Jeremy merely laughed. They said their goodbyes and Stella knew they wouldn't see each other again.

Sometimes things just weren't meant to be.

Chapter 21 - The Dismissal

Samuel

HE HADN'T EXPECTED her to leave a note. Or maybe he did, but he knew that whatever had happened between them last night was a one-time thing. It would not happen again. He couldn't jeopardize a case like this, and he didn't want to send her the wrong message. That he didn't care about her case. He hadn't felt this kind of collegial connection with someone in ages, if at all, and he wasn't prepared to risk that kind of relationship, even if the sex was better than he could have imagined.

People looked at him as if they knew what had happened. But it wasn't his first time wearing the same shirt to work that he had worn the day before. Instead of falling into paranoia, he lifted his coffee in greeting to his colleagues before pulling the chair out from his desk. He took off his jacket, hung it over his seat, and pressed the button on his computer screen.

He slurped another sip from his now-lukewarm coffee, waiting for his emails to update.

"You alright, man?"

Samuel turned around in his chair to look at the rookie he'd had a drink or two with in the past. Derek was a good kid, always friendly and up for a good time, but right now, he looked like someone had told him that his dog had died. Samuel's mind went through a mental checklist immediately. Was he supposed to meet up with him and forgot? He didn't think so, but whatever it was, it clearly upset Derek, who chewed the inside of his mouth.

"You look like your nana just died, Derek." It was supposed to take off the edge, but Derek's face stayed white, only his lips moving when he continued.

"I think you should go over to the Captain's office. He was looking for you and..." Samuel followed Derek's worried gaze over his shoulder to the Captain's closed door, then focused on Derek again, who continued. "He is not happy."

Luckily, Samuel didn't have enough time trying to wrap his head around this rather cryptic message. He heard the Captain's door swing open before a biting tone cut through the air.

"GREEN! My office. NOW!"

Samuel jumped at the mention of his name, suddenly understanding Derek's worry. What the heck had he done wrong now? Did he know Samuel had missed a few meetings? Not wanting to keep his boss waiting when he was in such a mood, Samuel got off his seat and sprinted over to the open door.

"Close the door behind you and sit down!"

Definitely a mood, Samuel thought, hoping he could ease whatever reason he had to be this openly upset. "You sound like you haven't had your morning coffee yet, Cap—"

"I'm not in the mood for your smug comments, Sam," Captain Holmes cut him short.

Samuel pushed the door shut behind him and walked over to the chair in front of his boss' desk. "What happened, Captain?" he asked, sinking down into the chair.

The Captain massaged his forehead as if he were plagued by a migraine. He opened his mouth twice, Samuel patiently awaiting an explanation, but didn't say a word. Instead, he got off his chair and walked up and down the small space behind it. Something Holmes had never done before. Even in the worst and most difficult situations, the Captain had always kept a cool head. Whatever was going on in his mind, it weighed on him heavily.

What if Stella's mother had died? No, Stella would have told him. Samuel took his cell out of his pocket to check for a message from Stella, but there were none. His eyes darted back to his boss. *Did something happen to Stella? Was that why he was acting so strangely? Was he about to deliver bad news about another death under his care?*

"Jesus, boss, you are scaring the shit out of me."

Holmes came to a halt in front of his chair. He leaned his elbows on the back of it and stared at his hands. He looked as if he had aged ten years since yesterday.

"You are done, Samuel." The hushed tone was a stark contrast to his earlier form of angry power.

Samuel blinked at the man in front of him. "Done with what?" he asked hesitantly, unsure if he even wanted to hear more.

His boss lifted his gaze and, to Samuel's horror, his eyes were filled with disappointment.

"You are sleeping with Stella Woodworth." Those words took the air out of his lungs.

"What?"

"I know you are sleeping with her."

"H-how?" Samuel asked, trying to make sense of what was happening, not even pretending to come up with an excuse to save his ass.

"Does it matter?"

It did to Samuel.

"I am not violating any code of ethics—"

"You know it's wrong."

He knew the second her lips had touched his that this could turn into a nasty situation.

Holmes shook his head and walked around the desk. He positioned himself directly in front of him. "I'm taking you off the case."

Samuel leapt out of the chair. "Now wait a second, Captain. Surely we can talk about this—"

"Don't make this harder on me than it already is, son."

Samuel couldn't believe his ears. "This is ridiculous, Captain. I mean, I've done way worse things, and this is the one you punish me for?"

"I am assigning you to another case. One that seems more suited to you and your *situation*."

"My situation? What is that supposed to mean?"

Holmes swallowed hard but didn't say a word. The shadow over his eyes said it all, though. He was threatening Sam with his relationship with alcohol.

This wasn't the Holmes he had known and worked with for years. This had Richard Woodworth written all over it.

Stella was right.

He took a step closer towards his mentor, who put a hand up in warning.

"Are you fucking kidding me?" Samuel's frustration ran wild.

"If you don't calm down, I will have to ask you to leave!"

This was insane. "You aren't even giving me an explanation? After I've done exactly what you asked me to do?"

Holmes' voice rolled over to Sam like thunder. "I did not ask you to get cozy with the daughter of one of the suspects!"

"Oh, so now he is suddenly a suspect?" Sam's heart was racing, trying to catch up with what was happening to him. The lunacy of this situation. "You are making this really easy on yourself, bending your own rules depending on where the wind is coming from. What exactly is it that this asshole Woodworth has over you that you are willing to throw all your principles out the window?" Samuel asked, fuming.

He had never expected his mentor and friend to throw him under the bus like that. And for what? For a man who didn't give a shit and would throw Holmes into the flames himself if it helped him?

Holmes looked down at his feet and for a second he looked like he carried the worries of the world on his sagging shoulder. Whatever caused him this moment of Weltschmerz, his own pain was part of it. Holmes had a secret and didn't want anyone to find out.

"I have nothing else to say to you," Holmes eventually said.

"What did you do, Captain?" Samuel asked his boss, hoping he'd open up, tell him and let him help him fix it, like he had done plenty of times for Samuel. "Talk to me, boss," Samuel begged. For nothing.

"There is nothing else to discuss. Miller!"

The office door opened within a second and Officer Miller's Crossfit-trained body took up the space in the door frame.

"You can't be serious? You are kicking me out?" Wide-eyed, Samuel stared at his mentor before turning to Miller. With an extended index finger, Samuel warned Miller, "If you touch me, I'll kill you."

Those words meant nothing to Miller. He probably heard them regularly from his own wife. With a reputation of losing it sometimes when he was under a lot of stress, Samuel knew Miller enjoyed this moment of power. Maybe even as much as he enjoyed kicking the shit out of his wife. Samuel had seen her face once, when she had called it in, and he was the first at the scene. He hadn't known Miller well at that point, but according to other colleagues, it hadn't been the first time and, unfortunately, it wouldn't be the last. He had tried to talk sense into him to stop this madness, but it had not gotten him anywhere. In fact, the only thing that had changed was that his wife didn't call the police anymore. She knew no one would stand up against their own. Samuel hated Miller, and that he has never been prosecuted but instead kept working here.

That Holmes used Miller to get him out of his sight hit him hard.

"Jesus, Sam. Have you lost your mind now?" Holmes asked, stepping between Samuel and Miller. "Miller is here to see me."

Samuel froze. He blinked at the absurdity of this situation. At his mentor, who looked at him as if he'd gone crazy, and at Miller, who couldn't wipe the smug smile off his face. The fucker enjoyed this too much.

"I think you should take some time off and sort yourself out," Holmes said, shaking his head slowly from side to side, but Samuel felt like Holmes was scolding him like a child.

"Are you suspending me?"

"Maybe taking a break from all of this is exactly what you need." Holmes said.

Taking a break from what? This case or his job?

Sam swallowed hard. Suddenly, his head ached and his hands felt like he'd put them in a hot pizza oven. Was he losing it?

This wasn't normal, though. His captain was overreacting. Sam had done everything he had asked of him. Why would he treat him this way if he wasn't trying to save his relationship with Woodworth?

Deep down, Samuel knew he was right. His gut was telling him and this time he would listen to it. He couldn't just drop this.

"Whatever your buddy has over you, I'll promise to find out what it is," Samuel assured Holmes.

"Sam, get out of here before you regret your next words." And he did.

Silently, he left the office. He passed by a trellis of involuntary spectators. His colleagues who looked at him in confusion, only Derek seemed fazed and sad. The rest of his team whispered behind their hands, about what they had just heard, about what they thought Samuel would do now and about how little some of them thought of him. Samuel felt like he was walking the plank, but with every step he took toward the edge, his determination to get to the bottom of this grew.

He would not have Richard Woodworth ruin his career.

Chapter 22 - The Intruder

Stella

KNOWING THAT HER FATHER had been aware of her mother's affair was more anti-climactic than Stella had thought. Driven by the need to confront her father about his marital failure, she felt hollow about the outcome of their conversation. Stella contemplated if she was suffering from PTSD after yet another horrific encounter with her father, which would explain this emptiness she was feeling instead of anger. It certainly had nothing to do with her conversation with Jeremy.

Or maybe she'd just gotten used to these kinds of exchanges with the man who had fathered her. The worst possibility was that she potentially enjoyed this masochistic tennis match.

How her father always got his way was beyond her. It was easy to believe only strangers or people he held something against would fall for this treatment, but Stella had to be honest with herself. As much as she knew what to expect, Richard Woodworth kept pulling the rug from under her feet. And this time she had landed hard on the concrete pavement of Fifth Avenue.

She meant what she'd said to her father. Enough was enough. This time, she wouldn't let him get away with this. She owed it to her mother, who was fighting for her life, to her brother Jonathan, who couldn't fight anymore, and to her sister, who still suffered from his reign. But most of all, she owed it to herself to stop the bully who had terrorized her for years from continuing to do so.

Manhattan mirrored her mood with heavy gray skies and a slight, but constant rainfall that soaked through layers of clothes. After straightening her ebony hair that had started to frizz, Stella walked into the lobby of her hotel and went straight for the bar in need of a drink. She sat down on a golden bar stool with a green velvet seat that matched the lighting fixture behind the bar and illuminated the array of alcoholic bottles available. Tinted in this Hulk light, they all transformed into Absinth.

She waved over the bartender, who was stocking the fridge with unopened white wine bottles, preparing for the evening when he'd have more than just one lonely morning drinker. One advantage of staying in a fancy Manhattan hotel: guests could drink around the clock without judgement. Definitely not the bartender who was hoping for a generous tip and therefore showed Stella his biggest and most confident smile. He leaned casually against the bar and listened attentively to her order before he picked both a short glass and a bulbous bottle with a golden brown content.

She gave him the number of her room to put it on, took the glass and downed it in one quick go, before she opened her purse in search of her phone. Getting drunk wasn't her goal. She still needed to be clear-headed enough to think about her next steps, and she had to update Samuel as well.

Forefinger hovering over her phone, she stopped from dialing his number, wondering if things between them would be weird now. Sex usually complicated things, which was why she shouldn't have gone down that road to begin with. Rubbing her eyes, she waited for some sign to tell her what to do, but knew all too well that she'd be gray and old if she waited for signs. If she wanted things to move along, she needed to act now and with someone she trusted would support her.

Things are only weird if you make them weird, right? She told herself before tapping on his name on her phone. The line started ringing. When his mailbox kicked in, she left him a quick message, mentioning that she had news and asking if he could meet her at her hotel. At the bar, obviously. She wouldn't make the mistake of taking him up to her room again.

She hung up and tapped her phone against the bar.

Her phone pinged a few minutes later. She smiled unknowingly when she read his response.

Hey, are you still at your hotel?

She typed a quick yes, followed by, *Is everything okay?*

His response came immediately.

Well, my morning has turned a bit crazy.

Tell me about it, was on the tip of Stella's finger, but she waited for the rest of Samuel's message to come through.

I need to talk to you in person.

Okay. I'm at the hotel. Are you sure you are okay?

She saw him typing for a while, unsure how much detail he would give her. Maybe this was about last night. She'd assumed he wanted to talk about their case, but what if he wanted to open an entire conversation about the night they'd spent together?

Stella suddenly felt nervous. There was nothing to feel uncomfortable about, right? They were two grown people who had slept together. They didn't need to talk this through. Or did they?

Her phone vibrated in her hands.

I'll be over in 20.

Twenty minutes was just enough to go up to her room, grab what they had collected, and come back down. It was probably better for them not to be in her room alone again. This way, they'd keep the conversation professional. She'd even have enough time to get another drink before Samuel arrived. No need to tempt him by drinking right in front of him.

She waited until she stepped out of the elevator on the fifteenth floor before trying her sister again, but only reached her voicemail.

Why is it always so hard to get hold of you? Stella huffed and typed a message before reaching the door to her room. Finishing her message in front of it, she pocketed her phone and held out the white keycard with the hotel logo printed on it to open her door.

Why hadn't Megan mentioned her last visit? Last time they spoke, she had made it sound as if she hadn't set foot in the mansion for years. Jeremy had said she'd had a fight with their mother. Did she know about the affair?

The door fell shut behind her as she marched straight towards the coffee table, hoping housekeeping hadn't messed up her papers by stacking them together.

They hadn't. Everything was still a mess only she could decipher. All the evidence they had collected lay splattered across the table. Luckily, the evidence of what else had happened in this room last night had been taken care of. Her bed was made up, slippers sat next to the left side of the bed, and a single piece of chocolate had been placed neatly on one pillow. Her pillow. There was no sign that another person had slept in her bed.

Her eyebrows furrowed at the unexpectedly hollow feeling in her gut. Maybe she was coming down with something. It couldn't be the memory of Samuel in her bed causing it. But maybe it stemmed from the masked intruder she looked at when she turned around, who blocked the way to the door with a shiny knife in his right hand.

Chapter 23 - The Attack

Samuel

FEELING UNCOMFORTABLY naked without his gun and badge, Samuel steamed like a Manhattan manhole on his way to Stella's hotel. His initial shock over his suspension hadn't evaporated. If anything, the march towards Fifth Avenue, dodging tourists and dog walkers alike, had made him even more agitated. He wanted a drink. His body ached for something strong to take the edge off.

But then his boss's face appeared before him, along with the memory of his words. No, he wouldn't give him the satisfaction and lean into the warm embrace of Johnny, Jack, or Jim. He'd keep his head clear to find answers to what was going on. And there was one person who could give him answers as to what Richard Woodworth could hold over his mentor. Despite Stella having been gone for years, she still knew her father better than anyone.

A smile had formed around his lips despite the anger inside of him when he listened to Stella's message. He was unsure how she felt about last night. Hell, Samuel was confused and unsure if things would be weird between the two of them now that they had slept together. Stella had sounded normal over the phone, her professional voice clearly entangled in whatever had happened with her father. Perhaps she didn't think last night was such a big deal. Hopefully. Samuel hadn't been with a woman in a while and even though he had enjoyed it more than he had thought, he knew someone like Stella wouldn't stick with him. As broken as she was, Stella was still out of his league. There was only one way to find out if they'd still be working well together.

He entered the lobby of her hotel, gazing over the bar area to see if she was down there having a drink. Luckily, she wasn't. He turned to the front desk and contemplated waiting for the guest to finish checking in before he'd register himself as a visitor. But when he saw the desperate look of the concierge, eyes wide with discomfort and playing with his collar that must have felt too tight while dealing with the meaty guest in front of him, Samuel decided to skip the line and go up to Stella's room unannounced.

Samuel reached her door and rapped his knuckles against the wood. Then he waited. And waited. He knocked once more, using his fist this time, just to make sure she'd hear him.

Again, nothing. Samuel checked his phone for a message, but the screen didn't show any missed calls or texts.

He was about to turn and take the elevator down again when he heard glass breaking inside.

"Stella?" An instinctive alertness that came with his job washed over him and he reached for the knob and turned it. Without a keycard, he was unable to open the locked door.

"Stella!" he shouted, pounding against the door, but the only response he got was a muffled grunt.

His hand instinctively went to his hip, only to find that his gun was no longer there. "Fuck!"

Intuitively, he jumped into action and against the door. His shoulder cracked when body met wood. He jumped again, but the door wouldn't budge. Samuel knew he could throw himself against it all day. He needed a different strategy. The commotion inside grew louder. Since going to the front desk for a keycard or waiting for backup would take too long, he searched around, hoping to find something useful to enter Stella's hotel room swiftly. All he spotted, however, were fragile chairs and ornamental hallway tables that would easily break, but not open the door. Then, his eyes fell on the emergency exit sign. He sprinted for it and for the red box he was sure would hang in the stairway.

The heavy door squeaked open, and he saw the emergency fire ax sitting neatly in its box. His elbow went through the glass quickly, tearing his leather jacket before he grabbed the ax. When he returned to Stella's door, a man stood next to it, his partner half hiding in the doorframe of their adjacent room. "What's going on there? We are trying to get some rest."

Samuel lifted the ax above his head and shouted a message at the man just in time.

"NYPD. Move aside."

The man jumped back into his room, fearing he might lose a limb if he stayed.

The ax missed the door handle but by the second hit, Samuel had gotten the hang of it. It only took him two more tries to lose the handle. He lowered the ax and kicked the door in.

Unsure what to expect, he prepared for the worst—like finding Stella bloodstained on the beige carpet. He stepped inside, ax raised, ready to attack anyone who would get between him and Stella. And then he stopped at the scenario in front of him. Shattered glass covered the floor, paper had flown around the room and there was blood, quite a bit, but it wasn't Stella's. At least not all of it. Stella had a masked stranger entangled on the floor, holding him down with her legs, which reminded Samuel of his wrestling years in high school. He had never been particularly good at it, but from the looks of it, Stella knew how to pin a man down.

In an unexpected turn of his body, the stranger freed his left arm while Stella's eyes found Samuel's. The stranger grabbed a knife that lay next to them. Samuel lunged forward, but the knife went into Stella's thigh before Samuel could reach her.

She let out an agonizing cry, her grip weakening just enough for the stranger to roll off of her and get on his feet, where he broke into a run. Samuel's fingers went for the attacker's arm, but they slipped off. A deep cut just under his shoulder covered the man's arm in blood, slicing through the zenith of a tattoo of a sun. And then he was out the door, followed by the frantic scream of the man next door.

Worried about Stella, Samuel turned towards her. She sat upright on the floor and leaned against the TV stand. Her hands were on her thigh, covering the stab wound. Crimson red liquid leaked through her white fingers. When he reached out to her, she brushed his hand away.

"Don't help me. I'm fine," she barked. "Go get him!"

He didn't need more. He sprinted into the hallway, followed the outstretched arm of yet another nosy neighbor, and pushed through the door leading to the emergency staircase. Taking two steps at a time, he flew down the stairway, the attacker's footsteps echoing off the concrete.

The trail of blood led him back into the lobby, past the shocked faces of guests checking in, and out through the revolving doors of the main entrance. When he reached the outside, Samuel bumped into a man wearing a neat gray suit. The man swore at him, disgusted by the speckles of blood Samuel's fingers left on his expensive suit, before he disappeared in the hustle and bustle of Fifth Avenue. Samuel scanned the area, attempting to find the direction the attacker had taken, but the man had vanished amidst a sea of suits. He let him slip away, taking with him a piece of the puzzle Samuel was determined to solve.

Chapter 24 - The Hunch

Stella

STELLA AND SAMUEL SLOWED down in front of a four-story building with sandstones painted white. The paint had cracked, revealing the original reddish brick typical of the few remaining authentic brick stone buildings in Manhattan.

"Sam, this isn't my hotel," Stella said.

After a night in the hospital, Stella craved a hot shower to wash away the dirt and memories of the previous day. They had forced her to stay the night. For observation, the doctors had said. Any kind of objection had fallen on deaf ears and when the first batch of pain killers had set in, Stella hadn't been that mad anymore and instead drifted off into an exhausted slumber. Her leg hadn't suffered significant damage. It hurt like hell but no artery was cut, and all that remained of her almost life-threatening stab wound were the stitches on her thigh that would require removal in a week or two.

"No, it's not," Samuel said, as if he didn't need to explain that he had basically kidnapped Stella. "You're gonna stay with me."

Stella turned to look at her abductor. "I'm going to do what now?"

He turned off the engine and unbuckled his seatbelt. "I'm not gonna have you stay alone in a hotel room when there is a guy out there who wants to kill you."

"So you kidnap me instead and take me to—" Her question drifted off while she pointed at the brick building to her right.

Following her gaze, Samuel smiled at her. "My place. I live here."

Her eyes widened. "I'm not just going to stay with you." She focused on his face and waited for a reaction that never came. Samuel just took his key out of the ignition and opened his door. Thinking he might come back, she jerked when he opened her door and held out a hand.

Her eyes moved from his hand, which she knew to be soft and rough, to his face. He'd recently shaved. There was a hint of a five o'clock shadow covering his strong jaw. Her mouth was suddenly dry. She shouldn't stay with him. She knew it was a bad idea. After everything they had been through. After the night they had spent together.

He smiled at her then. "You won't die if you take my hand."

I might.

When she still hesitated, he added, "I won't tell anyone that you needed my help, I promise." He crossed his finger over his heart like she had seen Boy Scouts do. His impish wink almost had her fall out of the car and onto the curb.

But he was right. She was a target, and who knew if the masked man would come back for her? And there was no one else she trusted more right now than Samuel.

Instead of staying in his car, she let out a desperate sigh. Sleeping in a car was never a good option. She leaned back, and grabbed her jacket from the backseat, and then slid her hand perfectly into his. He gently pulled her out of his

Dodge Challenger and waited for her to find her balance before locking his car.

Taking a step toward his building, he signaled Stella to follow him. She waited for him to unlock the front door and let her gaze wander up. From this angle, the building looked like something out of a DC Comics universe. The black fire escape hung precariously above her, taunting them with the possibility that the rusty screws would give way and cause the ladder or even the whole skeleton-like structure to fall down and crush their bodies.

Saved by Samuel unlocking the door, she followed him inside and up to the second floor. The stairs creaked under each slow step she took to reach his apartment door.

"I can carry you—"

"No, thanks!" Her leg throbbed, but she wouldn't let that stop her. There was no way she'd let him pick her up and get anywhere close to his face.

Sam's hands went up. "Alright. Just a friendly suggestion. The offer stands."

What she'd give to wipe that smirk off his face.

It felt like climbing Mount Everest, but she reached his apartment perfectly on her own.

It wouldn't have surprised Stella to find a gigantic rat sitting in front of his door. The hallway resembled the Copacabana of bugs. How people in New York still accepted living under such degrading circumstances was beyond Stella. No one should live like this, especially not in the most expensive city in the world.

To her surprise, his apartment was the opposite of the brokenness of the building. It was warm and unexpectedly cozy. It smelled of wood and pine trees, which presumably came from the candle on the small console next to the door. Samuel dropped his keys on a tray that had an open pack of Wrigley's Double Mint in it.

Stella let out a breath she had kept unintentionally. She was relieved his place wasn't a dump and her mind already started imagining her taking a hot shower when she stopped in her tracks.

"What the actual fuck?" Her eyes fixated on the black business suitcase waiting in the middle of the hallway and the single small sticker on the side of it. Luna, the black cartoon cat with the half-moon on its forehead, looked at Stella with her big anime eyes. This suitcase belonged to her, like the pile of documents that sat on top of it and that, as Stella knew, held all the information she had collected on her mother in the last couple of days.

"Did you take my stuff from my hotel room?"

"Yes, I did." Samuel took off his shoes and placed them under the coatrack beside the entrance. "Take your shoes off before you come in, please," he said and without further acknowledging the shock in Stella's eyes, he passed by her, grabbed the pile of documents and moved into the next room that was his living room. There he placed the papers neatly on his coffee table.

"You can't just take my stuff without telling me," Stella protested, following Samuel first into the living room and then into the adjacent kitchenette. "I didn't ask you to take my things."

Samuel grabbed two glass bottles of sugar cane Coke and moved over to a chest of drawers where he rummaged for a bottle opener.

"Drink this. You look like you are about to faint." He held out one bottle. Shaking her head either out of frustration or because she felt a sugar low, Stella took the bottle off him with a loud grunt.

"You have nothing stronger?"

"No. Got rid of it."

They were silent for a few moments. Each of them occupied with finishing their sugary beverages.

"I did tell you I'd get your stuff," Samuel said, breaking the silence.

"What? When?"

"You'd been out for a few hours and when you woke up, I told you I would get your things and that you could crash with me. You don't remember?"

No, she didn't. Stella searched her mind but instead of an answer she found a dark void where the last fifteen hours of her life were supposed to be. She must have been under the influence of the painkillers and she worried about what else she could have agreed to.

"You even told me to take the dwarf bottles from the fridge," he said with a smirk.

Shit. Did she really call the drinks in the mini bar dwarf bottles? She must have been properly out from the painkillers.

"And you didn't think I was in no state to make a coherent decision?"

"Well, I should have guessed when you told me where to find your underwear." Sam chuckled and Stella gulped the last drips of her cola. "It was quite cute."

"I wouldn't call a half-conscious woman cute, but then, I am talking to a man who owns pillows with horses on them." Stella retorted, pointing at the pillow on Samuel's sofa. The only one with a print. Three horses running, their manes flying in the wind.

"That was a present."

"Sure," Stella said and winked at him before she put her empty bottle on the kitchen counter.

"I'm sorry."

"What for?"

"I should have been there."

Stella scoffed, "No one could have predicted that." When he didn't react, she added, "Don't stress yourself over it. I didn't even get hurt that seriously." Which was true, but only because she knew how to defend herself. Without her Kung Fu training, this situation could have turned much worse than a stab wound.

"But I do. The moment you said you felt someone was watching you, I had this feeling but—" He ran his hand over his face. "I didn't listen to my gut feeling, and you got hurt."

After leaving the church, she'd mentioned to him she thought she saw a car following her, but until yesterday, she wasn't even convinced that was really the case. At first, she had believed her father had put one of his spies on her. Perhaps the guy driving the Suburban with the tinted windows, but there was no evidence that this person also entered her hotel room without her knowledge and attacked her.

"That's debatable. I think the guy might feel different with that big cut on his shoulder," she said, scratching the side of her arm. "Messed up his sunshine tattoo as well."

"Where the fuck did you learn to fight like that anyway?"

"Hong Kong," she said matter-of-factly, but Samuel wanted more background than that. "I've been training in Kung Fu and I'm happy to see that my money was well spent."

"Jeez, the guy never had a chance, did he?"

"No," she said smugly. "He wasn't an easy opponent, though. The fucker knew how to throw a punch and had a strong defense. I have to give him that much."

"I was worried," Samuel said, his voice turning soft.

Unable to reply to his statement, Stella shrugged and walked back to the sofa. Maybe staying with him really wasn't such a good idea after all.

Samuel followed her a few seconds later, pointing at the papers in front of her.

"So, back to square one. What do we have so far?" Stella asked.

"A lot of hunches, but nothing concrete and not enough to tie anything to your father."

She sank back into the sofa. "Bummer."

"I don't think you're gonna like what I'm about to say."

"Please don't tell me I should drop this."

"No, but I can't shake this feeling that we are staring at the wrong angle."

Stella looked up at him, a big question mark hanging over her head.

"To be honest, I don't think your father tried to kill you," Samuel pushed through his teeth as if he had held this idea in for a while and it finally got out.

"I know. That's why he hired someone."

Samuel shook his head, sitting down next to her. "I don't know."

"Come on! Did your boss get to you? It's obvious he is behind all this. Next thing you are telling me, he didn't try to kill my mother." Stella half-laughed at him, but swallowed hard when he looked at her.

"You've got to be kidding me, right?"

"Even if he has something to do with your mother's suicide, why would he risk everything he has built in his life?"

"He is angry. She wanted to take her share of the money and he thinks he is invincible. Isn't that reason enough?" she asked.

"But he is also smart," Samuel added.

"Unfortunately."

"Okay, I have to ask."

"Oh, boy, that doesn't sound reassuring," Stella said.

"I know you are convinced your father is orchestrating this evil scheme but—"

She raised her eyebrows at Sam in doubtful anticipation. "But what?"

It took him a few beats and a big exhale before he dropped the bomb on her. "Is this about helping your mother or just hurting your father?"

Stella looked at him in shock. She couldn't believe what she was hearing. Of course, she wanted to help her mother. How could he think anything less?

"Wow," she scoffed. "Didn't see that one coming." Focusing on the paper chaos in front of her, she shuffled pages around, occupying her hands.

"Stella, I have to ask. You are more involved than anyone in this case and I would get if that—'

"If that clouded my judgment?" Stella snapped.

"You know I am on your side."

"Are you?"

Taken aback, he sat down on the sofa, keeping his eyes on Stella. "Of course I am."

She knew he was. With a loud sigh, she sank down next to him and extended her throbbing leg, which matched the frantic rhythm of her heart. "If everything points at him, it probably is him," she said, leaning her chin on her hand, staring at the paper in front of her.

"But it's not all pointing at him," Samuel continued. "His alibis are bulletproof for each event. He wasn't anywhere near your mom or you when the two of you got attacked."

"I told you, he hired someone to do his dirty work."

"I just don't believe it, Stella. It makes no sense. If you had a client come in and present you with those facts, what would you think?"

Her jaw tightened, and she felt the pressure of her grinding teeth radiate through her face. Instead of acknowledging she might react the same if the roles were reversed, she stayed silent and leaned into the soft sofa cushions.

"Can you think of anyone else who would want to harm you or your mom? Anyone who could tell us more?"

Stella shook her head, pinching the bridge of her nose, right between her eyes, where she felt a headache approaching.

"What about your sister?"

Ignoring the growing pain in her temple, Stella's head spun around at the accusation towards another innocent member of her family. "Oh, now my sister is on your list, too? Seriously?"

Samuel rolled his eyes at her, but went on. "When you talked with her, did she say anything? I mean, she sees your mom regularly, right?"

"Megan hasn't seen her in ages—" She sat up straight as if stung by a wasp.

"What?"

Yesterday's conversation blared inside her mind. She had thought nothing of it then, but the possibility that came with Jeremy's innocent words grew bigger with each passing second. He had seen Megan and her mother arguing. What did he say? A few weeks ago? Or was it months?

Stella got up slowly and started pacing the small living room, trying to make sense of the noise inside her head.

"What's going on, Stella?" Sam asked.

Surely there is nothing to it.

Maybe she forgot to mention her argument with mom.

"Hey, talk to me," he pressed again, but Stella's mind was racing.

She wouldn't. She doesn't have any reason.

How well do I really know her, though?

Maybe she does have a reason?

She stopped in front of Samuel. "How fast can you get me upstate?"

"What? Why?"

"I think you might be right," she said, a big lump forming in her throat. "I think we need to see my sister Megan."

Chapter 25 - The Sister

Stella

TWO HOURS OUT OF THE New York City Metro area and one could easily be on the moon. The small town where Megan had settled down wasn't like one of those cute suburban neighborhoods people see on TV. Her street didn't have white wooden fences around meticulously cut lawns and flower beds. Her street consisted a metal grids of fences around small bungalow-style houses, and Stella wasn't sure if they were meant to keep people safe from the outside or the other way round. Every property created its own small prison. Front yards didn't exist either. The only greens that survived were endless varieties of wilted weeds that clung to life.

Stella felt a genuine shock when they parked the car in front of number 639, prompting her to double-check the address. The screen of her phone in which she had saved the address of her sister went black and Stella turned towards her window.

"And you are sure this is the correct address?" she asked Samuel, not taking her eyes off the building in front of her.

"I might not have been able to look up her address myself, but I trust Derek to type in a name and read the address off the computer correctly." He leaned in closer to Stella, trying to get a better look through the window on her side.

Samuel had to ask a favor of one of his colleagues. Since his suspension, he couldn't access the police databases. Luckily, Samuel's colleague Derek always liked him and didn't appreciate the way Samuel was forced to leave the precinct.

Samuel let out a whistle. "Jeez, this doesn't look very welcoming."

Stella nodded in agreement. But it could have been worse. There could have been a white chalk outline of a human body on the pavement. At least the house looked fine—the roof sturdy and no trash littered the property. It didn't, however, take away from the reality that this part of town was definitely not where she had pictured her sister to live in. A police car siren howled somewhere in the distance, setting off a dog in a neighboring garden.

"Only one way to find out if she is still living here." Stella pocketed her phone and clicked her seat belt off.

The whiff of chill air she felt when she exited the car sent a shiver to her core, but she wasn't convinced that the temperatures were to blame.

If they were lucky, Megan had moved.

Maybe she forgot to tell people, and that's why the police still had her old address.

The metal gate cried like a banshee when they passed through and Stella almost expected a huge Rottweiler to come running towards them from the back of the house. But everything was silent. The dog had stopped barking and not a single bird chirped.

Walking up the three concrete steps to the front door, she suddenly felt shy. Stella's fist hovered a few inches away from the wooden frame. Out of the corner of her eye, she glimpsed Samuel peeking into the window. The sides of his hands pressed against the glass, his face had vanished in between them.

Her knuckles hit the door twice.

With her ears on high alert, she waited for a sound or movement from inside.

Nothing. She glanced over at Samuel, who shrugged his shoulders. She knocked again, stronger this time. In the back of the house, a baby started crying, and Stella relaxed. Her sister didn't have a child. She had the wrong address, after all.

She heard footsteps approaching, and she readied herself to explain to whoever lived here why they had bothered them. That they were looking for the tenant who used to live here. If they might have an idea where she went. Then they'd say their goodbyes. Stella would apologize for the intrusion again and wish the person she was about to meet a good day before they'd follow the next piece of information to find her sister.

The door opened, and Stella lost her breath.

A ghost stood in front of her with skin as pale as a strawberry out of season. Burst blood vessels stretched across her cheeks like the arms of rivers visible from space. Her ashen hair hung lifelessly off her head and needed a wash. The shell of a woman in front of her shielded her eyes from the bright daylight that flooded towards her, casting a long shadow seemingly growing into the darkness of the room behind her. Under no circumstances did this woman resemble the gorgeous sister Stella knew Megan to be.

It was the sapphire blue eyes that gave her sister away. Through the worn out exterior, her eyes still showed what really lay beneath. How could this be her Megan?

Samuel cleared his throat, his voice steady. "Good afternoon, Ma'am. I'm Detective Green. We're looking for—"

"Meg?" Stella whispered, almost too afraid to hear the answer.

"What are you doing here?" Megan's voice was rough from a sleep she had been interrupted from and something else. A whiff of cold nicotine surrounded her.

"I need to talk to you, can we come in?"

Megan eyed her sister, then looked over at Samuel, who gave her a comforting smile. When she glanced over her shoulder, her eyes searching for something or maybe someone in the dark, Stella thought she saw her tremble for a second. The snort she let out made her sound like an animal, but Megan moved back into her home, leaving the front door open.

She vanished into the darkness of her home before Stella and Samuel followed her inside. The smell hit them like a bar opening first thing in the morning—stale, sour, and suffocating. Mixed into this was the stench of something rotting. Food molding away, small spores continuing to grow in what otherwise was an uninhabitable environment. Or worse, the corpse of a decomposing animal. Stella fought the urge to cover her nose. A flash of a memory of her pet hamster hit Stella. The one she had needed to hide from her parents and that had died an agonizing death of starvation when they had spent a week at their second house in the

Hamptons unexpectedly. She hadn't been able to take Henry with her and had worried all seven days, hoping he'd make it. He didn't. She disposed of him in the same manner he had come into her care. In secret, hidden in a small shoe box.

Megan returned from what Stella believed to be the kitchen with a black plastic bag and started to collect the empty cans and food containers from the table.

"You should have called. I wasn't expecting company."

"I'm sorry, but it was a quick decision," Stella replied, distracted by her surroundings and Megan's task of picking up dirt.

"I don't like when people show up unannounced."

A loud scream broke through the ceiling. "Mama is coming in a minute," Megan shouted over her shoulder.

"Mama?" Stella asked, confused, her head following the direction of the noise. "You have a child?"

There was no comment from her sister when she cleared the last item off the table and put a knot into the plastic bag.

Why hadn't her baby sister told her?

"How...?" This couldn't be true.

Megan raised an eyebrow at her. "Do you really want me to explain to you how this works with the birds and the bees?"

Her comment hit Stella right into her already tumultuous stomach. Why was Megan so angry with her?

"No. I'm just surprised you didn't tell me." Stella's remark hung in the air. Was she really that surprised? If the last weeks had told her anything, it was that she didn't know her family as well as she had thought. Or wanted to believe.

242

And that growing feeling in the depths of her stomach spread inside her again. If she had kept her own child a secret, what else was Megan not telling her and why?

"Did you know mom was having an affair and wanted to leave our father?"

Megan's face stayed portrait-still, hiding any emotion but for a small twitch that had her upper lip jump.

"She mentioned something, but I thought she was just fishing for attention."

It wouldn't have been the first time. Their mother had a tendency to declare she'd leave their father. That she would take all three of them and leave the mansion, the city, and even the state. Find a cute house in a friendly neighborhood. With a garden for them to play in and maybe even a dog. It had taken Stella many years to understand that those promises were only made when there was at least a bottle of Chardonnay involved.

"Why didn't you tell me?" Stella asked.

"I didn't think it was important."

"When did you last see her?"

For the first time since they had entered the place, Megan stopped and looked directly at Stella, her eyes boring into her.

"I don't know. Easter?"

It didn't add up. Jeremy seemed convinced he had seen both of them a few months ago. Twelve weeks, tops. What was going on?

"Why haven't you been to the hospital to visit her?"

Megan rolled her eyes and waved a hand around. "I've been busy, as you can see, and just haven't gotten around it."

Stella wanted to shake her sister. While she looked nothing like the young, vibrant woman she had known, she still had kept her annoying attitude of being a pain in her ass whenever she didn't give a shit. Why didn't this bother Megan more?

"Are you not at all worried about her?" Stella asked, her voice raised by an octave.

In return, she received a death stare from Megan, who had built a physical barrier between them by crossing her arms tightly over her chest.

"I don't know why you are suddenly so interested in her life or mine?" Megan snorted.

I have always been interested in your lives. Lay on the tip of Stella's tongue, but she knew that this was only partly true. Yes, she wanted to know her sister was well, hoped she was, but she also didn't want to be burdened with an answer that would tell her otherwise and make her feel bad. She didn't want to be responsible for her or anyone else in her family anymore. She wanted to be free from all of it.

"Like I thought." Megan read her mind. "And please don't say you are sorry."

Stella closed her mouth instead of apologizing to her sister.

"How are you then? Really?"

Megan took in a long breath before she answered, "I'm fine. Keeping busy, you know."

"Are you still working with—" Stella started, unable to finish the sentence because she didn't know what her sister's job was. If she had ever worked after moving out. Shame crept up her neck.

"Don't worry. I didn't expect you to know," Megan said. "I'm a nurse."

"A nurse?"

"Yeah, I wanted a job where I could help people."

Stella swallowed the lump that kept building up in her throat again. Her eyes fell on a picture on the mantelpiece that showed her sister and a baby, presumably her daughter. Both of them were smiling. Her sister looked healthier in it. Happier. And she saw the resemblance of her in her daughter. Before she had turned bitter. Or maybe her daughter had brought the best out of her.

"So, this is your daughter?" Stella asked, pointing at the photo. "I can't believe you are a mom."

"If you are here to make me feel bad that I didn't tell you, don't!"

"I am not." But Megan didn't seem to believe her, raising her eyebrows questioningly. "Meg, I am not here to judge you. I am just interested."

The eyebrows came down and Megan moved over to her sister slowly until she came to a stop next to her.

"She is cute. What's her name?" Stella asked.

Megan hesitated, biting the inside of her mouth like she used to as a kid. Old habits die hard. When Stella thought she'd stay silent, Megan gave up a name. "Mae." An honest smile washed over her face and lit it up like the first rays of sunshine of the day.

"What a pretty name." Stella lifted the frame and let her finger run along the glass and over the face that belonged to her niece. She was an aunt. How was that even possible? The last time she had seen her sister, she was only a teenager, and now she was an adult. And a mother. She wondered if Megan had told their mother, but even more why she didn't feel comfortable enough to tell her. It dawned on Stella then that she didn't know her family at all. As much as she wanted to convince herself that a call once a year could keep a relationship up, she knew she hadn't done enough to deserve to be included in this. Would she be able to be included again in the future? Did she want to be included again?

"Can I meet her?" she asked with the pride of an aunt. Her smile faltered when her sister took the photo off her and placed it back where it belonged.

"She doesn't feel comfortable around strangers. Maybe next time."

It was a punch to the gut. Maybe a deserved one, but nevertheless painful. Megan sniffed again, like a cold she was trying to overcome.

Her fingers trembled, and she cleaned something off from under her nails, using her teeth. Something felt wrong. Her sister felt off. It was suddenly so clear, but the realization still shook Stella to the core. *She's an addict.* Guilt washed over her. Guilt over not having cared enough about her sister and for abandoning her family. Megan didn't see a sister in her anymore, but merely another person she had known in a life long ago.

The floor above her creaked, and Megan's head shot up.

"Is someone else in the house?" Samuel asked, suddenly alert, his eyes scanning the living room they stood in.

Megan shook her head. "T-that's just Mae. I should probably check on her." Megan's voice trembled for a millisecond, but Stella immediately felt protective over her sister and niece. She mouthed the words, *Are you okay?* Hoping to signal to her sister she was here for them.

"Do you need a hand?" Samuel asked, taking a step towards her, but Megan held up her hand.

"No! Just give me a minute."

"Of course," Stella replied before Samuel could say another word. She watched her sister disappear into the hallway, listening to her footsteps making their way upstairs. Her muffled voice could be heard above them, followed by another voice repeated *Mama* like a battery fire.

Stella's eyes fell back to the mantelpiece. She smiled at the photos and the fact that she had gained another family member. Hopefully, one that would never have to deal with the troubles of what it meant to be a Woodworth. Stella wasn't a believer, but in this moment she prayed that little Mae would have an unburdened future. That whatever Megan was going through, she'd overcome it and ensure that the little blonde girl was happy and safe. And she made a silent promise to herself that she'd help her sister. Get her into a program. Get her clean and stable. And once this nightmare was over, she would change her life as well to keep that promise.

"What do you make of this?" Samuel asked, looking around, scanning the surroundings. Nothing was really that out of the ordinary, keeping in mind that her sister's life had changed more dramatically than she had known.

"What is taking her so long?" Samuel asked with a noticeable worry in his voice. Something had him on edge.

"Give her a moment," Stella said, but knew it was she who needed a moment to think, to take in everything that had just happened.

"Stella, this doesn't feel right." Samuel worried, and she felt it, too.

"I know," she answered, looking towards the stairway leading to the floor above.

"I'm gonna have a look around," Samuel stated when the sound of whispers traveled down. Stella put her forefinger on her lips and forced Samuel to stay. Listening to the sound from upstairs, she could make out her sister's voice but also someone else's. And that voice wasn't Mae's.

Stella's head turned to Samuel, her finger first pointing upstairs towards the ceiling and then adding a second finger to it.

Her sister and niece were not alone up there. What if her sister was in danger? What if the same person who had tried to kill her mother, and herself, was upstairs and threatened them?

She needed to get up there. She couldn't lose them before she had a chance to meet her niece and get to know Megan again.

Samuel's warm hand gripped her arm. Pointing to his side, he shook his head. "I don't have my gun."

She had almost forgotten. But she wouldn't need a gun. She had fought a man before, and despite her injured leg, she'd do anything to defend and protect her family.

As her eyes roamed around in search of a knife, a baseball bat, or poker, they suddenly stopped on another framed picture. It showed her sister in the embrace of a man with ordinary brown eyes that matched his ordinary shortcut brown hair. But what wasn't ordinary about him was the sun shaped tattoo on his right shoulder. The same tattoo Stella had recently cut through with a knife.

Samuel's eyes went wide at something behind Stella. Before she had time to turn, a shot rang out and her legs collapsed. She fell to the ground and a man, who smelled of pine woods and aftershave, immediately tackled her. Samuel.

He was up in an instant and tried the same method on the man Stella now knew to have been her attacker a few days ago.

Another gunshot pierced the air, followed by a moment of stillness. Stella's heart pounded so hard it felt like it might burst. Then, two lifeless bodies hit the ground. Upstairs, Mae screamed, scared by the sudden noise and violence happening in her childhood home.

Sam.

"I'm fine. I just need a second to catch my breath." He grunted through gritted teeth. Reading her mind again. Or maybe seeing the worry in her eyes.

Relief washed over her, and her attention turned to her sister again.

"I'll go looking for Megan," she told Sam.

She had just made it to the kitchen when the shiny razor-sharp blade of a steak knife cut through her jacket and pricked skin. Instinctively, she put her hand over the slash on her right forearm. Blood leaked out of her and fell in a constant drip, drip, drip onto the white-tiled kitchen floor.

Her eyes went up to meet her sister's now-enraged face.

"Why did you have to come here?" Megan shouted.

She is in on it.

The undeniable truth cut Stella deeper than the second slash. Shielding her face, her left hand took the cut and Stella screamed out in pain.

"You should have left us alone! You are going to ruin everything."

"Meg, please. Drop the knife!" Stella pleaded, but her frenzied sister went straight for yet another blow towards her face. One she ducked away from. She lowered herself down, feeling the stitches on her thigh rupture, opening yet another wound, and knocked her sister off her feet with one swift tip of her foot.

Megan hadn't even thought about protecting her legs. She went down, surprise on her face. Trying to stop herself from falling onto her back, she attempted to turn, but slipped on the streak of blood Stella had spilled. She hit the ground headfirst.

No! The world seemed to slow as Stella leaned over her sister and pressed two fingers against Megan's neck.

Please don't be dead. Through trembling fingers she couldn't feel anything but her own fear until, at last, she felt the faint beat of a pulse.

She took the knife from Megan's still hand and stumbled back to the living room, her pants now stained with the blood that had oozed from her newly opened wound.

"Sam, are you alright?"

Leaning against the bookshelf, he held his side and took in shallow breaths. "Don't be mad at me, but I don't think I'm fine." His eyes fluttered down to his side. Stella gasped as he lifted his hand and a surge of blood squirted out of him.

"I think the fucker got me."

The first shot. He must have hit him.

Stella reached for the phone in her inside pocket. It almost slipped through her bloodied hands. She caught it just before it shattered on the floor and dialed three digits, pressing the loudspeaker button, leaving a bloody print of her finger on the screen.

"911," a calm voice answered the line. "What's your emergency?"

"An officer was shot," she shouted, louder than she needed. Panic rose inside her. She couldn't lose another person. She couldn't lose Samuel. "He needs immediate medical attention," she said as calmly as possible while she pressed her hand on the entry wound on Sam's side that didn't want to stop bleeding.

When Sam closed his eyes, she pleaded into the phone, "Please, I need help" and "Don't you dare die on me" at a paling Samuel.

Chapter 26 - The Awakening

Samuel

THROUGH A CLOUD OF dizziness, Samuel noticed his surroundings. He wasn't sure for how long he had closed his eyes. It could have been hours, but when a head with hair as dark as coal had stopped in front of him, it couldn't have been more than a few seconds. He had just seen Stella kneel in front of him, felt her warm fingers on his arm. Afraid to take his hand off his side where the bullet had entered his soft flesh, he didn't lift his hand to touch Stella's face. But he wanted to, badly. He wanted to let his fingers run through her silken hair, like he had done just a few nights ago.

He remembered the burning pain from the gunshot. That fucker had hit him real good. He had felt dizzy for a few seconds before his legs gave out. He had known immediately that the sting of this bitch wouldn't be gone in a minute or two.

At that moment, he saw the face of his father in front of him, or rather a strange memory of him when he was in his early thirties and Samuel was just ten years old. He had just dropped him off at school and placed a kiss on his forehead before Samuel left. He hadn't thought about his dad for a while, especially not the last moment he had spent with him before a drunk driver veered into the oncoming traffic, hitting his dad's blue Subaru.

Maybe this vision of his dad wanted to tell him something his body had known already. Maybe it was his time to be reunited with him.

But the excruciating pain that suddenly exploded inside Samuel was surely not heaven. At least he didn't think so, because everything hurt, including taking a breath. That must mean that he was still alive. He had survived and was brought back to a world where pain was the essence of life.

"Samuel? Sam?" A familiar voice broke through.

Opening his eyes was hard and hurt like a motherfucker. The fluorescent light of the room he was in stung his retina. He blinked the harsh brightness away before giving it another try. A strangely blurred form appeared in front of him, reminding him of a painting from Gerhard Richter he had once seen in the Museum of Modern Art. All black and red and pale.

Stella. He thought he said it, but didn't feel his lips moving. Something was stuck in his throat, blocking him from speaking. He gagged. He couldn't breathe. There was no air. Panic rose inside him and he felt something wet run down his cheek and neck. A drop of sweat or a tear, he wasn't sure.

A nurse was called, who stood over him and said something about a tube in his mouth and breathing out. She held onto something on his chest, or was it his mouth? In one unexpected move, the blockage in his throat disappeared, and he took his first breath. With eyes wide in shock, he turned his head and saw a face he knew, had grown to trust and like.

Stella wore a smile of relief. Her hand clutching her throat; her knuckles had turned white. Her eyes were bloodshot, but he focussed on the green center.

He didn't hear the nurse telling him to take it easy. That he shouldn't talk yet. Or that more pain was predicted for him. He didn't realize he was put into an upright position with his head heavy on a white pillow because he was lost in the colors of the lush forest that were Stella's eyes. He felt her presence moving closer, sitting down on his bed, right next to him, taking his hand in hers.

It took him a few beats to understand that the coarse voice trying to ask what had happened was his.

"Is he okay?" Stella's head turned to the nurse with a comforting smile on her face. "Can he talk?"

"Now that the intubation is out, he should feel much better. He might have some inflammation in his throat, and it'll be painful for a little while, but his vitals look good. He can try to write down what he wants to say or whisper. Less straining for his vocal cords," she explained, placing a hand on Stella's shoulder. "But what he needs is rest."

Stella nodded at the nurse and waited for her to leave the room before she concentrated on Samuel again.

"How are you feeling?" she asked.

"S-shit—" he started and ended in a cough that rattled his body, lifting him off the pillow. Stella grabbed the mug from his bedside table that contained some ice chips and lifted the smallest one to his lips.

"Here. The nurse said you can't have proper liquids yet, but maybe this will help."

He let her dab his lips, thankful for each cool drop of water soothing the pain in his throat before settling back against his pillow.

"H-how l-long—" he tried again and then settled for whispering the rest of his sentence. "How long was I out?"

"A few days. You were in pretty bad shape and the doctors weren't a hundred percent sure if you...if you'd make it," she said, voice trembling.

The memory of the bullet entering his flesh came back as quickly as the guy had pulled the trigger. He'd felt it get stuck somewhere and hoped it had missed his liver. He wanted to touch that spot but was afraid of opening what the doctors had stitched together carefully.

"What happened?"

"The short version is you got shot. And the longer version is that it looks like my attacker was my sister's boyfriend."

Was?

He flinched at the memory of wrestling the man who had tried to kill Stella twice. Who would have killed her if Samuel hadn't intervened and taken the bullet.

"I know, insane. He didn't make it."

Of course he didn't, Sam thought. If he remembered correctly, he had shot him right into his chest with his own gun.

"And Megan?" he asked.

"The police took her in. I haven't seen her since." Stella stopped, clearing her throat. This was hard for her. He saw it on her face now. The dark circles under her eyes, the worried frown on her forehead, and the paleness that gave her skin an extra shade of white. Her head lowered, she struggled to get the next sentence out. "Sam, Meg was in on it. She attacked me. S-she—"

"W-why?"

"I don't know. I still can't get my head around it." She sighed, shaking her head as if she could get rid of reality this way.

"And your niece? What happened to the little girl?"

He heard Stella swallow long and loud. "Child Protective Services have taken her. I'm not sure where she is right now."

It took him some effort to lift his hand, but his fingers found Stella's hand and he squeezed it as tightly as he could do. "We'll figure this out. I promise."

"We? Who said I'd keep you around? Since I met you, I have been attacked twice," she replied with a smile on her face. It was good to see her smile, even if it didn't fully reach her eyes.

"I did take a bullet for you," he pointed out, much to Stella's dislike, who rolled her eyes at him dramatically.

"How long will you hold this one incident against me?"

"A long time," he said with a smile on his lips.

He watched his fingers play with hers, their limbs gently intertwining. She inhaled loudly, wanting to get something off her chest.

"What is it?" he encouraged her.

"I was worried about you." It was almost a whisper, but her words rang louder inside him than they could have if she had shouted them at him.

"Don't worry. It takes more than a bullet to take me down." The comment made her laugh and he could feel the tension in her body loosen.

"I'm going to let you get that rest now. I'll come back later, okay?"

He smiled at her and the promise that she would return.

The room felt cold and odd when she left and he tried to find sleep, but his head was running wild. He had been right about Stella's father. He didn't try to kill her and he also hadn't hired a hitman. But why would Megan try to murder her sister? There was no logic in it. And why would his own boss try to prevent him from finding out the truth if he wasn't somehow involved in this?

He needed to talk to Megan, get some answers, but while he made plans on what next steps to take, a darkness lulled him in and eventually his eyes fell shut for a rest his body badly needed.

Chapter 27 - The Cell

Samuel

"YOU KNOW I CAN GET in real trouble for this."

Samuel leaned over the counter, holding his side. Under his layers of clothes, his wound was still hurting, but he was on a nice cocktail of painkillers that helped him cope with his injury a week after the incident. So when he winced dramatically in front of Officer Stephens, it was more for show than actual pain. After listened to Samuel recount his heroic adventures for over fifteen minutes, she gave up. She rolled her eyes at him but pressed the small round red button he knew was on the side of the desk she sat on. A buzzer sounded, and he pressed through the security door.

Stephens stepped into the doorframe and handed him the paper he was looking for. While she monitored the entry hallway through which he had entered, Samuel skimmed through the official yellowish papers in his hand.

"Why was she transferred?"

"Check page six. You'll like that one," she said, not taking her eyes off the hallway.

He licked his right thumb before he returned to page six and frowned at the information presenting itself in the form of a signature. This couldn't be right, he thought as he looked up at Stephens.

"Fuck!"

"I know, right? Why would he do that?"

"Can I get a copy of that?" Samuel asked while he handed the papers back to her. When she dropped them on her desk, page six was still open, showing an almost completely blacked out section where the detailed information for the transfer request of Megan Woodworth was supposed to be.

Stephens hesitated, her eyes fixed on the official document. Samuel knew he was asking for a lot. He didn't want to press her, but he needed copies before the originals disappeared and they surely would.

"Whatever is going on here, I can and will figure it out. We are not like this. Like them," he added, knowing he'd get to her.

Being a police officer ran deep in her family and with it the pride of serving her country and each person living in it. So when she was transferred from the downtown precinct to this place a few months ago for reporting a procedural mistake by her superior, she was shaken to her core.

She exhaled loudly but nodded, making Samuel smile on the inside.

"I also need to speak to her."

"Figured you wouldn't just leave after this." She reached for her hip and unlocked a set of keys from the silver chain that was attached to her belt. Pointing to the left, she said, "Follow me."

They made their way down the hallway, through more security doors, and eventually into the small housing section. The sound of his shoes squeaking on the linoleum echoed through the corridor as he walked towards the cell where

Stella's sister was being held. At the end of the floor, the ceiling lamp flickered.

It hadn't been easy, but Stella had found out where her sister was taken and held for custody. It had taken her a week and a million calls to a good friend she had on the west coast, but eventually Stella had found Megan.

She'd been moved closer to the city, away from the local precinct in Pennsylvania. This wasn't normal practice. Someone must have specifically requested the transfer from Holmes, and he needed to know who was behind it and why his captain would throw all principles out the window. Luckily, he still had a few contacts that didn't believe his suspension was the right decision.

Working by the book in the past had given him an excellent reputation and even after the debacle last year, and to his personal surprise, plenty still stood by him. Even though Stella had done all the work in finding her sister, there was no chance for her to get into the jail where Megan was held. So, here he was, on his own.

Samuel hadn't even tried to reach out to his captain. After their last encounter and the radio silence he had received from his mentor despite being shot, Samuel could only assume how angry he must be at him. His instincts had warned him not to trust Holmes before, and now the discovery of his captain's signature on Megan's transfer request had confirmed his suspicion. He'd have to have a word with his boss eventually, but first, he needed to speak to Megan.

Reaching the end of the corridor, they stopped at a metal door to his left.

"Woodworth, I have a visitor for you," Stephens said while inserting the key and unlocking the door. She kept her eye on Megan as she pulled the door towards them.

In the dim light of this cell, he was confronted again with the person who had tried to kill Stella and who was involved in the hospitalization of her own mother.

As expected, Megan looked shaken. Her hair hadn't seen a brush or a comb in days. She was pale, with dark circles under her eyes from lack of sleep. The redness and dried-up crust at the corners of her eyes indicated she had just recently stopped crying. Her whole body trembled, and her gaze remained fixated on her fingers that she kept picking at. Megan was going through withdrawal.

"You'll have fifteen minutes. Not one minute more," Stephens warned. "And I'll be right outside."

"Thank you. I owe you."

"Don't thank me. Just make sure you finish quickly before someone sees you."

Samuel winked at her and stepped inside.

The door bolted behind him, but he kept staring at Stella's sister.

"Megan?" he said, but she didn't move an inch. So he stepped closer. "Megan, I'm Detective Green. I was at your house with your sister Stella."

At the mention of her sister's name, Megan lifted her head and her eyes were a pot of mixed emotions.

"Where is she? Stella?" she asked, her voice as hard as her eyes.

"She couldn't come—"

"Of course she didn't come," Megan scoffed, spitting out the words like they were venom. "I assure you she would have come, but even me being here is against the rules."

Samuel moved closer and stopped across from her, his back slightly touching the white wall, while Megan kept her eyes on him sitting on her single bed.

"Megan? Why did you attack us?" Samuel asked.

She looked at him but stayed quiet. Her fingers fidgeted with her bare ring finger when she suddenly asked. "Is Trevor okay?"

Trevor Peters was her fiancé and Samuel knew he was the man who had shot him, who had intended to kill Stella in her hotel room, and who had shown up in the hospital just before Stella's mother almost died. He knew Trevor Peters was a registered nurse, which made it easy for him to get into a hospital and take the coat of a doctor so he could enter a patient's room without raising suspicion. He also knew that Trevor had died in his own living room. Samuel had shot him with his gun. He had seen him die right in front of him and his family would put him to rest in the coming week. Samuel was surprised Megan didn't know, but he wasn't sure if her future in-laws didn't want to inform her about Trevor's death or if messages were kept from her while she was locked away. It wouldn't have been the first time for messages getting lost.

But he wasn't here to fix that part of the system. He needed to know why Megan's fiancé almost became a murderer.

But before he could get to that, he would have to do the decent thing and tell Megan the truth.

"I'm sorry, Megan, but Trevor was fatally shot when he attacked us. He didn't make it. He is dead, Megan," Samuel said.

A gasp escaped her mouth and her eyes shot up to meet Samuel's in shock. He hated this moment. It was one thing to tell someone about the death of a beloved person, but the deep and personal reaction everyone went through right after hearing the news was the most devastating and tough thing he had to do in his job. When the world of someone collapsed right in front of him and he couldn't do anything to help them.

"H-he is g-gone?" she asked with a shaky voice that slowly turned into a loud wail.

"I am so sorry, Megan. Please help me understand what happened," he offered, wanting to comfort her, but couldn't.

"What am I supposed to do now? I can't do this alone," Megan babbled.

Samuel took a small step towards her. "I promise you, I can help you, but you need to give me more information. You need to tell me why you and Trevor attacked us."

"Trust you?" Megan barked through sniffles. "I can't trust you. You are probably going straight to him."

"Who are you talking about?" Samuel asked, confused, as a sudden heaviness settling in his stomach. *Who else was involved in this?*

"Where is Mae?" Megan asked suddenly, a tremor in her voice.

He hadn't even thought about her daughter. The last thing he had heard was that she was with Child Protective Services until they could determine what to do with Mae.

"Don't worry, she is in good—"

"She cannot go to him," Megan interrupted him sharply, an urgency in her voice that had his hair stand up.

"To whom?"

Her eyes shone with tears in them, pleading. "He cannot have her."

"Who, Megan?"

"My father."

"Your father? Why would he—" It dawned on Samuel that Stella and her father could be the last family members and that Social Services would reach out to them before they'd place Mae in foster care.

"Please! He cannot take her. She is too young. He cannot hurt her." Megan was on her feet quicker than he would have expected and had closed the small distance between them in a second. Her hands reached for his arm. Instinctively, he wanted to move back, but only hit the wall. Tears ran down her face as she held onto him, drowning in panic. Based on what Stella had told him about their childhood, Megan's reluctance to have her daughter live with her grandfather didn't surprise him, but he believed that staying with family was better than entering the system. Megan's fear, however, felt primal. She was ready to protect her child at any cost, but what was she so afraid of?

His stomach tightened. "What are you so terrified of? I promise you I'll help you, but I need to know what's going on."

Her grip on him turned stronger, and he felt the tinge of pain when she pulled on his arm. Cracked lips moved closer to him. He felt her heavy breathing on him when she urged him on.

"You need to get me out of here. I need to be with my child. I need to keep her safe."

His mind flew circles in his head. Was this really worry in her voice, or was he talking to an addict? But he wasn't even in a position right now to get her out of here, and he surely couldn't just smuggle her out. Hell, she tried to have him and Stella killed. He shook his head and gently pushed Megan away, keeping her at arm's length.

"You know I can't do that."

"They'll try to get rid of me," she shrieked, droplets of saliva flying through the air.

Samuel ran his hand over his face. He knew Megan was in terrible shape and whatever addiction she had, it might have already clouded her mind to an irreparable extent. But her terror was genuine.

"Megan, no one is trying to get rid of you. I'm trying to help you. Your sister is trying to help you."

He saw Megan's demeanor change in her posture first, turning cold and stony. Her fingers curled into fists as madness crept into her voice.

"You are just like them! I knew it! You are all in on it!" she screamed, pulling at her own hair, a few blonde strands falling to the ground.

"In on what? Megan?" He wanted to help her, but how could he when she didn't make any sense?

She collapsed down onto her bed and pulled her legs into her, wrapping her arms around them. She cradled herself like a child. Like the child, she couldn't hold.

"Megan?" Samuel asked again, but she was gone. Lost in her own world.

When he left, he could still hear the echo of her voice.

"He can't have you."

"Mama's gonna keep you safe."

"I'll protect you, Mae."

What had her father done to her?

Chapter 28 - The Confession

Samuel

IT WAS TIME TO CONFRONT Holmes and demand answers.

While Samuel believed Megan was delirious and incoherent, he also sensed her fear was real. She didn't fake the panic that had risen inside her at the mention of her father's name. Despite Samuel's uncertainty about Richard Woodworth's potential threats against Megan and his reasons for doing so, Megan feared the harm he could inflict on her child or herself. If only he could talk to the one person who held more information, but the state of Stella's mother hadn't changed. Whatever light Beth Woodworth could shed on this situation was inaccessible because of her coma.

Samuel's guts churned as if they wanted to tell him what was going on, to gurgle an answer he couldn't decipher.

This case had felt off the second he had stepped into Holmes' office a few weeks ago. The sudden transfer and secretive behavior and now he had seen his boss' involvement in blackened out print. Holmes had a personal interest in this case and had gotten way too involved. But why? It didn't make any sense. Holmes was a great boss. A stickler for rules and supporter of the underdog. Whatever he was hiding and made him a pawn in Richard Woodworth's power game, he had to get it out of him. Even if he was on suspension and even if he had never felt more apart from his mentor and friend than ever before. Even the generic 'get well soon' card Holmes had sent him felt awkward and misplaced.

As if on cue Samuel received a phone call from the man he hadn't talked to in over a week. The incomprehensible joy Samuel heard in Holmes' voice almost knocked him off his shaky feet. He wouldn't have been surprised if Holmes did his little victory dance in the office, which Samuel had seen him do many times after closing a tough case. Holmes wanted to see him and, if his demeanor could be trusted, all the resentfulness of their last encounter had ebbed away like the ocean tide. Samuel, however, wondered when the next flood would arrive and what it would bring.

Entering the precinct, Samuel nodded at his colleagues on his way up to the fifth floor. It was odd being back here, even though it had only been a few days. Samuel felt more like a stranger now than when he came back after his first round-the-clock binge on Johnny Walker. Something had changed. He had changed and the way he saw his possibilities at the precinct.

Holmes' door was open, but Samuel knocked anyway. "Can I come in, Sir?"

His captain looked up and jumped off his chair. "Yes, yes. Come on in," he said gregariously, waving Samuel in like he hadn't basically thrown him out just over a week ago.

Halfway to the seat, Holmes met him with open arms. One hand went in for a shake while the other found Samuel's back. Even through his jacket, he felt the attempt at a fatherly slap on his back.

"How are you feeling?" Holmes asked, referring to the gunshot wound.

The bizarreness of this situation had Samuel almost forget his insides were still healing where the bullet had sliced through his flesh.

"The doctors say it is healing well. I probably won't be winning any baseball trophies, though."

Holmes let out a hearty yet unusual laugh while leading Samuel to his chair. Once Samuel seated himself, Holmes found his own seat.

"You've done an outstanding job," Holmes blurted without looking at Samuel.

Say what now?

"Ah, don't look at me like that." Holmes chuckled. "I know our last encounter was a bit heated, but there are no hard feelings on my side."

No hard feelings? Had Holmes been hit on the head?

Holmes attempted to look at Samuel like he used to, but it wasn't genuine. Underneath the smiles and laughter, Holmes was exhausted, and he wore the look of someone who could finally sit down, relax, and get a good night's rest.

"I'm happy to let you know that Miss Woodworth, that's Megan of course, not Stella, gave a full confession."

That got Samuel's attention, and he sat up straighter in his chair.

"She did what?" He couldn't believe his ears. He had just seen her yesterday and at that point she was far away from saying anything, nevermind admitting attempted murder. While she was clearly involved in all of it and most likely the driving force behind her fiancé's actions, Samuel doubted she would ever see it that way. Whatever she had done, Samuel was convinced she thought she had to do it. She felt desperate enough.

Holmes produced a sealed plastic bag with a yellow paper inside and handed it over to him.

"She wrote a confession last night."

Stunned, Samuel took the paper. How did Holmes have this document and why, Samuel wondered while trying to understand what Megan had scribbled down on the piece of paper in his hands.

"She'll be transported to another facility first thing in the morning," Holmes continued cheerily.

Megan's fate hung in the air for a moment while Samuel tried to make sense of it all. This was all going way too fast.

"Is she not going before a judge?" Sam finally asked.

"She has confessed to everything, Sam. She doesn't want a lawyer, so there is no need to drag this out."

Holmes pointed at the letter in Samuel's hand, and he continued reading. There it was, in black and white. Her confession. Samuel read it over twice, branding the short message into his mind. Megan had been on drugs and when she tried to get support from her family, they told her they'd help her get clean but wouldn't give her any money. She got angry and desperate and slipped. She didn't want this to happen. It wasn't like her, which is why she needed to better herself, take responsibility for her actions, and maybe in this way, she could make it up to her family one day.

"It's terrible what an addiction can make you do. How it can destroy your life."

Samuel let the hidden meaning slide off him without comment and concentrated on what was clear. There was no way Megan wrote this. There was no mention of her fiancé Trevor or her daughter Mae. Nothing about the attack on her sister. The woman he had seen yesterday would have never given up like this. She wanted to fight. Felt the urge to protect her daughter. How could she do that if she was in prison?

That meant someone must have forced her to sign this. Threatened and scared her enough to sign anything they'd put in front of her. And who had done something like this before? Richard Woodworth.

Was Stella right? Could her father have been behind everything and was now putting the blame on another vulnerable person? But why would he go through all this trouble? It didn't make any sense. What was Samuel not seeing?

Of course, Megan would need to atone for her actions, but right now she needed someone to help her because there was a man out there who wanted to destroy her so badly he'd be willing to shut her up for good.

"This means nothing," Samuel said, throwing the piece of paper back at Holmes. "If she is an addict, this won't hold in court. She needs to be checked by a doctor and psychiatrist. You can't just lock her away."

"Son, I know it's tough to let go of a case that seemed like there was more to it, and I know Stella has tried hard to find someone to blame. Sometimes, though, the answer is simple. Sometimes things just work out and thanks to you, they did. Even if your methods were a bit, well, unorthodox."

He meant because Samuel had done exactly the opposite of what his captain had asked him to.

"You should be proud of yourself," Holmes continued. "This will look great for you at your next evaluation."

His captain went on praising him, but all Samuel could think about was that this couldn't be it. There should be an investigation. He should be put on leave for disobedience. Holmes should at least shout at him.

Where was the right procedure in all of this? How could Holmes wash over this like it was nothing? He wasn't following any protocol. He simply wanted this case gone as quickly as possible.

"I think the word promotion might fall as well. At least as long as I have something to say about it."

Holmes' grin was wider than Samuel had ever seen it on him, but it didn't reach his eyes. Samuel studied his face, unsure what he was looking for. And when he thought his boss might actually mean every single word he just said, he saw the drop of sweat running down his temple. Slowly, like it didn't have a worry in its life, it slipped down to his ear and he wondered how much effort it took Holmes not to wipe it off.

The city hadn't turned on the heating yet, so one couldn't describe the temperature in Holmes' office like anything related to a warm or even tropical climate. It wasn't a fall heatwave Holmes felt. He was nervous. Holmes needed Samuel to believe him, to get this case closed and gone for good.

Samuel had sworn an oath. He knew this wasn't right, but he also knew he needed his badge in order to get his answers. And if that meant playing along, he'd do it. He got off his chair and held out his hand to Holmes.

"Thank you, Sir."

The relief on Holmes' face was real as was the firm handshake.

"Go out, celebrate. But not too much. I need you to get back in shape and then we can assign you your next case," Holmes said.

"The next case?"

"Yeah, you don't think I'll let you get back to your old desk after such a win?"

Of course not. How could he not have seen this? He just shook his life away and placed it in the Captain's hand. He needed to find out the truth fast or else he'd end up like Holmes. The puppet of someone else.

"Now that this is all behind us, I'm sure I can get you a seat here in homicide. Right next to me," Holmes said.

He wanted him near him so he could keep an eye on him. Holmes was still afraid he'd find something. As long as Megan was out there, she'd always be a threat to Holmes and the actions he took to make her disappear so he could protect his friend. And that put Megan's life at risk.

Samuel left the precinct without stopping at the desk he had vacated under Holmes' orders. He didn't wait for the elevator, but walked the five stories as fast as his healing body allowed him. He needed to make a call, and it had to be as far away from the precinct as possible. Who knew whom Holmes had placed on watching him? Observing his actions, listening to his every word.

A few blocks down the road, when he believed no one had followed him, Samuel called the one person he could trust.

Chapter 29 - The Jail

Stella

THE LIGHT TURNED RED, but Samuel put his foot on the gas and zoomed across the junction, barely missing a silver Mercedes. The long and frustrated sound of the horn followed him and Stella as they chased the next traffic light.

"You'll kill us if you continue driving like this," Stella shouted at him, one hand pressed against the roof of Samuel's Dodge while the other clawed into her seat.

"Do you want me to go slower?" he asked her without taking his eyes off the road in front of them. "I'm trying to get you to your sister as quickly as possible."

"I appreciate that, but I'd like to arrive in one piece. Preferably alive."

Stella flinched when Samuel flew by a truck, barely making it back onto his side before oncoming almost traffic hit them.

She had never understood the urge to race down streets in a car or on a motorbike. Was there really ever a need for speed or were people just never properly organized to make it to their planned destinations on time? But now she got it. She had tried to talk to her sister for several days, but all her requests were declined. Under normal circumstances, she would have been able to at least get access to her family member by phone or email. This procedure of deliberately shutting her out wasn't normal. It made Stella extremely uncomfortable. Why go through all these hoops just to stop her from talking to her sister?

"Tell me again why you think my sister is in danger?"

"It's my gut," Samuel replied.

"Your gut?"

When Samuel had called Stella, he sounded off and when she arrived in the pub where he had asked her to meet him, she was sure she'd find him drinking, but the glass in front of him contained only Diet Coke. He explained what had happened between him and his captain. Built-up frustration spilled out of him and collected itself in one strong feeling: Megan was in danger.

They approached a white Honda Civic that was going way below the recommended speed limit.

"Move!" Samuel barked, but whoever was behind that wheel was neither impressed by his flasher nor the blinking red-and-blue lights of his car. He slowed down behind the Honda, veered into the ongoing traffic, and retracted. There wasn't enough room. In the end, they had to wait for six cars to pass by before he could finally overtake the old and tiny lady who could barely see over her steering wheel.

"Is your gut also telling you to drive like *The Fast and The Furious*?" Stella asked while they passed the old, white-haired snail in the Honda Civic. The human dinosaur looked over at them through glasses thick enough to give a mole clear vision and gave them the finger.

"Loved that movie."

Of course he did.

"I really hope my gut is wrong, but if I'm right, we need to get to your sister before someone else does."

"Because your boss is trying to kill her?" The sound of her skepticism reverberated in her mind.

"I know it sounds insane, but you should have seen him. He is scared to death and with her gone, the secret he is keeping would go away as well."

It sounded like a made-up movie script, but it wouldn't have been the craziest thing to happen so far. They were still trying to figure out what happened to her mother and why. Every time they thought they had found another piece of the puzzle, another thousand pieces were added. It was frustrating to constantly work against those who wanted to keep the truth hidden.

They took a right turn onto a road with high security fences to their left and silently followed it for a few minutes until they eventually reached the jail where Megan was held.

"Your sister is the only one right now who can tell us what is really going on. Why she wanted to kill your mother. Why she had Trevor attack you. We need to get her to tell us. Tell you," Samuel said when he parked the car.

"I don't know if she will tell me, to be honest." Stella sighed, looking at the gray concrete building in front of her.

How could her baby sister end up in jail?

Why would you want to hurt mom?

After turning off the ignition, both of them got out of Samuel's car.

"She has to," he said. "However you decide to appeal to her, you must get through to her," Samuel urged before they walked the short distance to the entrance.

He had called beforehand to organize a visit for both of them. Lucky for them, Samuel's list of acquaintances was long. Under no circumstances would Stella, or anyone else for that matter, have been able to get a visit on such short notice. But he'd done it. Again. He also seemed to know his way around this jail, which made it easier for them to go to the correct windows and the right people.

Everyone always says it's hard to get out of prison, but today it felt just as hard to get into it. At least to Stella it felt like a never-ending process of asking questions, checking IDs, emptying pockets, and contacting superiors until both of them were deemed no threat and allowed to continue. On the other side of a heavy metal door, a tall man in a gray suit that matched his full gray head greeted them. He pushed the golden rim of his glasses up his nose before extending his hand to Samuel for a handshake.

"I'm Thomas Jenkins, the warden of this prison. What can I do for you today, Detective Green?"

It didn't surprise Stella he knew Samuel's name. Both of them had given their names to so many people, every prisoner in here probably knew they were coming. Samuel reached for the hand and gave it a firm squeeze while addressing the importance of their visit.

"Thank you for accommodating us. We really appreciate it."

"You made quite a fuss, but I'm interested to hear what this emergency is."

They weren't in yet. As much as Samuel had pulled strings before, this man was the one he needed to convince.

"We need to speak to Miss Woodworth. We believe she has important information on a case we are working on and we also believe this information is putting her at risk of being a target." There was clearly no use for playing around and only offering half-truths to this man.

"I assure you, none of our inmates are in any physical danger while they are in my jail."

"We really need to speak to her," Stella cut in and got Jenkins' attention for the first time. He turned to look at her and finally offered his hand to Stella as well.

"And you are?"

"I'm Stella Woodworth. I'm—" she started, returning the firm grip of his handshake.

"You are the sister, I see." For a split second, and only for Stella to see, something else but a friendly smile washed over his pale face. Confused, Stella withdrew her hand from the skeleton-like grip. Maybe Samuel's gut was right. Was her sister really in danger?

"Mr. Jenkins, can we please see her now?"

The warden noticed Samuel's demand, but he took his time, letting his decision to grant permission hang in the air.

"It would mean a lot." Stella's voice was honey sweet, and she even lowered her eyes a bit, timidly looking up at him. "I cannot believe what she did to my mother, and I just need to see her before she's taken away. She might tell me why she did it. Give me a way to find closure."

She wasn't sure at all if this would work. Jenkins looked like a man who enjoyed his power and not like someone who'd let others dictate what he was supposed to do. Samuel's straightforward approach might not have been the right way for this man.

The skeleton-hand touched Stella's forearm. "I'm sorry for what you must be going through. Such a tragedy. And while I'd like nothing more than to let you see her, I need to think about the safety of everyone in here. We have rules to follow and barging in like this..." Jenkins waved both his hands at Sam and her as if he was opening his arms to the sinners they were, teasing Stella and Samuel with absolution.

This man wanted to be treated as more than just the warden. He wanted to feel like the master over this institution, the incarcerated, and even over them.

Samuel clenched his teeth. This was hard for him. Stella knew how he felt. She wanted to show Jenkins what it meant to barge into a place but so far this approach hadn't gotten her as far as she had hoped.

She would give him what he wanted for the sake of her sister.

"Of course. We know you have your procedures that need to be followed. You have them for good reasons. It's hard enough to run a jail and I don't want you to break any rules. I just hoped—" She paused dramatically for effect, swallowing hard, looking up at Jenkins with worry in her eyes. "To see her one last time. I don't know when I'll see her again."

Jenkins still hesitated, but Stella didn't give him time to say no. Like rapidfire she threw words at him.

"I live in Asia and need to return soon. You know what it's like, right? This is probably my last chance to see her. I just need to tell her goodbye. Put this behind me."

She let the words that held more truth than she could admit to herself sink in. Jenkins didn't say no immediately. He just looked at her, hungry for more. What else could he want? She was practically begging. And thn she knew just what to say.

Her palm cupped his hand on her forearm, pleading, and her voice quivered when she said, "Please."

He'd wanted her to beg. She should have known it.

Next to her, Samuel treaded nervously from one foot to the other.

Finally, Jenkins gave his blessing.

"I am always happy to assist a colleague."

They weren't colleagues.

"Even without prior notice."

They did call.

"Sure, I can help you out with that." Jenkins smiled at her wryly, but Stella didn't care. She'd gotten what she needed. Let him think he'd won.

He asked them to follow him with a nod of his head and continued, "You'll be pleased to hear that just this afternoon I had a rather pleasant conversation with her. She seemed better than the last few days, and I was ready to have her moved from her solitary confinement."

"Solitary confinement? Why was she put in there?" Stella asked, surprised.

They stopped in front of a door, and Jenkins turned to her. "Miss Woodworth, your sister has shown a disturbing level of aggression towards the other inmates. We had to separate her for her own safety and that of others. But she was much better this afternoon."

Danger to others? Stella couldn't believe what she was hearing. She remembered Megan attacking her in the kitchen of her house. And while she still wouldn't consider her little sister a danger to others, the penny dropped. She really didn't know her sister at all. The young and happy girl with big dreams for her future had been gone for ages. At some point in the past, Megan had changed, while Stella was busy living her life in Asia. Megan would never talk to her.

The door opened, and Jenkins waved them inside. "I'm going to have her brought over to you. Take a seat."

Stella thanked him and waited for him to leave before she let out a sigh.

"Jesus, I didn't know you were such a good ass-licker," Samuel said, only to gain one of Stella's notorious eye rolls.

"Well, your strategy of charming your way inside didn't work, so I had to make sure we would get this done."

"Touché."

They sat down at a metal table in the center of the room. No windows. Just a fluorescent lamp above them that flickered every minute or two, just like Stella's heart.

What would she say to her sister?

Would Megan even talk to her?

"How are you holding up?" Samuel asked.

She raked her fingers through her hair. "I've been better, I guess."

Samuel shifted in his chair, trying to find a position that felt comfortable. He must have been on quite the cocktail of pain medication to make it this far. The suicidal car ride couldn't have helped him. He needed rest, but he kept insisting on following any lead they could find.

"How's the wound?" she asked.

"Okay."

She raised a questioning eyebrow at him.

"You didn't twist your ankle, Sam. You got shot. Not too long ago."

"I've been better, I guess," he repeated her own words and weirdly it made her smile. "Listen, there is something I wanted to run by you."

At the discomfort in his voice, Stella's smile dropped.

"What?"

He took a deep breath before he continued, "Do you not find it strange your sister tried to kill your mother when she is afraid of your father?"

"What do you mean?"

"Okay, so hear me out—"

"Oh God, now this sounds reassuring," Stella said, watching his thumb patting against the table in a staccato rhythm.

"I think your mother upset your sister," he pushed out and Stella's eyes went big.

"My mom? What did she do? She wouldn't hurt a fly."

"I have this feeling that—"

"Oh, is that the same gut that is telling you my sister is in danger of being murdered in jail right now?" Stella interrupted.

"Yes!"

He said it with certainty, and Stella knew there was no arguing with him about it. His gut had been right every time so far. And as much as she wanted to believe the system worked, that prisoners were kept safe, she knew that the system was broken. It was all Darwinian survival of the fittest in there.

She gave him the benefit of the doubt and thought his comment through. He didn't know her mother. Sure, she had flaws and hadn't always made the best decisions when they were younger, but she always tried her best, which, under the circumstances of being married to her father, was rarely easy. She had been to every school function, recital, or game. When Megan had basically dropped all her extra curricular activities at school, her mom had even tried to get her into something that was fun and wouldn't just look good on a resume. And when Stella had left, she couldn't have made it without her mother's secretive financial support to get her started. Whatever Samuel thought she had done, she surely didn't do it.

"You sound insane," she concluded. "This is all my father."

"Jesus Stella. You can't blame him for everything just because you hate him so much."

Samuel's truth hit her like a bullet. Fast and unexpectedly. Until now, she believed they were on the same page.

"What the fuck is wrong with you, Sam? You have met the guy."

"I know—"

"Well, clearly you don't. Or did he or one of his pawns finally get to you?"

"Of course not, but—"

"And what is your gut telling you she did, huh?" Stella poked.

"I don't know—"

"Aha, very convincing. I thought we followed real clues?"

"Goddammit, Stella!" Sam called, and she went quiet. "Will you stop focussing on your horrible father and listen to me for a fucking second?"

He had never spoken to her like this. Or raised his voice to her. His chest was heaving with anger and she saw how much effort it took him not to shout at her. The surrounding silence was painful, and eventually Stella gave in.

"Go ahead then."

Samuel took in a deep breath before he continued in a calmer voice. "Look at what your sister did. Who she attacked, not who she is scared of. Your mother is the center of her aggressive obsession, no matter how horrible your father is. Could your mother have done something to your sister to make her angry?"

Stella shook her head. "Why would she attack me then?"

"Collateral damage."

"Excuse me?"

"No, really. I believe you were in the wrong place at the wrong time. If you hadn't come home, you wouldn't have become a target. You are trying to save your mother, and Megan doesn't want you to succeed."

She opened her mouth for another remark on how ridiculous Samuel's idea was, but stopped herself. Instead, she thought through his comment honestly this time. Maybe Megan was angry about the affair. As absurd as this might be, maybe she had a reaction to the fact that the broken but only kind of family she knew was really falling apart this time? Maybe she was afraid to be alone? Maybe she thought she wouldn't get any financial support anymore? Their father would clearly not worry about financing her addiction, especially if he potentially had to pay some sort of alimony to his cheating wife.

Was this all just about money?

She ran her hand over her face and through her hair. If she had been trying to solve this for a client, she would have thought about more angles than merely her own father. Samuel was right. Megan concentrating on their mother could mean more.

Maybe.

But why were the police so invested in keeping this all a secret if they weren't deep in her father's pocket?

She had to talk to Megan.

"Why is this taking so long?"

"They probably have her in the furthest corner of this place. He'll get her," Samuel reassured Stella while she got up from her chair and started pacing the small space.

"I don't know. Something feels off." According to her watch, they'd been in here for almost forty-five minutes. Maybe this was all normal. Maybe Jenkins took his sweet damn time with them again, but Stella didn't think so.

She really needed to see her sister.

Right on cue, the door opened and Jenkins appeared ghostly pale, followed by no one. Stella looked over his shoulder, waiting for her sister to appear, but when Jenkins closed the door behind him, her hopes died.

This felt bad.

Next to her, Samuel got up from his chair and moved over to her side.

"W-where is my sister?" Stella stammered while she felt Samuel's shoulder touch hers.

Jenkins took a tentative step towards her. "Miss Woodworth, I think you should sit down."

She didn't want to sit down. She wanted to see her sister. Where was Megan?

"What's going on?" Sam asked when all Stella could do was stare at Jenkins, who had trouble swallowing. Whatever he had to tell her terrified him, and therefore Stella.

"I-I am very sorry, but I have to inform you there has been an accident."

No!

"An accident? What kind of accident?" she asked, but dreaded the answer.

She is fine.

"I have to insist we see Megan Woodworth, now!" Sam's demand almost drowned out the nasty little voices inside of Stella's head.

Someone hurt her.

Samuel was right.

They are trying to get to her.

"I am afraid that is not possible."

Stella's hand found the back of the metal chair. Her knuckles went white under her tight grip. Megan was the last one left. She couldn't lose her, too.

In a heated exchange in front of her, Samuel tried to get Jenkins to tell them why, but the master of this jail had become even more uncomfortable.

"For fuck's sake, tell me where my sister is or I swear I'll go looking for her!"

The men went quiet. Silence shrouded the room.

Jenkins straightened, and when he found his courage, he told her exactly where Megan was.

"Your sister is dead."

Chapter 30 - The Aftermath

Stella

HUNCHED OVER AND STARING into the distance, Stella sat Jenkins' office. Next to her, Samuel approached her with a cup of water. Her fingers were still shaking, and she spilled some of the water on her pants.

"Shit."

She struggled to fully comprehend the magnitude of what had just taken place. Unconvinced about the reality of this situation, she'd tried everything she could to see her sister, but protocol didn't allow her to get close to the body.

Samuel had assured her they'd go down to the morgue together, identify the body, figure out what had happened, and say goodbye. She wasn't sure she could handle the sight of her sister's lifeless body, though.

The images of Jonathan's lifeless body ran on repeat in her mind like a broken record, torturing her already fragile state. She had tried for a long time to shove the traumatizing memory of his death into the depths of her subconscious. Try as she might, though, she remembered every detail. When she had entered his bedroom, her brain had not made the connection between death and her brother's body dangling from the ceiling in his en-suite. At first she had thought he might be playing a trick on her, but when she had touched the unnaturally cold skin between his faded jeans and royal blue socks, she had known something was wrong. All the shaking in the world hadn't woken him up.

Somehow, she had assumed this experience would prepare her for death.

But nothing could have prepared her for this.

In her mind, a war raged on about the senselessness of this situation. She could have avoided Jonathan's death if she hadn't been so consumed by her own anger, if she'd only paid more attention to the people in her life. She could have avoided her mother's hospitalization if she hadn't fled the country and left her alone to deal with her own anger, fear, and grief. And she could have prevented Megan's death. That one hurt her the most because she should have known something was off. Should have heard it in her sister's voice. But she had been too slow and too distracted by herself.

She ran through every scenario in her head, trying to figure out what she did wrong and where she could have done something differently.

This is what Samuel must feel like since he lost that girl Melanie.

Knowing that he didn't do enough.

No wonder he is drinking.

She was an only child now.

Stella's chest tightened, and she found it suddenly difficult to breathe.

A hand fell gently on her shoulder.

Sam.

"Are you okay?" he asked and Stella blinked herself back to the living.

"How is this possible? You saw her a few days ago."

Settling himself next to her, Samuel sighed. "It's not uncommon for inmates to commit suicide," he said, watching her while his words settled into her brain.

"Are we even sure she did that?"

Jenkins had told them he'd found her lying lifeless on the jail floor, her wrists cut. Thankfully, he'd spared her the gruesome details. But it was his word alone. What if someone had killed her? Sam had believed she was in danger and then she suddenly killed herself? What were the odds of that happening?

"She was agitated when I saw her last. Who knows what was going through her mind?"

Stella looked at him as if he was trying to convince her the world was flat.

"What the fuck, Sam? What happened to Holmes trying to get rid of her—"

"Keep your voice down." Samuel gritted his teeth, trying to keep a blank face. "I am on your side, Stella. You know that, right?"

While his face didn't show any emotion, his eyes were as warm as his body next to hers. Yes, Samuel was on her side and it made Stella feel safe to know there was at least one person left she could trust.

"So you don't believe that she committed suicide?" Stella whispered.

"No, but that's what they think happened," he said with a nod to the cluster of important men and women gathered outside the warden's office.

"And they will write this in their reports. The truth will never come out," Stella added in defeat. *This was it.*

"Maybe not."

"You have something in mind?" Stella asked.

"I talked to one of the first responders and got the address of the coroner where they are taking her body. I know the guy. Fred is good. He'll do a thorough job," he reassured her and let his hand rest on her thigh.

"And you believe that will help us find the truth?"

Samuel took in a long breath. She knew what was going on in his mind. He felt rundown and defeated. Like her.

"Maybe you were right," he said, dropping his gaze. "Maybe we'll never find out what really happened. I might have underestimated your father. It feels like we get further and further away from the truth. I honestly don't know. I just really wanted us to get ahead, but there is no one left who could tell us the truth."

"So this is it? He won?"

Samuel shrugged, not giving her an answer. Behind him, Stella watched the group of four men standing in a circle in the hallway. Jenkins was one of them. His hands casually hidden in his pressed suit pockets. He didn't show any emotion about the tragedy that had just happened on his watch. But Jenkins kept glancing over at her while answering questions from the police officer in front of him. The other two looked like prison staff. There was a lot of friendly nodding and smiling going on between them. She hated this inner circle buddy conversation that was going on. Probably reassuring each other that everyone had done a great job, that no one could have predicted this or even prevented this awful unpleasant situation. By tomorrow, everything would be back to normal, and her sister would be forgotten, as if she'd never existed.

This has to stop.

Jenkins patted the shorter officer on his shoulder in a fatherly manner before they shook hands and said their goodbyes. Then it was time to attend to her. In a few long strides, he had made his way over to them and came to a halt right in front of her.

"Miss Woodworth, I'm very sorry for your loss, but let me assure you that—" Jenkins started in his professionally unemotional tone that brought Stella's blood to a boil. She'd had it. She had reached her limit of playing nice. It hadn't brought them any closer to figuring this out. What if they wanted to shut her up or take her down? At least they'd have to do it with her burning down the house they were hiding in as well.

"Cut the crap!" she interrupted with no sympathy for this so-called competent man.

Jenkins was taken aback. His eyes searched for something from Samuel. Support or understanding, but Samuel merely shook his head at him, a big smirk around the corners of his mouth. He knew what Jenkins was about to endure.

"How the fuck can someone commit suicide in your jail and you don't know about it? Where did she get a razor blade from? Why wasn't she under watch when it was you who put her in solitary because you were afraid she might hurt others or herself?" Stella asked with such power in her voice, Jenkins took a step back.

"What kind of pathetic institution are you running here or are you the fuck-up who is too incompetent to do his job?" she added.

At this point, Stella had captured the attention of every single person who was still gathered outside in the hall. Everyone had heard her scold the warden, probably even the inmates. Jenkins treaded from one leg to the other and cleared his throat before he explained himself.

"As I was saying, I assure you we follow the highest standards of protocol—" he tried a second time. But in vain. Stella's anger had burst through and was running wild.

"Your standards can kiss my ass. My sister died on your watch and we both know this wasn't a suicide." At this statement, one that could cost him his career if ever proven correct, he started to lose the color in his cheeks.

"I-I don't know what you are referring to—" he stuttered and while he should have seen the interruption coming, it still took him by surprise. Or perhaps it was Stella's quick jump off the chair that startled him. Whatever it was, he took another step back from her, her extended index finger pointing at him like she was ready to pierce him with it.

"I don't know if you are blind or just playing dumb, but I'll make sure the medical examiner will find the reason behind my sister's death."

Her phone rang inside her jacket pocket, but she wasn't done with Jenkins yet. She needed him to know that this wasn't over. That she would do anything to find out the truth. Even if it was the last thing she'd ever achieve in her life.

"I am done playing nice and being silenced by all these men who think they are beyond justice," Stella said, pointing at the men behind him. "If I have to examine her body myself, I will do so and I swear if I find any evidence of her murder pointing in your direction, you better run for your life, because I will find and destroy you. I'll drag ruining your life out for as long as I can and trust me when I say that I will enjoy every single second of it!"

Her phone went off again and saved a pale and sweaty Jenkins from the heart attack that was imminent.

"This isn't over," she finished, then stepped aside and pressed her finger on the green button on her screen. "Who is this?"

"Miss Woodworth, hi. I'm calling from St. James' hospital. This is concerning your mother."

Please give me a break.

Stella closed her eyes. The adrenaline had instantly run dry. She wasn't sure if she could handle yet another tragedy. The day had been tough enough. She rubbed her temple, feeling the first pricks of a headache as she listened to the voice on the other end.

Her legs suddenly shook. She reached for something to hold on to and found Samuel's arm. Her phone slipped through her shaking fingers and dropped to the ground, the voice on the other line still calling her name while it lay motionless on the linoleum floor in front of her.

"What happened?" Samuel asked, steadying Stella. She felt the urge to wrap herself around him in a comforting embrace, getting lost in his warmth.

"It's the hospital," she mumbled instead, almost impossible for Samuel to hear.

He leaned in closer, his warmth spreading around her. She saw the worry in his eyes, saw his Adam's apple bobbing up and down like a nervous pinball.

When she met his eyes, hers were foggy, and she found it hard to sharpen her view.

"My mother woke up."

Chapter 31 - The Mother

Stella

"CAN YOU GIVE ME A MOMENT alone with her?" Stella asked.

She hadn't realized that Samuel's hand was still holding hers. His warm fingers covered her trembling limbs like a cozy blanket. He sighed, and she imagined him debating this in his head. They'd gone through a lot together. She couldn't have done it without him, and he knew it. She wouldn't want to be left outside now that her mother was awake.

And while part of her wanted him at her side, Stella needed a moment with her mother. She hadn't seen her in so long and the feeling of going in there with a stranger— a detective—might overwhelm her mother. She was stable for the moment, but who knew what could happen.

Samuel finally gave in. "Sure," he said, his thumb still circling her knuckles absentmindedly. "I'll be here."

Knowing he would wait for her was comforting. Stella wasn't used to relying on someone else, but her self-imposed wall of protection had started to crack. She felt more at ease around Samuel and with each supportive touch and word, another brick crumbled, leaving her more exposed. Hopefully she wouldn't regret this, but right now she was glad about every bit of support.

Stella was unsure what to expect when seeing her mother. Would she be lucid or not? Had the coma damaged her? Would she still be her mom?

The fact that she was the last of her siblings shook her and made her shiver. Very soon, she would have to tell her mother. She hadn't always been able to show how much she loved the three of them, but she had tried in her own ways. Telling her Megan was dead would crush her.

Stella registered herself at the front desk and let the nurse bring her to her mother's room.

"Your mother was asking for you," the nurse said over her shoulder, and Stella sighed in relief. At least she was aware of her surroundings. But in the back of her mind, she wondered how her mother knew she was in town. Maybe it was true that people in a coma could still realize what was happening around them. Had she heard her? Did she feel Stella's touch?

The door to her room stood open and there she was, displayed in this monstrosity of a bed that almost made her disappear between the sheets. The nurse moved over to her, stroking her arm gently to wake her up. While her mother blinked away the sleep, the nurse helped her into a more upright position. The buzzing of the bed's mechanism was the only sound in the vacuum of the room.

"Your daughter is here," the nurse said and placed a pillow behind her head.

Her mother frowned but a wave of relief passed over her face when she turned her head towards Stella.

"Megan?" Her voice came out hoarse.

Stella's worst fear came alive in front of her. She'd been wrong. Her mother wasn't in control of her body. Her body had woken up, but her mind hadn't.

"No, Mom, it's me, Stella."

Stella's mother still looked weak, but her cheeks had a light pink hue and her eyes had a sparkle of anticipation in them. A good sign that she was on the mend. But once their eyes met, that sparkle turned into confusion.

"Stella?" Relief washed over Stella. The woman holding out her veiny hand with a drip latched on to her was her mother indeed. "What are you doing here?"

Stella dropped herself next to her mother, took her hand like she needed to make sure she wasn't dreaming. Careful not to mess with the drip or cause her mother any pain, she pressed her mother's palm to her own face and placed a soft kiss on her wrist cautiously.

"I came to see you, of course." A tear of relief escaped Stella and landed on the white blanket covering her mother's chest, leaving a short-lived darker halo.

Eyebrows drawn together, she looked at Stella with a big frown on her face. "All the way from Hong Kong?"

Stella found it challenging to keep looking at her mother. She averted her eyes to the golden cross around her mother's neck and swallowed hard. She would have journeyed to the moon or crossed the galaxy if she had to. Maybe it had been a mistake to distance herself so much from her family. She could have made the effort to speak to her and to Megan more regularly. Still be a part of their lives and let them into hers. She had lost the chance to do that for Megan, but she wouldn't make the same mistake with her mother. She would cherish the time she had left with her.

"Is Megan with you?"

Stella's eyes shot up to meet her mother's. "Megan?" Her chest constricted.

"I need to talk to her," Beth said.

She couldn't bear to tell her that her youngest child had met the same fate as her eldest. That she was left with the middle child that had tried so hard to get as far away as possible from her. Guilt and worry tangled in Stella's throat. In her line of work, she had been in the uncomfortable position to inform others of their beloved's demise. Sometimes she had to hold their trembling bodies, but it never really affected her. This felt different. This time, she was part of the family.

"I have to apologize to her. Can you get her to come?" her mother demanded.

Oh God.

She would need to ease her mother into the reality of her situation. "Do you remember anything from your attack?" she asked instead, her finger stroking her mother's hand gently.

"Attack?"

Maybe she didn't remember what happened to her. This happened to victims of trauma. Possibly her brain's self-preserving mechanism had kicked in, trying to guard her and heal itself before having to deal with the reality of what had happened.

Under her fingers, her mother's hand got colder. A light shiver made her limbs shake. Stella felt her mother's pulse quicken through her own fingertips. Her breathing grew more ragged and Stella's pained eyes remained fixed on her mother's ghastly face.

"Where is Megan?" her mother asked again, her voice unusually strong for the weak state she was in.

Stella couldn't bear to look at her. She dropped her head on her mother's hands, her words muffled by the hospital sheets underneath.

"I'm so sorry."

It was all Stella needed to say for her mother to understand. Somehow Beth Woodworth knew she had lost yet another child. A light tremble started in her body and reverberated through her and into Stella. When she looked up from her mother's hands, she saw the devastation on her face.

"It's all my fault."

The thought completely took her aback. That her mother would claim to be responsible for her sister's death. She had as much to do with it as with Jonathan's suicide.

"I should have stopped it," Beth said. Her gaze drifted inward, like she was fighting a conversation in her head. Her eyeballs zoomed sideways and up and down like a computer game, just that this was no game to her.

What did she mean by stopping it? Samuel's words echoed in her head. Could she have done something to Megan?

Stella's gut churned. A shadow spread inside her, poisoning her and grabbing at her heart. Her mother's reaction felt different, the tone in her voice hinting at more than grief.

"What are you talking about?" Stella asked through a suddenly dry mouth.

Her mother's shaking worsened, spreading from her hands to her shoulders and into her chest and Stella feared she might have lost her mind in the end.

"It's all my fault. I should have stopped him." Her voice came out chased and high pitched.

A heaviness dropped in Stella's gut. "Stopped whom?"

But her mother didn't even listen to her. "I've been so scared." Her hands curled into fists on the crisp linen. "I should have stopped him when she came to me."

"Mom, what are you talking about?" Stella demanded, her hand on her mother's trembling fist.

"He is a monster and I should have gone to the police when she told me what he was doing to her at night— that he touched her."

No!

Dizziness made Stella's head spin.

Anything but this!

For a second, Stella's world went silent. Her mother's lips continued to repeat the last words over and over, but all Stella heard was white noise. Maybe she was suffering from acute hearing loss. Or maybe her body was trying to shield her from a truth she didn't feel ready to hear. Acid burned Stella's throat as bile rose up.

This can't be happening.

Her mother's icy grip around Stella's wrist jolted her back to reality, but her gut fell from a skyscraper when her mother spoke. "I have to stop him!"

She knew who her mother was talking about. Deep down she knew there was only one person capable of doing such an unspeakable thing, but her brain didn't want to believe the unfathomable.

Yes, he's horrible, but even he couldn't be this horrible. Right?

She wanted to run. Out of this hospital, this city, back to Hong Kong or even further. But Stella was done running from her family. She needed to finish this, and she needed to hear the name of the accusation.

"Mom, who was it?"

Her mother's eyes went white and with a clearness to her voice she hadn't heard in ages, Beth Woodworth said, "Your father."

Chapter 32 - The Statement

Samuel

SAMUEL PUSHED ASIDE the yellow police tape that cautioned every person in close vicinity to keep out. With the other hand, he turned the metal doorknob and opened the door to Megan Woodworth's home. He went in first, giving Stella a moment to take a breath before she followed him into a house that would most likely haunt her with traumatizing memories for years. He knew firsthand what that felt like and he wished she didn't have to go through it.

He handed Stella a set of blue latex gloves and waited for her to put them on before he did the same. Forensics had done a thorough job inside, wiping every surface for fingerprints, turning every cushion and opening every book, trying to find answers. Which surprised him, because everyone involved in this case seemed determined to rid themselves of any evidence. Maybe there was still hope for truth seekers.

Behind him, Stella cleared her throat. She looked wiped out. In the last couple of hours, she had not only lost a sister but also opened a chest of family secrets no one should ever have to deal with. How she was still standing was beyond him.

"This place gives me the creeps," she murmured to herself, while putting one of her sister's family frames back upright that forensics had missed. On it, Megan had left butterfly kisses on the tummy of a smiling Mae.

"Let's try to get this done quickly. Any idea where your sister could keep her diary?" Samuel asked.

Stella didn't need to be in here for longer than necessary. She'd relive what had happened here for the rest of her life.

After Beth Woodworth had told Stella about what her husband had done to his daughter, she had mentioned the last conversation between her and Megan. How they had fought over her mother's decision to leave their father and start a new life with Paul. Megan had blamed her for everything, for the abuse, the pain she inflicted on herself, and the carefree future she would never have. She threatened her own mother to tell the truth, to hand in her diaries as written proof of the accusations. Beth Woodworth apologized, but she had already made up her mind. She'd start fresh, and that decision had flipped a switch in Megan. According to Stella's mother, Megan had turned to stone. She had left without another word and a few weeks later, a man had entered the mansion at night and had attacked Beth Woodworth. She had thought she'd die when he put his gloved hands around her neck. She had tried to fight him off, but the mix of antidepressants and sleeping pills she had taken shortly before made her drowsy. Beth Woodworth had lost consciousness eventually, and the next thing she remembered was waking up in a hospital bed.

Samuel assumed Megan's fiancé Trevor had been interrupted, which is why he let go of her—perhaps thinking he'd already killed her. There was no one left to give them this piece of the puzzle. If they were very lucky, the police might find something in Stella's childhood home. Hair or skin, but the chances were low after weeks of having a cleaner vacuuming and mopping up potential evidence.

"My guess would be her bedroom," Stella said, snapping Samuel out of his thoughts. "And you are sure your guys didn't take in anything that looked like a diary?"

He confirmed his earlier statement. "Nothing was brought in." But even he knew this meant nothing. If Stella's father knew anything about a diary, he would have destroyed it. Though he didn't think so. From what he had learned, Megan had kept her home a secret from him. Richard Woodworth didn't have a clue where she was living, or maybe he had convinced himself his daughter would tell no one.

And he wasn't so wrong about that. Megan had bottled up the abuse, attempting to keep it hidden from everyone, including herself. However, when her mother decided to divorce her husband for another man instead of for the sake of her own daughter, Megan erupted in anger. Without Paul coming into Beth's life, Megan might have never started this chain reaction of events.

The stairs creaked beneath their feet, each step echoing the weight of their dread. Megan's bedroom was small, but it felt suffocating as they crossed the threshold, the air heavy with the secrets it held. They checked the obvious places first. Her dresser and nightstand. They lifted her mattress and Samuel even lay down on the floor to check if anything was under the bed. Stella went as far as knocking on the hardwood floor, in case there was a hidden compartment underneath one of them.

"Does she have a safe?" Samuel asked, already reaching for one of the paintings hanging on the wall, tilting the seaside scenery to the side, hoping to reveal a built-in safe. But there was nothing but daisies on the yellow wallpaper.

They went on lifting rugs, moving furniture, and even knocked on walls. Just in case. But nothing brought the hoped outcome. Maybe they were too late, and it was already gone.

"I think I have an idea where it might be," Stella said suddenly.

When Samuel turned from the wardrobe he was currently inspecting to look at her, she was staring at the open door. He moved closer to her, followed her gaze to the room across from them. The door had three big wooden letters in the colors of the rainbow glued to it. Painted unicorns and butterflies framed the pieces that spelled the name Mae.

With heavy, deliberate steps, Stella crossed the hall, Samuel right behind her. The pink bedroom visibly tortured Stella—innocence and happiness captured in pastel shades, mocking the trauma that had taken root in her family. She stood in the middle of it, her fists clenched in helpless anger.

Fucking families.

Sam wanted to support Stella and the only way he knew how was by finding the diary. So he went through the room with the same vigor as he had done before while Stella tried to come to terms with what her sister had endured as a child and how she had clearly tried to give her own little girl only the best of memories growing up.

307

When he reached the wardrobe, his eyes immediately fell on a red shoebox on the top shelf. He grabbed the box, took it down, and opened the lid.

"Stella," he said. "I think I found them."

Stella dropped the book she had taken off the shelf and strode over to him, where she accepted the box. She swallowed hard, frozen in place.

"I think I need to sit down."

She lowered herself onto the small fluffy pouf next to Mae's doll house, resting the box on her lap before selecting a worn-out diary with faded stickers on the back. With shaking fingers, she skimmed the pages of the first one, then went on to the next, her eyes going wider with each page. In the diary labeled 2022, she found a folded envelope at its center.

"This is a letter from my mom," she said, looking up at Samuel.

"What does it say?"

Stella placed the box on the ground in front of her and opened the letter. Whatever she was reading must have made her sick. She went pale, all the blood leaving her body. He glanced at the panda-shaped basket near Mae's bed, wondering if he should pull it closer—unsure if Stella would faint, scream, or simply break down right there.

She handed Samuel the paper, unable to continue. "He raped her the first time when she was just fourteen."

"Fuck! I'm sorry," Samuel said and took the paper from her.

There it was, the unspeakable truth of Megan's agony in black and white. It read like something nightmares were made of. But worse because it wasn't a fictional story. He felt his blood go cold, and a shiver made his hair stand up. Melanie appeared in front of him again. Why did this have to happen?

"Your mother knew all along?" Samuel sounded surprised reading it, even though Stella had told him about her mother's confession. Megan's mother had been aware of the truth from the start, but kept it hidden for many years after Megan's abrupt change of heart and assurance it had all been a lie. That she was merely looking for attention. Why Beth Woodworth's instinct wasn't to question her daughter for changing her story was beyond him. She didn't feel the need to go to the police or get Megan a therapist. Instead, Beth Woodworth closed her eyes and let her husband leave their shared bedroom at night to rape his child.

He forced himself to keep reading and suddenly froze.

This can't be right.

He read the sentence on the back of the letter again, trying to figure out if he had misread the information. But he hadn't. His heart pumped loudly against his chest and he felt dizzy.

"Did you read the whole letter?" he whispered.

"I got the gist, thanks," Stella said, getting off the pouf and walking to the window, in an effort to bring distance between her and the truth.

"I think you should check the back side again." He didn't give her a chance to say no. In fact, he needed her to read this and confirm he wasn't imagining things, even though he was hoping he was wrong.

Brows furrowed, Stella snatched the letter out of his hand, immediately turning it over.

"Your sister went to the police," Samuel said while she fought her way through the heartbreaking lines.

"I know. I read that. She changed her mind though and didn't go through with it."

"No, I mean the second time."

Stella reached the last paragraph on the back of the letter. Her eyes caught a name that was all too familiar. She looked up at Samuel.

"Detective Holmes?"

Samuel nodded.

"As in your boss?"

"The one and only," Samuel said, the boulder in his stomach forcing bile up his throat. His gaze went to the panda basket, contemplating if he would need it.

"Holmes was involved in this?" Stella sounded as irritated and confused as Samuel felt. This explained why Holmes had tried so hard to get this situation sorted.

"It was my boss who told your sister to stop lying and who scared her into keeping her mouth shut. My boss covered for your dad."

Her legs turned to jelly and Stella sank onto Mae's small bed. Samuel wanted to do the same, but he couldn't. He had to stay focused.

For Megan.

For Stella.

"How was all of this possible? How could all these people turn away when a young girl was molested right in front of their eyes?" Stella asked, but Samuel didn't have an answer. He had wondered about the exact same thing for years. Families should help each other, not be the pit of despair. And how Holmes, his boss and mentor, could have done this. Going on like nothing had happened, he'd gone home to his own daughters every night, tucking them in, kissing their foreheads while Megan endured her father's abuse.

Samuel pinched the bridge of his nose. His eyes burned. *Don't lose it now.*

"Ah shit," Stella blurted, and Samuel opened his wet eyes.

He could hear her swallow hard, and while he didn't think it possible for Stella to turn even paler, she now looked the same shade as the white paper she held in her trembling hands.

"What?"

"S-she—" The words wouldn't leave Stella's mouth. She rubbed her forehead and took in a few breaths until she finally managed to finish her sentence. "She was fourteen when all this started."

"I know, it's terrible."

"That's not what I mean." A tear ran down her cheek. "I-I was still here," Stella whispered, and it dawned on Samuel what she was referring to. "I lived in the same apartment, slept just a few rooms away."

He knelt in front of her and took the letter from her, then placed it on the night table. His hands found her trembling thighs. "Don't you dare go down that road, Stella. This was not your fault. You were just a kid yourself."

She fought more tears from falling, pressing the balls of her hands into her eyes. Samuel took her in for a hug. Damn protocol or whatever had happened between them. He wouldn't keep his distance from her when her world collapsed around her. Then she leaned into him and let her anger and sadness run. They sat like this for a while, until she had dried her eyes and calmed her nerves as best as she could. She took out her phone and photographed the diaries and her mother's letter.

"What are you doing?" Samuel asked.

"I'm emailing them to myself. I won't risk losing this evidence. This is the ultimate piece that will bring him down."

He grabbed the evidence bags from his inside pocket. "I know it's hard, but let's do this the right way. Make sure your father gets what he deserves." The letter from the night table vanished in the bag and Sam reached for the diary Stella still held. "I will not let this evidence out of my sight. I promise."

She looked at him through teary eyes, her bottom lip trembling. Then she let go of the diary.

Though it was a relief to finally had something substantial against her father, Samuel didn't feel victorious. How could he? There were no winners in this situation. The monster had won again. He'd lost another girl.

"It is time to kill this beast once and for all," Stella announced, her voice strong and determined. She was right, Samuel thought. Richard Woodworth might have been able to get away with it until now, but enough was enough. They'd be able to give him what he deserved and maybe this way they could bring justice to Megan.

Chapter 33 - The Truth

Stella

DARKNESS HAD SETTLED over the city and a light drizzle covered Stella and Samuel. The dampness crept through their clothes and into their bones. She blinked at the sharp raindrops pricking her eyes when she looked up to her father's apartment. The upper half of the concrete tower had vanished in low-hanging gray clouds. Like a monster of biblical proportions, the massive building loomed over her, ready to bite off her head or swallow her whole.

Behind her, traffic had almost come to a complete standstill thanks to the chaos of the wet streets. The aggressive honking of vans, taxis, and cyclists formed one intense cry of agony Stella could relate to. She wanted to join the pack of metallic wolves and howl towards the heavens.

Both of them stepped into the dry and warm lobby. Samuel shook his limbs, sending raindrops splashing around him. They moved towards the desk and closer to the face behind it. A young blond man sat there, his eyes glued to the screen in front of him. White buds poked out from his ears. So absorbed in his phone, he failed to notice their approach. Only once they stopped right in front of him did he lift his head. He jumped in his seat, as if he was looking at two ghosts and not simply two late visitors.

One earbud fell out of his ear, landed on his desk, rolled off the side, and plummeted to the ground. The soundtrack of *Hamilton* echoed off the tiled flooring.

"Are we stopping you from anything important?" Samuel asked with a smug smile while the young man got off his chair, grabbed the other bud from his ear and shoved both of them into his oversized jacket pocket.

"I'm sorry. You spooked me. How can I help you?" he asked, finding his professionalism.

Stella read the shiny golden name tag. Chad Walker.

She pointed at his name. "You are new."

Chad followed her gaze to his chest, nodded and smiled back at the two of them. "Yes, I just started."

"Where are you from?" Samuel asked.

"Ohio, Sir."

Oh boy. Stella didn't need to hear more to create a picture of musical loving countryside boy Chad. He wouldn't survive his first week in this place.

"Well, Chad, I need to get up to my father's apartment."

"Sure, which floor, Miss?" he asked, settling himself in front of the computer screen, ready to type something into the system.

"The penthouse."

Chad's fingers hovered over the keyboard. His mouth opened slowly, making him look like a fish on dry land trying to catch air. His tongue snaked out and he wet his lips.

"Y-your father—I mean, Mr. Woodworth—has made it clear no one is allowed to come upstairs." There was a hint of a nervous stutter in his tone. "Specifically his daughter," he added, looking around as if he expected her father to be standing right behind him.

She felt for Ohio-Chad, but she really didn't have time for this. Her fist landed on his desk with a loud thud and Chad jumped for a second time this evening.

"Let me tell you what's about to happen. You're in the fucked-up situation of having agreed to work for my father. Unfortunately, this puts you in an even more fucked-up position because no matter what you do now, it will result in you having to find a new job in the morning."

Chad's eyes darted from Stella to Samuel, probably hoping for some sort of reasonable explanation.

"She is right," was all Chad got from Samuel before Stella snapped her fingers in front of him.

"You are screwed either way. So open the top floor for us and let us do our jobs," she added.

Samuel took out his leather badge holder. He flipped it open in front of Chad, whose eyes went big when he saw the shiny NYPD emblem. He swallowed hard. This evening had not turned out the way he'd expected. But this was Midtown. Police showing up at fancy residences counted as normal in New York City. Poor Chad just didn't know this yet.

He studied the badge a bit too long.

"Are you sure you want to hinder an active police investigation?" Samuel asked.

Chad's face turned into a red tomato. He clearly didn't want to say no to the police, but he also didn't go for the elevator button. Instead, he leaned closer, which had Samuel and Stella lean towards him as well. He flicked his gaze to where Stella knew the security camera to be.

"But I'll get fired if I do that."

Maybe Chad wasn't as clueless about the real world as Stella had first suspected. She sighed and decided to give him another portion of reality, since the first time had fallen on deaf ears.

"I'm sure you thought a few years of working as a concierge would bridge the gap for you to finally make it, become a star on Broadway and someday have enough money to live in a building like this." Her hands went up towards the surroundings and the way Chad lowered his gaze confirmed her assumption. "It's not going to happen for you and the sooner you realize that, the better. You won't be discovered singing in the lobby of my father's building, like in a *GLEE* musical. In fact, my father hates musicals."

Again, Chad turned towards Samuel, but all he got was a nod confirming Stella's prophecy.

"Getting away from this building and my father will be the best decision in your life. Believe me. You'll be able to actually make a difference if you let me get up there and protect this city from a monster like him."

She wasn't sure what made Chad change his mind, but the young man swallowed hard, straightened up, and finally pushed the button for the private elevator. Within seconds, a chirpy ping announced its arrival.

Stella thanked Chad, and Samuel nodded at a young man, who had just aged by a decade. Hopefully, it would harden him for the real world.

Once the elevator doors shut and it moved up, Samuel faced Stella.

"You know Chad is calling your father right now. He's probably waiting for us the second these doors open, ready to bite off our heads."

Stella would have been disappointed if Chad didn't at least try to save his job. She'd assumed he'd call her father the moment they were out of sight, but it didn't matter.

She squared her shoulders. "Let him. I'm not scared of my father."

He could threaten her as much as he wanted with destroying her, having her thrown out, or even attempting to call the police. They had come prepared and this time, her father would not be able to escape. Sam would put him in handcuffs and escort him to the police station. For all of Manhattan to see. She ensure it by tipping off Mark Fullerton from the New York Times to be at the mansion at the right time. Richard Woodworth's life and reputation would be ruined. He just didn't know it yet.

The ding of the elevator door announced they had arrived at their destination and Stella cracked her neck, readying herself for her father. To their surprise, the hallway was empty when the doors opened. There was no fuming man waiting for them. No shouts echoed off the floors. Samuel peeked his head out of the elevator, looked left and right, and shrugged.

"The coast is clear," he said to her.

"Don't let him fool you. He is here. This is the calm before the storm." The storm that would drown the captain of this sinking ship.

Instead of him throwing his usual and predictable tantrum, Stella barely heard a faint noise coming from his

317

office. He moved quietly, like a predator. Only the clacking of his heels on the hardwood floor in his office proved someone was in the otherwise lonely penthouse.

His unusual behavior was enough warning for Stella. He knew something was going on. They had to act fast.

They made no noise when they moved towards the open office door, their bodies hidden in the shadows of the nearly dark hallway. How the roles had changed. The predator had become the prey.

Stella stopped right under the doorframe. Samuel was two steps behind her, still swallowed by darkness. In front of them, Richard Woodworth sat in his leather chair. Too distracted by his fingers swiftly scanning a deck of paper.

What was he looking for?

Maybe a way to get out of this mess? Maybe he was already ten steps ahead of Stella, planning his next escape, but something in the way his lips moved silently while rustling through the papers told her he knew they were coming for him.

Clearing her throat, she addressed her father. His fingers froze. He took a deep breath and when he looked up, his face had returned to his usual emotionless self.

"Of course it's you," he puffed, his tie slightly crooked. "And you brought company." He nodded towards Samuel.

Maybe she was wrong, but did he expect someone else? Did Chad not call him to let him know his deranged daughter had entered his home? Kudos to Chad, if that was true. She did not think he'd have it in him, but maybe the shiny NYPD badge had convinced him of the importance of their entry and doing the right thing.

"Detective Green, tell me, what can I do for you?" he continued too chirpily, looking at a spot behind Samuel, as if he was waiting for more people to arrive. That's when Stella put the pieces together and then it came to her. He thought his buddy Holmes might have arrived, with his pet Samuel in tow.

He doesn't have a clue what's happening.

It was almost comical.

"I believe you are aware of why we are here," Stella said, drifting towards him slowly.

"I don't think I am. So please, enlighten me," he said to Samuel, who didn't move an inch and let Stella lead this situation.

God, even on the brink of his doom, he was still a dick.

The flicker of a frown washed over his face when he realized Samuel wasn't here as a friend. Only then did he look at Stella.

"We can do this the easy way or the hard way. Me personally, I'd prefer the hard way, by dragging you out of this building in handcuffs while all of Midtown sees you being placed in a police car. But since I won't be the one putting those handcuffs on you, he is," she said with a nod towards Sam. "I assume he might prefer to go by the book and have you come with us voluntarily and without all the fuss."

"Is that so?" Richard Woodworth scoffed.

"I have a few other ideas of what to do with you, but none of them will lead to you making it to the police station," she added and erased the smirk from his face that had settled in because men like Richard Woodworth believed they were untouchable. This time and just for the blink of a moment, he believed she could, and it sent a surge of power through her.

She could do this, and she would. For her baby sister.

Instead of giving his daughter another useless comment, he straightened his tie and looked over her shoulder. "Nothing you want to say, Detective?"

"I think your daughter summarized your options pretty well. And for the record, I prefer the hard option as well," Samuel said with a supportive wink towards Stella.

Richard Woodworth's face went sour and it all suddenly made perfect sense. After everything Samuel had told her about his last encounter with his boss, the praise, the possibility of a promotion, the urgency to stick with Holmes. Her father thought he had bought Samuel's silence. Just like Holmes'.

When she turned her head to the right and looked at Samuel, she saw a man who wasn't anything like his boss. Samuel had integrity. Samuel had kept his promises, had told her the truth even when she didn't want to hear it. She had to smile at the comforting thought that he would do anything to bring justice to her case. She wasn't alone. He had her back and one day she'd return the favor.

"I didn't kill your mother, and I didn't kill your sister," Richard Woodworth blurted.

Of course, he knew Megan was dead.

Technically, he was right. He didn't try to kill her mother. That was Megan's boyfriend. And he didn't kill Megan. His buddy made sure all evidence against him and her father would disappear. Including the victim. It would be ruled a suicide, thanks to glitches, favors, and lost evidence. But she would get him for a crime without a statute of limitations. Her father would be held accountable for child molestation.

"No, you did much worse. You raped your own daughter and used your power to cover it up," she said and let her statement travel to him.

He didn't even flinch when the truth hit him. Maybe he even thought he was innocent. In his own perverted mind, he might actually believe he didn't hurt his daughter physically and mentally.

"How could you do this to her? She was your daughter. You should have protected her, not raped her," Stella pressed when her father didn't respond.

"You don't know what you are talking about." Annoyance dripped off his lips, as if Stella was stupid and he had to remind her she had gotten everything wrong.

"Mom knew and she won't keep her mouth shut anymore. She woke up."

A flicker of something washed over her father's face. Irritation maybe, possibly panic.

"Your mother is delusional. She doesn't know what she is talking about. None of her gibberish will hold in court."

The fucker knows exactly what he has done. He doesn't even bother denying it.

If Stella had been in the possession of a gun, she would have shot him and his narcissistic ego right then. Even if she wanted to put him behind bars, the world would be so much better without him. But she didn't have a gun or a knife or any other sharp object that could slice through his skin and make him bleed out in front of her.

She had something else, though.

"I wouldn't be so sure about that," she said with a triumphant smile on her face. In her hand, she held the copy of her mother's statement.

In an instant, her father turned pale. He opened his mouth, only to close it. There were no witty remarks, no nasty comments. For the first time in her life, someone had shut him up. She had defeated him. He suddenly looked small.

"I will not go to jail," he said stubbornly.

"I don't think there is any other option," Samuel said, his hands going for the cuffs attached to the back of his belt.

When Stella's father saw the small metallic mechanism that would brand him a felon, he realized there was no way out. He even relaxed a little. The built up tension in his shoulders loosened. He let out a sigh and leaned into his chair, his eyes playing ping-pong. He was trying so hard to think of a way to get out of the mess he had created. But there was none. This was it. The end of the road.

"Richard Woodworth, you are under arrest—"

"You want a drink?" Stella's father asked out of nowhere, interrupting Samuel. He didn't even wait for a response, but went straight for the bottom drawer of his desk.

Samuel's hand went to his hip. "Stop right there, Mr. Woodworth."

Stella's father did no such thing. He laughed at Samuel for grabbing his gun as he conjured a bottle of bourbon.

"You startle too easily, Detective," he said while he poured himself two very generous fingers. "Sure you don't want one? I know you are quite fond of it."

The audacity of this man.

"No one wants a drink, for fuck's sake," Stella yelled. "I want an apology or an explanation why you would touch your own daughter," she demanded, her heart racing. But did it really matter why? What would it change? Her sister would still be dead.

When no one said another word, Richard Woodworth lifted the glass to his mouth and swallowed everything in one quick movement. The empty crystal landed loudly on his desk.

"Then I guess there is nothing else to say." In a swift movement, his hand vanished in the same drawer, but this time it came back out holding a shiny .357 revolver.

"No!" Samuel shouted, jumping towards him, but the barrel already pointed at Richard Woodworth's own temple. Stella didn't move an inch. She stayed perfectly still, watching in slow-motion as her father's finger pulled the trigger. A bullet escaped the revolver and entered her father's skull. His head shot back into the armchair, splattering blood and brain against the dark leather and onto the desk.

Then there was only silence.

Chapter 34 - The Mentor

Samuel

SAMUEL WAS ABOUT TO do one of the hardest things in his career. Even his addiction felt easier than what he was about to do.

Despite witnessing Stella's attempts to calm her nerves by inhaling sharply, holding her breath, and releasing it, the technique had little effect on him.

With his head hanging low, he reminded himself that this was the right thing to do.

His fingers curled into a fist and he knocked three times on the yellow door in front of him. Then he took a step back and waited. Over his shoulder, he glanced at the two police officers he'd forced to join him, including Derek, the rookie, who nodded in agreement and support. Once Samuel was inside, they would make their way in as well. Slowly, giving him time and making this situation a little less traumatic than it could be.

Finally, he heard movement inside and when the door opened, he looked at the surprised and tired face of Gloria Holmes. His stomach dropped.

"Samuel, what are you doing here? You almost frightened me to death," she said with a relieved smile on her face.

"I am so sorry to bother you this late."

"No, no, not at all. Come in." She took a step aside and made room for Samuel to enter.

When she saw the other two officers approaching, confusion returned to her face.

"Gloria, is the Captain here?"

"Y-yes, he is," she said, eyeing the men behind Samuel. "What's going on?"

"I really need to speak with your husband."

She searched Samuel's face for anything but realized quickly Samuel wouldn't tell her more, so she asked him to follow her.

"He is in his study."

Samuel felt like a dog being dragged to his castration appointment. He wanted to turn around and run away, but he had to do it. It had to come from him.

They stopped in front of Holmes' study. He had been in this room many times before, but it had always been under much more pleasant circumstances. The last one had been Holmes' birthday party a few months ago.

Gloria knocked but didn't wait for Holmes to ask her to come in. "Honey, Samuel is here, and he needs to talk to you," she said while turning the knob and opening the door.

When Samuel entered, he saw a surprised Holmes sitting at his desk, glasses halfway down his nose.

"Green. What are you doing here at this ungodly hour?" The fatherly smile on his face was honest and made this situation so much more difficult. The man didn't have any idea what was about to happen.

He dunked a tea bag up and down into a white mug with the NYPD emblem printed on it, still waiting for a response from Samuel.

"I know what you're thinking, but my wife told me that tea in the evening would be better for my heart. What can I say? I love my wife," Holmes said with a wink at her.

Samuel didn't want to do this. He wanted to sit down and have a chat with the man he had learned so much from. He never admitted it, but Holmes had been like a father to him when his own was gone, someone who provided sense and discipline. If only he could turn back time, maybe he could have done things differently. Maybe he could have made a difference. But there was no time travel and even if he had known earlier, it would have still ended with him having to put a stop to this.

As much as he adored the man in front of him, the thought of what he had done made him sick to his stomach.

"Thanks Gloria. If you could give us a minute?" Samuel asked, his voice low and soft.

She didn't want to. She knew something was seriously wrong and that she should stay and support her husband. But Samuel wondered if she'd still feel the same once she learnt about how her husband had ruined a young girl's life? Would he disgust her or make her furious? Would she think about her own daughters who were just a few years older than Megan was when their father intimidated a child into silence and a fate worse than fighting a monster in the public eye?

"I'll be outside if you need me," she said and eventually left them.

Samuel closed the door behind her and leaned against it.

"Sir, I have to talk with you." He swallowed loudly before finishing his sentence. "It's about Richard Woodworth."

The tea bag slipped into the mug with a splash. The light green droplets going everywhere. It reminded Samuel of the crimson blood he had seen a few hours earlier splashing across half of Mr. Woodworth's desk.

Holmes cleared his throat, fished the tea bag out with two fingers and threw it into a black plastic bin. Only then did he look up and at Samuel. A stony expression had replaced his former smile, his face a wall of secrets, not letting any emotion through.

Samuel was sure he knew whatever he wanted to talk about with him would be bad, but he doubted Holmes realized what had happened to his friend. From the looks of him, he also didn't expect Samuel knew the whole truth.

Samuel pushed himself off the door. "I'm sorry to inform you that Mr. Woodworth has taken his own life earlier this evening."

Holmes' mouth dropped. "What are you talking about?"

"I'm saying that Richard Woodworth is dead," he answered, slowly taking step after step closer towards Holmes.

Samuel could see the machinery in Holmes' brain working, taking the information in and creating connections with what else this could mean for him.

"This can't be true. I just spoke with him earlier." Apparently, the initial shock hadn't cleared the path to the full extent of Richard Woodworth's demise.

Holmes rubbed his face with both hands, one of his fingers leaving a small wet trail from the tea bag it had touched.

He sat silently for a few beats, only his eyes moved loudly from side to side, his lids occasionally closing. As if he had been searching for a target, he suddenly focussed on Samuel, who had made his way across the study and was now standing right in front of his desk.

"What exactly happened?" he asked, through his fingers, half his mouth covered by his hands.

For a split-second Samuel thought he saw the flicker of a tremble on them, but then it was gone and Holmes' expression returned to concrete.

"When confronted with evidence proving his involvement in Mrs. Woodworth's hospitalization, he ended his own life instead of facing legal steps."

"What evidence?" Holmes interrupted.

"We have recently gotten our hands on a new piece of evidence confirming his connection to the attempted murder of his wife."

"This is ridiculous. Richard didn't try to kill his wife."

"No, he didn't…" Fishing for a small folded document in the inside pocket of his jacket, Samuel handed over a copy of the letter Stella's mother had written. "But he is guilty of another crime connected to this case."

This time, the tremble was clearly visible. Holmes had to hold the letter with both hands to steady himself. Samuel folded his hands in front of him and gave Holmes time to read the words in his hand.

Not finishing the full letter, Holmes placed it on his desk. Unable to let go of it, he pressed his palms onto the piece of paper and stared at it silently.

A few minutes ticked by until Samuel addressed Holmes again.

"You should read the back of it, sir."

Holmes clearly didn't want to. He knew what the other side would say. But eventually he turned the letter over. With each line his eyes flew over, his face turned another shade darker. By the end of the letter, when Holmes arrived at his own name spelled out, he had turned crimson.

"This is ridiculous!" He ripped the paper and threw it into Samuel's face. One torn piece settling itself on Samuel's sweater.

"You know this is a copy." He sighed, picking the piece with his fingertips before he dropped it on the ground.

Anger danced on Holmes' face, while he tried to find a solution to the mess he had created for himself. Samuel watched as his captain grasped the gravity of his situation when stillness settled into his wild eyes and he exhaled a defeated sigh.

When Holmes focused on Samuel again, all his energy was gone. He looked tired and maybe even a little relieved the charade was finally over.

"I've helped your career on so many levels and this is how you repay me?" Holmes said with a soft shake of his head.

"That's why I am here and not just any detective. As a friend, I am asking you to come with me voluntarily."

Afraid Holmes might consider the same route out of this scenario as Richard Woodworth, Samuel kept an eye on him, ready to pounce and stop him from doing something stupid. But he didn't need to worry.

"I knew this was coming."

Samuel didn't need him to explain why. There'd be enough time later to go through the details, but Holmes needed to ease the burden he had carried.

"I didn't know she was telling the truth. You have to believe me," he continued, his voice trembling. "Megan had always been very imaginative. What she told me didn't make any sense, and then she changed her mind. I-I truly thought she had lied."

Samuel shook his head in disbelief. "A fourteen-year-old girl comes to you and tells you her father touched her and you ask her if she is sure this really happened? You question her if she is only looking for attention and made this up? If she understands the consequences this will have on her family's reputation?" The words from her diary and what she had experienced when opening up to the police were engraved in his mind. "What did you expect that little girl to say?"

Holmes swallowed hard and hid his face in his hands.

"I know, I know. I-I should have followed up. I-I should have. But Richard assured me he had never done such a thing, and she never came back..." His voice trailed off.

"She was fourteen. It wasn't her job to come back to you. It was yours. You should have done the right thing!" Samuel exclaimed loudly, making his boss jump. Samuel's blood boiled with built-up anger, but when his mentor lifted his head and he saw the pain he had carried for decades in his red eyes, he knew Holmes was not only aware of what he had done. He knew he had to pay for what he'd done.

Holmes got up, sniffed his shame away, and dried his palms on his pants before he walked up to Samuel.

"Let's do this," he said and followed Samuel out of his office. When they stopped in the living room, Derek and Officer Martinez rose from the sofa where Gloria had seated them and where they had been sipping on the tea she had offered them.

"Sir," they said in unison, moving closer.

Gloria jumped from her seat immediately when she saw her husband's raw eyes.

"Honey, what is going on?" Her voice trembled, and she barely kept the tears from spilling. Before Holmes could say anything, she grabbed Samuel's arm. "Sam! What's happening?"

"Can I have a minute with her?" Holmes asked.

Samuel looked at the man who had taught him everything and the woman who had always made him welcome in their home. "Of course," he said and nodded at Derek and Martinez. "Let's give them a moment of privacy." He waited for Holmes to take his wife's hand off his sleeve before he followed his colleagues outside.

"You think that's wise? He could make a run for it."

Samuel looked at Martinez like he had lost his mind.

"He is our Captain! He helped every single one of us to become who we are. No matter what he did, we can never repay him for that. But we can do one thing and that is give him a moment to say goodbye to his wife because they will never have a moment like this again. Their lives are about to change irreversibly and it's gonna be long and painful years ahead of them. So, let's give this man a last moment of peace, will you?"

Suddenly shy and embarrassed, Martinez scratched his boot on the wooden porch and lowered his gaze. When Samuel told him and Derek to wait in their car, they moved without a single word.

It took Holmes almost twenty minutes to let go of his wife. Through the window, Samuel sneaked a peek occasionally. He watched Holmes kiss his wife and talk to her. He saw the change on her face when she realized what was about to happen. What her husband had done that had ruined spending the rest of their lives together as a happy family. She cried, shaking her head in an attempt to ward off reality. When she handed him a framed picture of him and their daughters, he let his fingers glide over the glass and his children's printed faces before he returned it to her. He knew he wouldn't be allowed to keep it where he was going. Holmes placed one last kiss on her cheek before he turned around and left.

Samuel waited for him at the front door, but gave him room to put on his jacket and dry his eyes. Silently they walked to his car side by side, like so many times before, but it had never been this quiet. He would miss his captain and their conversations.

The back door of the car opened and Holmes stopped, one hand on the frame.

"Thank you, Sam." His voice resounded with sorrow.

Avoiding glancing back at the house, Holmes kept looking straight ahead, not focusing on anything in particular.

"I know it's too late, but I am truly sorry," he said.

A lump formed in Samuel's throat, blocking his airway. His eyes stung, but he sniffed it away.

"I'm sorry Captain. I should have...maybe I could have..." Samuel didn't know how to finish the sentence. What could he have done? Nothing.

A big hand landed on his shoulder, followed by a fatherly look he had grown so used to. "You've done good, son. No matter how this ends, I am proud of you. You are a hell of a detective."

Then he got into the back of the police car and closed the door, leaving Samuel out in the chilly night air. Samuel took a deep breath and wiped the dampness from his eyes.

If he did the right thing, why did he feel so terrible?

With a heavy heart, he moved around the car, got into his seat and drove Holmes away.

Chapter 35 - The Goodbye

Stella

THE *New York Times* edition of the day flew past Stella when she opened the door of her mother's hospital room. It hit the wall before landing on the floor, sections sprawling everywhere, and was followed by a grim sentence that including several f-, a-, and c-curse words from her mother.

What a foul mouth you have, Stella thought.

At least it seemed like her mother had regained her energy since she had woken from her comatose state a week ago. She wore a pair of comfortable but formal dark blue slacks, combined with a red cashmere sweater, and for the untrained eye, didn't show any signs that anything unusual had happened to her. She had always known how to dress her part and she obviously wouldn't start making an exception now.

"Hello, Mother."

Beth Woodworth turned away from the window overlooking the hospital garden where, according to the nurses, she'd been strolling through every morning for a refreshing start to the day and faced the distant voice belonging to her daughter. She still had her arms crossed in front of her, but her angry demeanor changed when she saw Stella. A smile flashed over her face.

"My darling." With extended arms, her mother took her into a warm embrace and placed a kiss on each cheek. Stella let her hug her, but the stiffness of her body had Beth loosen the motherly embrace and take a step back.

"How are you?" Stella asked as her mother's concentration switched back to the leather overnight bag and the few pieces of clothing that sat on her hospital bed.

"Better," she said, taking one sweater and folding it neatly. "They will release me today. I only need to wait for my doctor to do his midday rounds, and then I can leave."

"That's great," Stella said politely.

A shy chortle escaped her mother's lips. "I'm scared to go back."

"You don't have to go back. You can be with Paul now."

That comment had Stella's mother freeze for a second. Her focus wavering.

"Paul doesn't want to talk to me anymore." She gestured with a nod of her chin to the headline of the *New York Times* that lay scattered on the floor. "They made sure of it."

Unsure of what her mother wanted her to respond to, Stella bent down and picked up the newspaper. A photo of her father and Captain Holmes stretched across the front page. Every newspaper in the city had this one or another photo of them published.

"What did you expect?" Stella let out when she placed the newspaper on the birch coffee table and sat down in the chair next to it.

"I know I made a mistake, but I don't deserve to be dragged through the mud like this."

Stella cringed under her mother's opinion of her rights. She was referring to the comments about her having supported her husband's unspeakable crime. There was a strong connection made to her being another Ghislaine Maxwell. People wondered how a mother could keep something like this a secret and if she really was innocent. Most news media didn't think she was a victim herself. Stella didn't think so either, which was why she hadn't visited her for the last seven days. Why she wouldn't visit her again in the future.

Today would be the last time she saw her mother.

She watched her for a few seconds, hoping for any sign of remorse. Not that it would make her change her mind, but it would help her believe there was something good in her family. Beth had moved on to retrieve her creams and lotions from the small bathroom that was connected to her private hospital room. How she had gotten those delivered here and made herself comfortable was beyond Stella. A deep fold ran straight down her mother's forehead, right between her eyes, as she fixed her gaze on a bottle of body lotion.

"I could swear this bottle was much heavier this morning. Do you think someone used it while I was out for a walk?" Beth Woodworth asked, shaking the bottle in front of her.

How could Stella have missed the real Beth Woodworth? The person who was so much more like Stella's father than she could have ever believed. She really didn't know her family at all. A part of Stella blamed herself for not having been able to see that earlier. Stella didn't reply to the impossible statement her mother had just given, so Beth Woodworth shrugged off her daughter's silence and put all items into the same bag.

Getting up from the chair, Stella shook her head at her mother's ignorance. "Well, I just wanted to come and say goodbye."

Beth Woodworth looked up immediately. "You are leaving?"

"Yes." Stella nodded back without a hint of remorse on her face or in her voice. She had made up her mind and the longer she stayed in the presence of her mother, the more sure she was about her decision.

"I had hoped you'd stay a while." Beth's finger fidgeted with the zipper. "I haven't seen you in so long and I thought it would be nice to spend some time together." She pulled the zipper all the way up and sank down next to her bag. "We are the only ones left."

Stella frowned at her comment.

Could it be true? Does she not know about Mae?

It was probably better for everyone that Mae wasn't dragged into the shitshow she called her family. Mae was better off as far away from the Woodworths as possible. But her mother's plea surprised Stella. The sadness in her voice. Her mother was scared because this would be the first time in a long while she would truly be alone. Stella was over feeling sorry for her mother, though.

"Do you really believe I'd stay here with you after what you did to Megan?" She pressed her reaction harshly through her thin lips and hit her mother right in the gut.

"I tried," Beth said innocently. "You have to believe me. I didn't want her to suffer."

"Well, that didn't work out, did it?" Stella cut in sharply, shocking her mother. One did not raise their voice in the

Woodworth House, even if they had all the right to bring down a building. The blanket of undeniable trust Stella had placed on her mother had been lifted, showing her the ugly truth. Her mother wasn't a victim. She was an instigator and had always been one. Stella had just been too blind to see it. Like her siblings, both her parents had played her.

Offering her daughter a comforting smile, Beth moved closer to Stella. "I know I made a mistake, but I asked her again if she still thought something had happened and-and…"

"And what?"

"She said she had made it all up."

The ease with which her mother explained her inability to act pushed Stella over the edge. "And you let her off? Just like that? Without questioning your fourteen-year-old? Without getting her to the police. Or to a doctor? You probably never even confronted your husband, am I right?"

Beth said nothing. Her face had turned darker and her eyes were shiny, but there wasn't remorse on her face. Anger had spilled across her like red wine from a knocked over glass.

"It's not that you did anything to help her, either. You left us, too," she eventually blurted in a moment of suppressed emotion erupting from within. A hiccup more than a full explosion.

"I am not her mother! You were!" Stella shouted back and her mother jumped at her daughter's harsh tone. It seemed almost unfathomable to Stella that her mother genuinely believed she had done nothing more outrageous than make a simple mistake. "It was your responsibility to protect her, but you let your own husband rape her for years!"

Beth opened her mouth to justify herself and counter her daughter's opinion but closed it immediately at the death stare she received from Stella. The fury inside Stella made her form fists. She wanted to plunge them into the wall. A dark part of her wanted to slam them into her mother's face. But she didn't let her rage get the better of her. She wasn't like the rest of her family. She wouldn't give in to such violent urges. Instead, she would find peace in knowing the people who had harmed her sister and brother had gotten what they deserved. Even her mother.

She could continue debating whose fault it was, but Stella knew her mother would never see reason. She had said what she needed to say. There was nothing left.

"Goodbye, mother," she said instead and strode towards the door.

"You can't just leave me. What am I supposed to do now?"

With one hand on the doorknob, Stella turned one last time toward her mother to offer honest advice.

"I think you should hire an excellent lawyer."

Then she left.

Chapter 36 - The Farewell

Stella

AN ENORMOUS SIGH ESCAPED Stella's lips when she walked through the automatic doors and out into the crisp Manhattan air. She was finally out of that stuffy hospital and able to breathe again. In just a few hours, she would be on a plane back to Hong Kong. Only a day away from returning to the normalcy of answering work emails and dealing with stubborn Hong Kong authorities. Something to look forward to, a statement she never thought would cross her lips. But after this ordeal, anything would be easy to handle.

Maybe she should take some time off. Clear her mind before returning to work. Agnes had suggested she'd find a therapist and talk through everything that had happened. Not that she wanted to live through it again. She had lain awake often the last few nights. Replaying all the information that had been dumped on her in only a few days. She had calculated dates in her mind, trying to figure out how long her sister had been in agony while she planned her escape to Hong Kong. And one night, a thought occurred to her. Had her brother, Jonathan, known? His room had been right next to Megan's. Counting out the dates in her head, she was certain now. Jonathan had killed himself just a few months after all this had started.

Stella had always thought he'd killed himself because of the pressure of her father to form him into the next Richard

Woodworth. But what if that wasn't the reason? What if her brother killed himself because he knew what was going on and couldn't do anything?

A car beside her honked and snapped her out of this dark thought. In the end, it didn't matter. They were gone. She couldn't change the past. But she could look ahead and try to do better in the future. Maybe therapy wasn't such a bad idea.

The black SUV that would bring her to Newark Airport waited patiently on the other side of the street. But before dropping her there and leaving her old life behind, she had one thing left to do. She was about to cross the street when she heard a familiar voice to her right.

"Leaving without saying goodbye?"

A knowing smile erupted on her face, but she played it cool when she turned.

"Big goodbyes aren't my thing. I'm more of an Irish exit kind of girl," she said, remembering their call the night before. Sam had made a big deal of wanting to know what she'd do before she left. She had told him she would see her mother, but she hadn't expected him to show up here. They had exchanged their pleasantries of "See you" and "Take care."

But she was glad he was here.

"No time for a last drink?" Samuel asked.

He looked good; alcohol had clearly not been on his menu for a few days, and she was proud of him. She also knew that he wasn't offering to go to a bar. There had been a moment the last time they had seen each other. After she had given her statement and when he'd walked her out of the precinct. Right there, in the middle of Midtown Manhattan, she had almost leaned into him.

Part of her wanted to say yes now, but that wouldn't be a good idea. She didn't want to admit it, but along the way, Samuel had become more important to her than just being a colleague.

"Actually, there is something I wanted to show you. Do you have time?" She laughed when Samuel frowned in confusion. "I promise I won't waste your time."

"Spending time with you is never wasted," he said, his face turning a shade redder. She guessed he hadn't planned on being this open. He even seemed a bit shy.

"Can I catch a ride with you?" she asked and Samuel nodded, pointing at his car. She asked him to wait and went over to her driver, Giovanni, whom she instructed to follow them before she returned to Samuel.

He opened the door for her, but she pointed at the fire hydrant next to his front wheel.

"You know you can't park here," Stella said.

"I'm a police officer. I can park wherever I want." Samuel wiggled his eyebrows at her.

"Is this how you win over the ladies?"

He chuckled at her remark. "I'm funny, good-looking and have a sense of justice. That usually does the trick. The free parking is just an extra perk I offer."

"If I remember correctly, your sense of justice got you a black eye the last time and not a telephone number," Stella said with a satisfying smirk on her face.

He thought about her words for a mere second before he winked at her. "I might have gotten a black eye, but you did give me your number."

Her answer came quickly. "After you forced me to give it to you with your shiny police badge?"

"Minor details if you ask me," he said and shrugged off her explanation with one shoulder.

Ready to deliver another snappy retort, she looked him up and down, fixated on his steel-blue eyes and closed her mouth without as much as making a peep. Instead, she got into the passenger seat, swung her legs inside, and looked up at him.

"What?" he asked.

"Nothing. Come on, Roger, let's do this," she said and slammed the doors shut before Samuel could curse.

He rolled his eyes at her, which made her smile, then walked to his side of the car. They settled into his car, and she breathed in that familiar smell of leather and Samuel, while she directed him out of the city and into the suburbs of New Jersey. She'd miss riding with him.

"Still not telling me where we are going?" he asked after taking another left turn by her instruction.

"We are almost there."

In the back of the side mirror, Giovanni was still following them like a ghost.

"I'm not sure you have heard it yet, but Megan's death was ruled suicide. With the camera glitch and no other evidence, there just wasn't enough. I'm sorry," he said and looked over at her, probably worried how she'd take the news.

"Hm, they'll always win, won't they?"

"Well, at least the truth is out, right? That's something."

It was better than nothing and she reminded herself to send Mark Fullerton an email once she'd arrived at home. He'd done a good job of bringing the truth to the public. The Woodworth empire was crumbling, and she was more than happy about that.

"I heard you got a promotion. Congratulations, Sergeant."

Samuel shuddered at the mention of his title. "Thanks." His hand went to the back of his head, scratching the part where his hairline ended and the skin of his neck continued.

"Did you want a bigger promotion?" Stella chuckled at his discomfort.

"God, no," he blurted quicker than he could finish his thought. "I just—"

Stella cocked her head at him. Her eyebrows went up when she realized it wasn't modesty that had him trail off.

"Oh, this is a bigger question," she said. "You don't want the position."

"Gee, how do you do it?"

"What?"

"Read me so well. We've only known each other for a few weeks."

"Comes with the job, I guess," she said with a shrug, even though she knew there was more behind it than that. She had never seen another person as clearly as she saw Samuel. The authentic version of him, not the one he tried to make everyone believe.

Samuel squinted at her, probably trying to read her mind.

"Hm, sure. If you say so." He took in a long breath and held it in for a second or two before releasing it. It was the same breathing technique Stella had perfected to calm her nerves or stop her from saying something she'd immediately regret and she wondered what he tried to keep to himself.

"I think it might be time to try something new," he said eventually through another breath. "Yeah, this whole debacle made me consider my options."

Having to arrest his boss and mentor hadn't been easy on him, and Stella could see how one would want to distance themselves from their usual life. Get some perspective. See what else was out there than the same desk and the same coffee mug.

"Anything in mind yet?" she asked him, intrigued to know what else Samuel Green could be interested in.

"Nah, I'll take my time."

"We can always use a talented man at our office," she offered, only partly as a joke.

"And move across the globe?" He laughed. "No, thanks. But I appreciate the offer."

Stella checked her phone and realized they were almost there.

"How about you?" Samuel asked.

"Hm? What do you mean?"

"Are you ready to go back to your job?"

She thought about it for a second. She had never considered not returning to her job. What else would she do? She was good at her job. Enjoyed it.

"Yes. I couldn't save Megan, but hopefully I can make a difference in someone else's life. Help them find the truth." It was a noble idea, but the truth. She couldn't imagine not helping others. There were plenty of Megan's and Jonathan's out there fighting against their nightmares, and someone had to stand up for them if they couldn't.

"You know what happened wasn't your fault," Samuel said.

She knew that, but it would take her heart some time to catch up with her head.

"And you saved Mae."

Mae.

She'd thought about what would happen to her little niece. It had kept her up at night, if she was honest with herself. She knew Child Protective Services had taken her after the attack in Megan's home. It had only taken her a few phone calls to figure that out. But the last time she had checked, the only information given to her was that she'd been placed in foster care.

"Do you know what happened to her?" she asked.

"To Mae? Only that she was placed with a family who is looking after her now."

It was probably good news. She was still so young; she might not even remember what had happened. Hopefully, the trauma of losing her parents hadn't scarred her for life. Surely, she'd find a loving family that would create many happy memories for her. She'd be fine. Right?

"I can ask around and see where she is, if you want?"

She thought about it for a second and replied, "Yes, please."

Samuel turned right under Stella's direction and took in a loud breath once he'd straightened the car.

"Stella, where are we?" he asked, but slowed down the car and stopped in front of a blue two-story house with white roof trimmings and red and green holiday decorations in the windows. Christmas was just around the corner.

He turned off the engine and looked at Stella.

"I couldn't have done this without you. While I'm still going through shit trying to understand what happened, I found closure, thanks to you. You could have run off, but you didn't. You kept your promise and stuck with me through all of it. And now I'm thanking you for giving everything to help me."

Samuel swallowed hard, his eyes wandering from Stella to the front porch.

"I don't think I can do this," he said in a shaky voice.

"Yes, you can." She put a hand on his trembling fingers. "I'm here. You are not alone."

Slowly, they got out of his car. Samuel walked over to Stella, his eyes glued to the house, unable to move towards it.

"What if they don't want to see me? I've ruined their lives."

Stella took his hand and gave it a gentle squeeze. "You didn't ruin their lives; Melanie's uncle did. You did everything you could, and you gave them back their baby girl."

It had taken her some time, but she had eventually found out where Melanie's parents lived. She could never repay Samuel for everything he had done for her. This was the only way she knew how to thank him and give him a bit of peace.

"It's time for you to find closure now, Sam," she added and gave him a gentle push. It was all he needed. His feet did the rest.

Halfway, he stopped and looked back. "Thank you."

"Look me up if you find yourself in Hong Kong. I know all the good bars you can start a fight in," she added with a smirk, remembering the moment they'd first met.

"Take care of yourself, Stella."

"You too, Sam."

And that was it. She settled into the car, and through the window she watched Samuel approaching the front door gingerly. It took him three tries to find the courage to knock on it. Every time his hand was up but then he chickened out until he finally let his fist fall on the door. After what must have felt like eternity to him, the door opened and a slim woman with long brown hair appeared. At the sight of Samuel, her mouth fell open, and she dropped the tea towel she'd held in her hands. She shouted something into the space behind her while Samuel wrung his hands in agony. When a tall, broad man arrived next to her, Samuel stiffened even more.

Please don't punch him in the face.

He didn't. Instead, Melanie's father lunged toward him with extended arms and took him into an embrace that lasted forever. They were still hugging when Stella told her driver Giovanni to start the car and as she passed them, she knew Samuel would be okay.

And so would she.

Stella

"LOOK, MOMMY."

The little blonde girl had followed Stella around the house with a piece of paper in her hand. Her curls bounced up and down as if a puppeteer held them, as she waved the paper carefully by her thumb and index finger, making sure her treasure didn't get squashed. This game of being Stella's shadow had been going on all of this beautiful Saturday morning.

"I see it, honey," Stella said with a quick glance at the colored paper. She patted the girl's cheek with her left hand, and pressed her iPhone to her ear with the other.

"No, really look." There was a firm and determined tug on Stella's white blouse sleeve.

"Mae, I'm on the phone. Just give me a minute, okay?" she reprimanded and was rewarded with a dramatic sigh of annoyance, worthy of an Oscar nomination.

After over two years of living with this tiny creature, Stella had gotten used to Mae's strategies for getting what she wanted. She also knew when not to give in, which was why she didn't bend down to the now almost-sobbing face, but winked at her and won a few more minutes of peace in return.

Stella concentrated on the other person being part of this conversation and spoke into her phone, "So, it will arrive today?"

The representative on the other line started a monologue of explanation while Stella tucked her hand under her arm and gazed out the window at the San Diego Bay in the distance. After several "uh huhs", the answer Stella had been hoping for was finally spoken.

She hung up, a sudden giddiness having her throw both her hands up in the air as if she had just won the Super Bowl and not just the administrative fight of having her bed delivered with a six-week delay. She felt her back relax immediately at the thought of not having to spend another night on the inflatable mattress upstairs. They could call it deluxe and more luxurious than any other air mattress as much as they wanted. In the end, sleeping on air would twist even the strongest spine into a knot.

Another tug on her blouse had her look down onto the small human who was fighting her own minor battle of attention, hoping to win this one now.

"Can I show you now?"

Mae's determination was admirable, and with her little hands on her hip, there was no way Stella could say no. So, she let Mae lead her over to the kitchen table where a minefield of color pens had exploded. At almost four years old, she was currently obsessed with drawing. One of many obsessions, but at least this one kept her busy and gave Stella time to complete everything around the house and at work.

Her attention was firmly concentrated on a drawing showing three people holding hands and standing in front of a house that had the same black window frames as the one they were currently standing in. The back of the drawing was all blue and most likely depicting the sea they could see on those clear days they had so many of in San Diego.

She smiled at Mae, and her heart tightened. She still couldn't believe she was a mother now. Stella stroked Mae's hair and tucked a strand behind her ear.

"I think this is your best so far. A masterpiece indeed. We should call MOMA and tell them to make room in their collection."

The eye roll she received was out of this world, but Mae's big green eyes still lit up with pride.

"Yeah, me too." Her smile was big and in moments like this, Stella could really see her sister in Mae. The soft lips she could pout to perfection when she wanted something or the cute little dimple that formed only on her left cheek whenever she smiled. And Mae smiled often. She was a happy child and to Stella, the little family they had formed was more than she could have ever wished for. Mae had changed her, and she was happier for it.

At times, the memory of nearly departing New York without her caused her to shudder. But a few miles shy of Newark Airport, her gut had her tell her driver to turn around. She'd given Samuel a call and asked for the address of the foster family that had taken Mae in. A day later she had stood in front of a Long Island townhouse with paint flaking off and windows so dirty there had been no way of peeking into the house, never mind anyone looking outside.

Her stomach had churned at the first impression and while the outside had been more neglected than the inside, she hadn't been a minute too early to take Mae out of there. Maybe that slightly elderly couple would have been good to

Mae, but her doubts had been dispelled when another three foster kids in their care had zoomed around like they were high on LSD while Mae had cried loudly somewhere in the back of the house. She couldn't have left her there.

The couple hadn't even argued. And once Mae had been placed in Stella's arms, she had stopped crying, leftover tears rolling silently down her chubby, red cheeks. She had rocked her from side to side until the last tears had dried-up. Right at that moment, she had known she'd fight anyone who'd even think of taking Mae away from her.

But no one did. As a blood relative, Social Services had been quick to transfer legal guardianship to Stella. Paperwork had never been processed quicker. She'd assumed Samuel had something to do with it, since he had known the caseworker assigned to Mae.

The white phone on the similarly white counter top of the kitchen island vibrated and Stella said a silent prayer, hoping it wasn't the contractor giving her more bad news.

But it wasn't Bob's number that lit up her screen.

"Hey," she said with a big smile.

"How are my ladies doing in San Diego?"

"We are great. Doing some arts and crafts while getting ready for your arrival."

"Has she been drawing another masterpiece?"

"Yes, she has, and this one included you again," Stella said.

"Well, you can't argue with an artistic genius like her, can you?"

"No, you really can't." Stella giggled into the phone, taking in the comforting voice on the other side that always calmed her.

"Sam calling?"

"Here, hang on. Someone is very eager to talk to you."

Stella handed the phone into Mae's small hands and, like a pro, she held one end to her ear and started babbling into the other end. Whatever they were talking about, Mae was highly interested. Her face was a mixture of hard concentration and delight. Whatever Sam was telling her, she liked it.

Sam had been a constant part of their life after they had left New York and somehow, in those two years, their friendship developed into something more. Samuel had spent many weeks with them in Hong Kong, using his annual leave to be with them and figure out what he wanted to do. What they wanted to do. The idea of opening their own private investigator company had formed one night as a silly idea after they had put Mae to bed the evening before he had to return to New York. The long distance and constant traveling from one time zone to another had been hard on them from the beginning, but neither wanted to ask the other to drop their life and move half across the globe. That's how San Diego came up. As the town nearly in the middle of both their current homes, it seemed to be the perfect spot to start fresh. That Stella's friend Agnes had been nagging her to move there and start working with her had also made the decision and start easier.

"Here, Mommy."

Stella took the phone and watched Mae dance back to her drawing table, occasionally looking over and then giggling mischievously into her hands.

"What did you tell her? She looks like she is about to explode," Stella asked Sam, and Mae rolled her eyes dramatically at her, her little eyeballs almost popping out of their sockets, but she stayed seated on her yellow chair.

"Only that I have a little surprise planned for the two of you."

"Oh great, a surprise. What is it?"

He knew how much she hated surprises. Of all the things that had changed in her life, her need to know what was going on had stuck. In fact, caring for a child had only intensified that feeling, but she was working on that.

"If I tell you it's not a surprise, is it?"

"Just promise me you won't show up with a puppy or pony when you arrive?"

"You don't trust me even a little, do you?" Samuel said, in playful shock.

"I just know you too well," Stella retorted. "So, did everything work out with your place?"

When Samuel told her he had sold his apartment instead of renting it to someone else, she had almost choked on the dumpling she was eating that night. His explanation made complete sense. He wanted to start fresh, and that meant cutting old ties that would only keep him from moving on. She didn't fully believe him, but he had done it.

"Yeah, I got the last of my stuff out yesterday and handed over my keys. Can't believe I'm moving to San Diego."

"You'll love it here. The weather is warm, and the people are actually nice."

"Sounds terrible. But as long as I have the two of you, I'll be fine."

Her heart jumped at his comment, like it had done so many times in the last two years.

"I have one more errand to run, but then I'm ready to head over."

"It's blowing my mind that you are going to drive across the country instead of taking a plane. And I thought I'm the one being afraid of flying."

"I'm not afraid of flying," Stella rolled her eyes at the explanation to come. "I just don't want to get ripped off by some moving company."

"You know I could have paid for it and there are pretty decent companies out there who'd move your precious stuff."

"Yeah, but I guarantee they'd forget or break some of my stuff. I've done this before."

"Says the one who hasn't moved from Hong Kong to San Diego and had their stuff stuck in a container for weeks."

"It'll be great. I've never done a road trip, and it's only a few days. That should give you enough time to really be sure you want me to move in."

"Getting cold feet?" she asked, with a hint of worry about what his answer might be.

"Nah, I'm sure we are a great team. In all aspects. I've never been more sure about anything in my life."

And her heart skipped another beat.

There was a knock on the door.

"Hang on a second, my bed is finally being delivered and I won't risk the delivery guy to just leave again."

"You mean our bed?"

"Get here and we'll see if I'll give you some space in my super deluxe premium king."

With Mae right at her heels, she walked over to the front door. When she let the warm afternoon sun hit her face, it blinded her for a second. Then she dropped the phone as she stared at the man standing in front of her.

"SAM!" Mae squeezed past her and went straight for Sam's leg, wrapping her arms around it. But only for a second. Sam bent down and took her into his arms. He pressed a kiss to her forehead while she clung to his neck like a little monkey.

"Hey, princess. How have you been?"

"What are you doing here?" Still shell-shocked, Stella looked at the two, unable to move.

"I told you Mommy would like this surprise," Sam said to Mae, pinching her tummy and making her giggle in his arms. Then he turned to Stella.

"I couldn't wait to see you two, so I paid an outrageous amount of money to this dodgy moving company—"

Stella didn't let him finish. She closed the distance between them, pressed a kiss on his lips and joined in on the group hug.

"Welcome home, Sam," she said.

And finally, her family was perfect.

The End

Acknowledgments

BACK IN 2020, I STARTED my author journey with a romance novel. At that point Stella Woodworth wasn't even a thought. But here we are. Four years later, the romance novel is shelved and Stella is making her and my debut. And I couldn't be prouder of her and the journey both of us have taken.

I have always dreamt of writing and publishing a book but it is so much more work than I expected it to be. From daydreaming first ideas, writing in my second language (yes, english isn't my mothertongue), learning about structure and development of a story, finding a community to share your insanity with, seemingly endless rounds of edits (and you'll still have typos in your published version), to uploading the whole book online for publication, this journey has been a rollercoaster. And I wouldn't have it any other way. I've learnt so much over the last four years and met and worked with incredible people who helped me make this dream come true.

Thank you for going through this with me. The amount of positive feedback *The Perfect Family* has received is incredible and really makes my heart swell. It is one of the biggest honors of an author that so many people like (or dislike) the characters I've created.

A huge thank you goes to all the readers who love this story. Without you there would be no reason to have this book.

I couldn't have done this without a group of talented authors who kept me sane throughout writing Stella's story. To Jamie, Kathrin, Soleah, Victoria and Sarah for being my cheerleaders, brainstorming partners and therapists. Our weekly online meet-ups have been and still are a blast. Coming up with creative ways for the perfect crime is research, right? You are amazing and I'm so grateful I found you. Hopefully we'll meet IRL soon.

To The Write Practice, the best writing community in the world, and especially to Joe Bunting and Sarah Gribble, for teaching me how to actually write a book. I can say with all honesty, without you, I wouldn't have been able to pull this off. Thanks for your endless support and encouragement to sit down to write and get this book published. (Check them out if you want to write and publish a book, they know what they are doing.)

A huge thank you goes to my first beta readers. To the ladies in my book club in New York, Shelly, Patricia, Jenny, Lauren and Claire. You made me feel like a real author for the first time. Anita was incredibly gracious with her time, fact-checking all my medical lingo. For my crime and jail scenes, as well as police procedures, Tristan made time in his busy schedule to ensure that what I wrote actually made any sense.

Thank you Kim, for your developmental edit of the first, second (or was it the hundredth?) draft of *The Perfect Family*. The story is so much stronger thanks to your input and expertise.

To my book coach Solar, who had to deal with me trying to get a synopsis done in one try. I failed miserably but you were patient enough to work through rounds and rounds of edits until both of us were happy.

The amazing cover for *The Perfect Family* was designed by James. You captured the essence of my story perfectly and I couldn't be happier with the final result.

To the talented Kathrin for taking up the task of copy-editing the whole book. I don't know how you did it but you did an incredible job and surely have found a calling as editor. World, watch out.

I cannot thank my ARC readers enough. Spread across the whole globe, you decided to immerse yourself into the world and the characters that I've created and tell the world about it. The amazing ladies in my book club in Dublin even insisted on reading *The Perfect Family* as our monthly pick. Your support on the day of the launch was crucial to make the publication a success. You are my heroes. As promised, a big shoutout goes to three geniuses who found the majority of my last typos. Clio, Gerry and Krysten, thank you for being so nitpicky days before the book launched.

To my parents, who gave me my first typewriter and who like and comment on every single book related Facebook post I leave, even if they don't speak english and have no clue what they are liking. An meine Eltern, die mir meine erste Schreibmaschine schenkten und jeden buchbezogenen Eintrag auf Facebook liken und einen Kommentar hinterlassen, obwohl sie kein Englisch sprechen und keine Ahnung haben was sie da so toll finden.

To all of you who bought a copy of *The Perfect Family* on the day it launched. You really made my day. I am officially making money from writing. That's insane!

And last, but definitely not least, to my amazing husband Shane. You've always encouraged me to follow my heart and do what makes me happy. I want to tell everyone in detail how wonderful you have been throughout this whole adventure but that would be a book in itself. So trust me when I say I couldn't have wished for a better life-partner. You are my rock, my biggest fan and the best shoulder to cry on when I start to doubt myself as a writer.

To any other indie-author out there, writing a book is hard work and it takes a village to get through it but along the way you'll make friendships for life. So don't give up! Sit down and write your story. Make your dream come true!

Also by Denise Weiershaus

• • • •

For the most current list of Denise's titles, please visit her website
www.deniseweiershaus.com.

About the Author

DENISE IS A GERMAN native who has lived on three continents so far. Paying the bills working for the Government, her true passion has always been to read and create stories and share her experience with others. She writes crime thrillers, contemporary romance and dystopian climate fiction short stories, foreshadowing dark climate scenarios that might soon become our new reality. Her stories always include strong female characters.

When she doesn't write or read, you'll find her with a camera in her hand or hiking boots on her feet, exploring the country she currently calls home. At the moment, she is living in Dublin with her Irish husband and Confucius, their not-so-wise rescue cat from China.